STALIN'S PRIESTS

Rita and Erik Brandin

STALIN'S PRIESTS

iUniverse books may be ordered through booksellers or by contacting:

iUniverse
1663 Liberty Drive
Bloomington, IN 47403
www.iuniverse.com
1-800-Authors (1-800-288-4677)

ISBN: 978-1-5320-3746-7 (sc)
ISBN: 978-1-5320-3747-4 (hc)
ISBN: 978-1-5320-3748-1 (e)

Library of Congress Control Number: 2017919272

Printed in the United States of America.

iUniverse rev. date: 04/03/2018

Contents

Book 1
The Children of Fátima

Book 2
The Teacher and the Boy

Book 3

The Priest

Book 4

The Man of God

BOOK 1

THE CHILDREN OF FÁTIMA

THE INQUIRY

August 6, 1917

As Father Carrera entered Ourém, a small hilltop town built around a centuries-old Moorish castle and surrounded by vineyards and farms below, he saw a group of around thirty villagers, mostly farmers, standing outside the city hall.

"You there!" he said to one of the farmers. "Why are you out here and not inside?"

"The courtroom is full," he said.

"Shhh! The inquisition has already started," said another.

"Crazy kids," said a third.

Father Carrera dismounted his horse, asking one of the men to watch him, and pushed his way through the crowd into the city hall to the courtroom. The lack of breeze in the room intensified the heat of the August afternoon, and many of the onlookers, mostly men from the surrounding villages, had taken off their jackets and hats and were fanning themselves and brushing away the flies.

Above the heads of the bystanders, Father Carrera could see that the child named Lucia Marto was on the stand. The bishop had sent Father Carrera to find out if the three children claiming to have seen the Virgin Mary were safe—and if the visions were true. He knew from visiting the families that Lucia was the only one at court. She'd arrived with her father

1

when summoned; the other two were still at home. He knew from the bishop that the mayor summoning these children and running the court was no friend to Catholics or even to children.

The grumbling of the onlookers made it hard to hear exactly what Mayor Santos was saying, but it sounded as if he were interrogating the child, as each time the mayor spoke, the men would yell out their own answers, and many laughed derisively when Lucia spoke. Father Carrera nudged through the men to get a closer look at the proceedings.

He was immediately impressed with the bearing of this ten-year-old girl. Lucia was clearly one of the peasant working class, but her black-and-white plaid dress was clean and pressed although threadbare. Her head was covered with a coarse cotton shawl that exposed her tan face and highlighted her broad forehead and dark deep-set eyes. Lucia sat tall and straight with her hands folded around a rosary in her lap, looking not at the mayor but at the crowd of unpleasant men in front of her. She showed no fear or anger as they taunted her.

Although he was not a physically imposing man, Mayor Santos was wearing a black suit and a bright blue satin apron and collar, both intricately embroidered in gold thread and tassels. Such formal attire was out of place in the rural town, but it was obvious to Father Carrera the mayor was dressed that way to intimidate the child—and to impress all the villagers in the courtroom.

Positioned on each side of the mayor was a man similarly dressed, each holding a flag emblazoned with a gold triangle formed by a compass and a mason's ruler square, signifying that they were members of the Freemasons.

Seven years earlier, the Freemasons had staged a governmental coup in Lisbon and defeated the constitutional monarchy, proclaiming a Masonic republic. The Masonic government had passed many anti-Catholic laws that undermined the teachings of the church and promulgated the harassment of priests and nuns, causing fear in the religious citizens. This intense religious persecution had been focused in the larger cities, such as Lisbon, Porto, and Braga, but had not spread to most of the rural villages or counties, such as Ourém. Father Carrera remembered the warning from Bishop Vidal about the anti-Catholic sentiment of the mayor, who had just been elected grand master of the Masonic hall in Ourém. He had heard more about the mayor from his friend Father Mendoza during his overnight stay in Cartaxo. He had learned that the mayor of Ourém had been in politics since his youth, and although he was of meager education, he had gained tremendous power in the county as chief magistrate, wielding a heavy hand in not only administrative matters but also judicial matters. Santos was also the publisher of the local newspaper, which he used to undermine the Catholic church with the intention of quelling the religious fervor of the people in his county.

Father Carrera made it to the front of the room just as Mayor Santos stood up to tower over Lucia.

"So this woman you say you saw at the Cova da Iria—who do you think she was?" Mayor Santos asked.

"She told me who she was," the girl said, betraying not the slightest trace of humiliation as a few of the men laughed.

One shouted, "She's lying! She just wants attention!"

"Who did she say she was?" the mayor asked.

"The Blessed Virgin," the child responded, still looking not at the mayor but straight ahead as the laughter increased.

"And this blessed virgin—what else did she tell you?" the mayor said with a leer.

"She told me secrets," Lucia answered.

"Secrets! And what were they?"

Father Carrera could see Mayor Santos's face redden as he paced back and forth in front of Lucia.

"I cannot say," Lucia said without looking at the mayor.

"You refuse to say?"

"She told me not to say," Lucia whispered, looking straight ahead.

"But I am the mayor, and you are in my court, and I order you to say."

"No, she told me not to," Lucia said softly. She looked at the mayor as he pushed his face toward her.

"Do you know where you are?"

"Yes."

"And you refuse to tell this court one thing that this so-called virgin said to you?"

Father Carrera saw Lucia shuffle in her seat and then sit up taller. She seemed to be thinking about the mayor's question in a new way.

"Yes, I can tell you one thing. She said she wants to meet me again at the Cova da Iria on the thirteenth of this month." Lucia took a deep breath and smiled as she looked out at the crowd of men and then back at the mayor.

"I order you to tell this court what else she said to you!"

"I will not."

"Do you want to go to prison?"

The aggressive behavior and the threat of prison were more than Father Carrera could bear. Forgetting himself, he stepped forward.

"What kind of a trial is this, where a grown man bullies a child in front of a group of laughing jackasses?" Father Carrera boomed.

Mayor Santos whirled around to confront the person who had just insulted him. "This isn't the Vatican," he spat. "Your collar carries no weight in this court of law, Priest!"

Father Carrera removed his collar and stuffed it into his pocket. "All right," he said, trying to control his own anger and maintain a sense of poise equal to that of the child on the stand, who was already an inspiration to him. "Let us all forget our ranks and titles and talk to one another as human beings and citizens of a great nation. I was sent from Lisbon by Bishop de Lima Vidal to ensure that this child has an advocate, an adult who can protect her rights and defend her dignity."

"And that should be you?" the mayor sneered. "What about the girl's father, who is sitting in this very courtroom without raising the slightest objection?"

"If he's here, why don't you put him on the stand and threaten him with jail?"

"Because he has been cooperative in every way," said the mayor. "But if it will shut you up, I'll do it."

Father Carrera tipped his head slightly to signify his appreciation and stepped aside to let the mayor return to his chair above the witness stand. The mayor appeared to have calmed down and took his time reseating himself and organizing the papers on his desk.

After a few minutes, the mayor looked over at Lucia. "Girl, you go sit by your uncle while I talk to your father," he said. Afterward, he called Antonio, Lucia's father, to the stand.

Antonio rose slowly from his seat in the first row and, looking back at

Lucia, removed his hat to comb his hair away from his forehead with his fingers. He was uncomfortable and sweating in his brown woolen suit. He walked quickly to the chair at the front of the room and slumped as he sat looking down at his lap, where he fingered his hat.

"Do you believe that your daughter has told us the truth here today?" the mayor asked Antonio.

Antonio looked at his hat, tapping it on his knee, and muttered something unintelligible.

"I'm sorry, but could you please speak up?" the mayor asked. "In your opinion, is your daughter telling the truth?"

"She has a very active imagination, like most children," Antonio stuttered.

"Please answer the question," demanded the mayor. "Did Lucia and her two cousins, in your opinion, meet and converse with the Blessed Virgin?"

"Of course not," Antonio admitted with a polite shrug, looking up at the mayor for the first time.

Father Carrera stared at Lucia to see how her father's timidity on the stand affected her. To his surprise, he found that Lucia was paying no attention to what was happening in the front of the room. Instead, she was looking right back at him inquisitively, as if she'd recognized him and could read his thoughts.

"Do the people of Fátima believe these children are telling the truth?" the mayor asked.

"Oh no, sir," Antonio insisted. "These are tales that the women sometimes tell. Nobody takes them seriously."

The mayor seemed satisfied with Antonio's answer. However, the man Lucia had gone to sit by was not satisfied with his brother's answer, and he jumped up to confront his brother as well as the mayor.

"Put me on the stand," demanded Ti Marto. "I am Lucia's uncle, and I believe what she says. My two children were there and say the same things about talking to Our Lady. You summoned them here today, but I would not let them come."

"So you admit that you have flouted the law?" the mayor asked.

"I admit nothing of the sort. I simply made the decision that my two small children have no business being questioned in a court of law, and after seeing how you've treated Lucia, I was right not to bring them. I have come in their place, and I am prepared to answer for them. May I take the stand?"

"Please do," the mayor said.

As Ti Marto walked toward the stand, Antonio stepped down and paused to look at his brother. Neither one spoke, but Ti Marto shook his head as he took Antonio's place.

"Do your children tell the same story as the girl?"

"They do," Ti Marto said.

"They claim to have seen the Blessed Virgin at Cova da Iria?"

"They do."

"And what do you say?"

"I say what they say."

"I beg your pardon?"

"You ask me what they say. I have answered truthfully."

"Do you believe what they say?"

"Yes, sir, I do."

The men in the courtroom laughed, and a few whistled at Ti Marto's answer.

"Perhaps I should throw you in jail," said the mayor, more irritated than before by this peasant.

"What would be the charge?" Ti Marto asked.

"Yes, exactly," echoed Father Carrera. "On what charge?"

The mayor waved his gavel in dismissal. "I see that in your case, your children come by their delusions honestly," he said, receiving an appreciative laugh from the crowd. "I order you both"—the mayor pointed at both fathers—"to discipline your children and keep them from spreading these dangerous lies that make people very upset. And I want your promise that you will keep your children indoors on the day of August thirteenth."

"I will promise, sir," Antonio muttered.

"Good. Then get your daughter back home, where she belongs," said the mayor.

"I do not promise," said Ti Marto. "I will take my children to Cova da Iria on that day if they want to go."

Father Carrera could see that the mayor pretended he didn't hear what Ti Marto said, but he noticed the mayor pulling at his collar and then wiping sweat from his forehead. The two men next to the mayor had stepped down from the platform. Just as Lucia and her father stood to leave, the mayor pounded his gavel so hard that everyone in the courtroom froze. Father Carrera rushed forward as the mayor rose from his seat and jabbed his gavel toward Lucia with a sneer.

"Girl, if you go to the field on that day, your disregard for my orders may cost you your life."

Lucia's father hung his head but said nothing to this man who had just threatened his daughter's life. Ti Marto squeezed Lucia's arm and pushed her toward the door through the crowd of men standing along the aisle of the courtroom.

The mayor's threat to Lucia infuriated Father Carrera, and he bolted toward the mayor as Santos stood to leave.

"You just threatened to hurt a child," Father Carrera said to the mayor. "How could you, with any conscience—"

The mayor whirled around and shook his fist at Father Carrera. "Priest, I'm warning you. Go home, and stop meddling in the business of my municipality, or you will be in jail yourself!"

Father Carrera said, "My concern is only the safety of these children."

"You come from Lisbon, and you don't know the ways of our parish!"

"The bishop sent me to ensure that the children are not harmed. You just threatened her. Surely even you do not wish to harm the child!"

"I am the authority in this municipality, not you, not some bishop, and certainly not the Catholic church!" The mayor signaled to two men from the crowd, and all three quickly disappeared to the back of the courthouse through a bolted door.

Father Carrera pushed his way outside through the crowd, where Antonio was placing Lucia on top of a burro.

"It seems to me that a grown man just threatened your child," he said to Antonio.

Antonio waved him away and packed his burro.

"I hope you keep an eye on her," said Father Carrera. "I do not think she is safe."

"Please don't worry about me, Father," Lucia said with a proud smile. "Our Lady will see to my safety."

Father Carrera watched Lucia as she rode away with her father. She looked back at him with the same inquisitive intensity he had seen from her in court. He knew the matter was far from settled, and he would need to stay in Ourém until August 13 to help protect the children if they went to the Cova da Iria again.

THE INTERSESSION

Father Carrera rode to the residence of the parish priest, Father di Pietro, with a note from the bishop that introduced him and requested that he receive lodging for as long as he wanted to stay. By the time he arrived at the old stone church across from the large square in the center of town, Father Carrera found that word of his behavior at the courthouse had preceded him.

"Father, it is not wise to cross the mayor," blurted out Father di Pietro when he met him. "For the good of every Catholic in this municipality, I beg you to hear me."

"I'm here on a mission," Father Carrera explained.

"You must not talk to the mayor or challenge him the way you did today in court," Father di Pietro insisted.

"Why should he be allowed to mistreat and threaten those children?"

"You don't understand how cruel he is. He has used the power of the Masons to gain control of Ourém. He controls the newspaper. He's printing endless propaganda to get people to forget about religion. In so many little ways, he makes life for these people hell, and keeps them in fear. He seeks to rid the entire nation of the church in all its forms. The last thing he wants is a miraculous sighting of the Blessed Virgin in his own municipality."

"It may not be something he can control."

"Those children are lying, and they are causing us all a lot of trouble."

"Maybe they are making things up or imagining things," Father Carrera said. "Children do that. But we do not hurt them for that. Do we?"

"Who said anything about hurting them?"

"The mayor did. In court today, he threatened to hurt them if they returned to the Cova de Iria."

Father di Pietro shook his head and sighed. "Dear God, it is worse than I thought." He handed Father Carrera a key. "You can stay in the room in the back of the rectory. Please do not cause any more trouble than you absolutely have to."

Father di Pietro showed him to his room and then disappeared back into the rectory.

After Father Carrera washed up, he prayed before eating the snack he had brought with him: "Our most gracious Father, thank you for guiding my journey to Ourém. Please give me the wisdom and strength to protect these children who believe they have talked with the Virgin Mary. Help me to understand your miraculous ways, and thank you for this nourishment. In the name of the Father, the Son, and the Holy Spirit. Amen."

As Father Carrera ate his meal, his thoughts drifted back to the courtroom and Lucia's resolve. He was perplexed by the mysterious, brave little girl who had faced those jeering men that afternoon. He knew that Lucia and her cousins needed his help. He was also intrigued by the apparitions as well and wanted to see firsthand how the crowds of faithful reacted to the children when they showed up in the field for their monthly conversation with the Virgin.

AUGUST 13

When the sun came up on August 13, Father Carrera mounted his horse and rode to the home of Ti Marto, where a crowd had already gathered. Ti Marto's wife, Olimpia, was calling him in from the fields. Mayor Santos had arrived shortly before Father Carrera. Father di Pietro was there too, standing timidly at the side of the mayor.

Ti Marto went first to shake hands with Father Carrera. "I am certainly glad to see you here, Father," Ti Marto said.

"It seems I have come not a moment too soon," said Father Carrera.

The mayor impatiently stepped forward and offered his hand to Ti Marto, who reluctantly shook it.

"To what do I owe the pleasure of your visit, Your Honor?" Ti Marto asked the mayor.

"Are your children planning to go to Cova da Iria today?" the mayor asked.

"I believe so."

"I will take them in my wagon then," the mayor said.

"That is not necessary," said Ti Marto. "I will take them myself."

"Why should you lose a day's work, when I am perfectly happy to take them?"

"I will take them," Ti Marto insisted.

"Let the mayor take them," Father di Pietro said. "I will go along too. We will stop at the church after our visit to the Cova da Iria. It is my wish, as their parish priest, to question them about what they see today, and the church will be a safe place to do so."

"I will take them," Ti Marto said.

"I assure you they will be safe," Father di Pietro promised. "I give you my word."

"I want him to go along too." Ti Marto pointed to Father Carrera.

Both Father di Pietro and Mayor Santos shook their heads.

"There is not enough room in the wagon," said the mayor.

"I have a horse," Father Carrera said.

"This questioning should be private," Father di Pietro said.

"You are a priest; he is a priest. What is the problem?" Ti Marto asked.

"I can keep a secret," Father Carrera assured the crowd.

"This is not your affair," the mayor insisted.

"But they are my children," Ti Marto said. "They cannot go with you unless this other priest rides along."

Father di Pietro and the mayor looked at one another. It seemed to Father Carrera that they were coming to some silent agreement.

"Yes, fine," the mayor said. "We are wasting time here. Let him see what we see and hear what we hear so that he can put an end to this nonsense for his bishop in Lisbon. Let us go."

All three children—Lucia, Francisco, and Jacinta—were loaded into the wagon, and the group set off for Cova da Iria with the mayor at the reins. Father Carrera intended to ride alongside to keep an eye on the children and watch the mayor to make sure he did not threaten them again.

Most of the crowd who had gathered outside Ti Marto's house followed the wagon on foot for the journey from Aljustrel to Fátima. Father Carrera saw a few older women on burros led along the rocky road by their husbands, but most of the men and other children walked almost in single file. He noticed one group of women, each with a rosary in hand, cross themselves and begin a prayer as they walked. Although he couldn't hear them over the bumping of the wagon, he could see that they were mouthing in unison, and he guessed they were reciting the Hail Mary by the way their fingers worked their rosaries. The wagon stalled several times, caught in deep ruts leftover from the late-summer rainstorms, and each time, men from the crowd would rush forward to lift the wagon while the mayor urged the horses forward with a tap of his whip.

Father Carrera didn't know that route to Fátima and was surprised to see so many small stone farmhouses along the ride. As they came to each dirt road leading to another farmhouse, whole families and other farmers joined them, each silently waiting for the wagon to pass to join the large group from the rear. Thirty minutes into the journey, Father Carrera looked back and realized he could no longer count the swelling crowd.

When Father Carrera turned back toward the wagon, he saw that the wagon had stopped at a fork in the road. The crude wooden sign pointed left to Cova da Iria and right to Ourém. It seemed odd to Father Carrera that the mayor would hesitate. Then, suddenly, the mayor cracked the whip harshly on the horses' flanks and jerked the reins to the right toward Ourém.

The crowd was quiet for a minute, confused at first by the wagon's sudden turn to the right. As the wagon sped away, they shouted and yelled at the mayor, thinking he must be confused and hoping to stop them from going in the wrong direction.

Father Carrera immediately kicked his horse, Quieto, with his spurs and leaned forward to urge him to gallop. Quieto's stride was long and fast, and Father Carrera loosened the reins so he could pick up more speed. Gaining on the wagon, Father Carrera galloped to the right of the horse team. He was almost there; he had to go just a little farther. Then he pulled the reins across Quieto's neck to steer him toward the wagon. He reached down, grabbed the bridle on the lead horse, and pulled both the wagon and Quieto to an abrupt stop.

"Where are you taking these children? Cova da Iria is the other way!" Father Carrera yelled through labored breath, still gripping the horse's bridle. He pointed at Father de Pietro and glared at the mayor. "Can't you see the crowd of people waiting for you at the fork?"

Father Carrera quickly dismounted his horse and looped the reins around the harness to the cart. As he walked to the back of the wagon to check on the children, he saw Father di Pietro get down off the wagon to meet him on the other side.

"Could I speak to you confidentially, away from the children?" Father di Pietro asked with a frightened look on his face.

Father Carrera knew that with Quieto standing alongside the other horses, the wagon could not be moved, so he followed the priest some distance away so the children would not hear their conversation.

"I now believe that these children are in danger," Father di Pietro whispered, and Father Carrera noticed that his hands were trembling.

"Of course they are in danger," said Father Carrera. "I told you I didn't trust the mayor, but you wouldn't listen. That's why I came here today—to make sure the children made it to the field."

"Perhaps you could convince them to stay away from Cova da Iria today." Father di Pietro grabbed Carrera's arm with an urgent squeeze.

"Do you think they would listen?"

"I don't know. It may be our only hope. But there is one thing you need to know before you talk to them."

"What's that?" asked Father Carrera.

Father Carrera never heard Father di Pietro's answer. Something hit him hard in the back of the head, and his world went black.

FINDING THE CHILDREN

Father Carrera awoke on a cot at the parish rectory in Fátima. A doctor was tending to him. Father Carrera pushed the doctor's hands aside. The dim light in the room told him some time had passed. Father di Pietro sat on the other side of the room, covering his face with both hands.

"Where are the children?" Father Carrera said as he sat up. The back of his head was pounding.

"Thank God you are awake, Father," said the doctor.

"Father Carrera, thanks be to God you are awake and safe," Father di Pietro whispered as he crossed himself and wiped his nose with his sleeve.

"Where are the children?" Father Carrera repeated.

"I had no idea the mayor would do this to you," said Father di Pietro. "You must believe me."

"I believe you. Now, tell me—"

"You must think me a horrible coward. I have to live here under the thumb of that man while he does horrible things to scare my parishioners."

"Where are the children?" repeated Father Carrera.

"There were more than fifteen thousand people at Cova da Iria today. People came from all over Portugal, and I heard that some even came from other countries. The word of these apparitions has spread throughout Europe. They were all waiting for a miracle. And of course, the miracle never happened. The people who came out believed it was because the children were not there. They blamed me, and they thought I'd conspired with the mayor to kidnap them."

"Where are the children?" Father Carrera asked one more time.

"I am afraid that if I tell you, you will mount your horse and ride, and you are in no condition to do that."

"For the love of God, man. Tell me!"

"The mayor has imprisoned them in his home."

Father Carrera was off the cot at once, buttoning his shirt and dusting himself off with his hands. He sat down, waiting for the dizziness to pass. When it did, he accepted the glass of water Father di Pietro offered him, and he felt much better.

The doctor stood in front of him. "You've had a blow to the head. I don't think you—"

"Where is the mayor's home?" Father Carrera demanded of the doctor.

"It's right there on the outskirts of Ourém. It's the biggest house in town. But you can't go there now. Your head—"

"Where's my horse?" Father Carrera demanded. Realizing none of them would answer him, he grabbed his coat from the end of the bed and walked outside to find Quieto.

Father di Pietro followed. "Please, Father, you must tell those children to stop spreading these silly stories about seeing the Blessed Virgin. Look at all the trouble they have caused. This is just the beginning of it if they won't stop."

"Children sometimes tell silly stories simply because they are children. But they do not deserve to be treated like criminals," said Father Carrera as he tightened the cinch on Quieto's saddle. "It is our duty as men of the cloth to protect them so that they can grow to learn better."

With that, Father Carrera mounted his horse, gave him a quick kick, and galloped west toward Ourém.

5

BOILING OIL

It was early when Father Carrera found the mayor's house on the outskirts of Ourém. A farmer taking his vegetables to town for the next day's market had given Father Carrera directions and a better description of the mayor's house.

The house was surrounded by a massive granite block wall, not the usual rock material used in that part of Portugal. The iron gate was locked, but he could see the large two-story villa between the rails. He could see that someone was home, as light filtered from a second-story window, and smoke curled out of the two chimneys on the roof.

Father Carrera tied Quieto to a nearby tree and climbed the wall, using the cracks between the large granite blocks as handholds. When he reached the top, he threw one leg over the top to straddle the wall. He paused to make sure there were no dogs to hamper his descent, and seeing none, he lowered himself halfway down with the strength of his arms and then jumped to the ground, slightly twisting his ankle when he landed. He stood there silently for a moment to let the throbbing of his ankle and his head subside. A shadow passed by a window on the upper floor. Taking a deep breath, he strode up to the front door and pounded on it with his knuckles.

After minutes of pounding, the door opened, and a servant quickly led the three children out onto the front landing. As the servant backed away, she brushed a stray hair away from her forehead and then stopped to look at Father Carrera with tears in her eyes.

"I pray for forgiveness, Father. These children do not deserve this treatment from Mayor Santos. I believe them. I do." She crossed herself and backed away from the children.

Lucia, Francisco, and Jacinta ran to Father Carrera. He inspected each one and found them unharmed. In fact, they were elated.

"We did not betray Our Lady," Lucia said, beaming with a beatific smile.

"He said he'd boil us in oil!" said young Francisco.

"Open that gate!" Father Carrera demanded of the servant. The servant ran toward the massive front gate to unlock it, and Father Carrera led the children to Quieto. He helped Lucia and Jacinto onto his horse, but Francisco refused to be hoisted, so Father Carrera took his hand as he led the horse by the reins on foot. The pains from his twisted ankle, bruised knuckles, and throbbing head went unheeded as he focused all his efforts on the arduous task of bringing the children home.

As he ambled along, Lucia spoke from atop the horse. At first, it seemed she was talking to herself. Then he became aware that she was talking directly to him.

"He told us we had to tell him the secrets the Blessed Virgin told us. And when we refused, he told us we would go to jail. When we still refused, he threw us in the basement. It's like a jail down there, with little rooms that have doors with metal bars on them. It's cold and musty and smelly. He put us all in different rooms and told us if we didn't tell him about what she said, he would—"

"Boil us in oil!" Francisco said, interrupting Lucia with great enthusiasm. "He said he would boil us in oil!"

"He took Francisco back up the stairs first, and I heard him crying, and then I couldn't hear him anymore," Lucia said, rubbing her eyes with the backs of her hands. "He came back later and told us that Francisco was dead. He said Francisco would not answer his questions, so he'd thrown him into a vat of boiling oil. And Jacinta said—"

Jacinta interrupted. "I said that my brother was happy now because he was with Our Lady. I said for the mayor to put me in the oil too so that I could be happy."

"We never once betrayed Our Lady," Lucia said proudly.

"But he didn't really boil me in oil." Francisco giggled as he squeezed Father Carrera's hand. "He yelled at me a lot and used bad words when

I wouldn't tell him what she said to us. He was only pretending that he would boil me!"

Father Carrera was furious that the mayor had threatened the children but amazed that they didn't seem to be the least bit afraid of the mayor or anyone else. "Children, you have been blessed to witness the glory and goodness of God through Our Lady's visions, but Mayor Santos does not believe. He is the evil in the world that Our Lady was trying to warn you about."

"Our Lady will protect us," Lucia said.

Father Carrera patted Quieto's neck, and as he and the children came to the fork in the road that led back to Aljustrel, he saw a crowd of people up ahead, led by Father di Pietro.

Father di Pietro ran ahead of the others and embraced the children as he lifted them down from Father Carrera's horse.

"Thank God the children are safe and unharmed!" Father di Pietro exclaimed. He knelt in front of Father Carrera and took his hand. "Thank God for you, Father Carrera. You have saved the children. I was wrong and very afraid. You knew no fear and did what had to be done. My life has been changed by your example. Never again will I let that bully of a mayor touch the children. We were on our way to the mayor's house to demand that he release the children. We were prepared to burn his house down if he did not let them free. Look how many have gathered! Can you believe it? We will put him in his place."

Antonio, Lucia's father, came forward, lifted his daughter off the priest's horse, and held her in his arms.

"Thank God you are safe," said Antonio. Then he turned to Father Carrera and said clumsily but sincerely, "You did what I should have done. I am shamed because I did not protect her, and she could have been gravely harmed. I will never let that happen again, Father; you can take my word for it. I am forever in your debt."

6

THE VISIT

The next morning, Father Carrera walked with the children the short distance to the Cova di Iria, a small valley in the hills near the hamlet of Aljustrel.

"My father says this land has been in our family for four generations," Lucia said proudly as she skipped ahead. "I am in charge of tending our family's sheep with Jacinto and Francisco's help. The well for watering the sheep is over there." She pointed toward the base of a rocky slope. "We sometimes climb up to those rocks. That's where we have lunch, and we can see the entire meadow from up there."

"Oh, Lucia, that's where you like to hide from the sheep." Francisco laughed as he grabbed Jacinta's hand, and they ran ahead toward a holm oak tree. "This is the place where we saw her," Francisco said as he excitedly circled the tree, dragging Jacinta with him.

Father Carrera could see that while Jacinto and Francisco were excited to show him the holm oak, Lucia had become quiet and serious as they reached the tree.

"Lucia, can you tell me of your experience here?" Father Carrera asked softly, hoping she would trust him with the details.

"The three of us were tending the sheep, as usual. That first day she came to us, we were scared. It was time for us to climb the rocks to eat our meal, when there was a flash of lightning," Lucia said with a strong and steady voice.

"I was the most afraid," said Jacinta. "I started to run because the thunder was so loud, and I did not want to get wet if it rained."

"Jacinta is right. The three of us were ready to run home, but then we saw her just above the oak tree. She was a beautiful lady made of light, and she was holding a rosary in her right hand," Lucia said as she concentrated to remember the details of that day. "She spoke to us that day. She could see that we were afraid, but she said she had come from heaven, and we did not need to be afraid."

"Did she tell you her name?" Father Carrera asked delicately, not wanting Lucia to feel threatened.

"No, she didn't, but we knew she must be special when she told us she had come from heaven. She asked us to come back to this very spot for six months, on the exact day and at the exact hour, and said she would tell us more about where she came from and what she wanted."

"Is that all she said that day—that she would be back to tell you more?" Father Carrera asked. There was little meaning. Why would the Blessed Virgin come to earth only to tell them to come back?

"Oh no, Father, she said a lot more. She asked us if we were willing to make sacrifices and bear suffering as reparation for the sins that offend God and for the conversion of sinners," Lucia said with more intensity.

"I was really scared when she asked that!" Francisco said. "I'm just a little boy. I don't know how to do those things she asked."

Lucia reached out to comfort Francisco, and he took her hand. "Francisco, tell Father Carrera about what happened next," Lucia said as she squeezed his hand.

"The beautiful lady opened her arms, and a light glowed from her," Francisco said.

"She then taught us a special prayer before she left, and all three of us have practiced it and said it every day," Lucia said as she motioned to Jacinta. "Jacinta, come stand by Francisco and me, and we will say the prayer together."

Lucia, Jacinta, and Francisco recited the prayer in unison: "O my Jesus, forgive us our sins, save us from the fires of hell, and lead all souls to heaven, especially those in most need of thy mercy."

"That is a very serious prayer," Father Carrera said. "And the three of you recite it very well. What did you do after she left?"

"We were very quiet and knelt down together. None of us could speak for a long time," Lucia said softly as Jacinta and Francisco nodded. "We agreed to keep it to ourselves until we could see her again."

"I was sad a little," Francisco said. "Because she told us that God was sad and was offended by the sins of people."

"But she also said that if we prayed the rosary like she asked, it would cause peace in the world. I think that might help God not be sad," Jacinta added.

"So you went home that day after seeing her and promised not to talk to anyone about what happened?" Father Carrera wanted to know how their story, which now had the mayor so angry, had gotten out. "How did the mayor find out then?"

"It was my fault," said Jacinta sheepishly. "I was so happy when I got home that I told my mother and father the whole story. My mother cried and was happy too, so she prayed the rosary with Francisco and me that very night."

"Yes, and then when our aunt and uncle came for dinner, my mother asked Jacinta to tell the story again, and then I told them about how beautiful the lady was. When we went to Mass on Sunday, it seemed that everyone had heard," Francisco added.

"You visited with her two more times, didn't you?" Father Carrera said.

"Yes," said Lucia. "We came back to the tree on the thirteenth of June and July, like she asked. She came to see us, as she had promised, but there were more people here that second time."

"Did she tell you more the second time you saw her?" Father Carrera asked.

"Yes. I asked her if she would take the three of us to heaven with her, and she told me that we could not go now, because she needed our help, especially mine. She said that soon, though, she would take Francisco and Jacinta, but I had to stay here for some time because Jesus wanted me to help with establishing a devotion to her." Lucia spoke plainly and showed no sadness that Jacinta or Francisco might die.

"She said I could come to heaven with her and Jacinta too," said Francisco, who did not display any fear of dying.

Lucia smiled at Francisco as she continued her story. "She told me not to worry or lose heart when Francisco and Jacinta went to heaven with her. She promised she would be here with me and would lead me to God.

She reminded us to return the next month, and then she rose into the sky and disappeared like the first time, but when she left that time, there was a loud crack—like thunder."

"None of the people here that day could see or hear the lady like we could, but they heard that loud sound when she left." Jacinta giggled. "My mother and her sisters fell to the ground and started praying the rosary."

"When we came back on July thirteenth, there were thousands of people here," Lucia said. "My mother told me that people all over Portugal were talking about our visits with the lady from the sky. She said some people who came to the field believed us, but some of them came to shame us for making up a story."

"Had she revealed who she was to you yet, or did she in July?" Father Carrera asked Lucia. The details, he knew, pointed to either an elaborate hoax or a true story. He had to hear the details to know for sure.

"No, she had not told us yet. But she promised that when she returned in October, she would tell us who she was and what she wanted. She promised to perform a miracle so that all the people who were there, especially those who doubted us, would see and believe.

"That time, when she visited, we were terrified. When she opened her arms, a great light came out, and she showed us a sea of fire, with demons and souls in human form plunged in the flames. They were floating in and out of the flames as they shrieked and groaned with horrible sounds of pain and despair." Lucia looked directly at Father Carrera.

"That is a very terrifying thing to see. What did you do?" Father Carrera asked.

"We looked back at the lady's face and asked what to do," Lucia said. "She told us that she had shown us hell, where the souls of poor sinners go. God wanted to save them by establishing a devotion to her. She told us again that if more people practiced their devotion to her, the war would end. But she said that if people did not stop offending God, another war, an even worse one, would break out, and if we saw a night illuminated by an unknown light, that sign meant God was about to punish the world for its crimes with more war, famine, and persecutions of the church and the Holy Father, our pope. But she said if the pope and all the bishops of the world would consecrate Russia to her Immaculate Heart, Russia would be converted, and there would be peace. She said that if Russia is allowed to continue to spread evils throughout the world, wars and persecution of the church will be worse."

"Lucia, this is quite a difficult load for the three of you to bear. Do you even know where Russia is?" Father Carrera asked sadly. He doubted the children could have made something like this up on their own, which left one explanation—one he was honored to report back to the bishop. But one thing still troubled him. "How does she expect three young children to help with such serious consequences of sin in the world, like wars and the Russian dictators?"

"She is simply telling us her message so that we can warn the leaders of the church," Lucia said.

"Why then have you not told Father di Pietro so that he can help?"

"He has not believed us from the beginning, and he is old and nervous and afraid of the mayor. I think we were waiting for you to arrive, Father Carrera." Lucia smiled and went forward to hug Father Carrera. "You are here, Father, and you saved us and believe us. That will give us strength to stand up to the mayor and to those people who do not believe."

Father Carrera was moved by Lucia's hug. He could hear the conviction with which the children spoke.

"Come now, the three of you. Let's say the rosary together like the lady instructed. I must leave tomorrow to return to Lisbon to report back to the bishop, and our reciting the rosary together will give me strength for the long ride on Quieto." Father Carrera motioned for the children to join him as he knelt beside the holm oak.

"Hail Mary, full of grace. The Lord is with you ..."

Two and a half months later, Father Carrera read in the Lisbon newspaper reports of a great miracle at Fátima. It said that in spite of torrential rains, seventy thousand people had gathered at Cova di Iria in October and witnessed the three children as they had a vision of the Virgin Mary, who identified herself as the Lady of the Rosary and asked for a chapel to be built. Many had observed a column of bluish smoke rise over the heads of the children and evaporate. The Virgin Mary was reported to have appeared once again to the three children. After Lucia's request that Our Lady give the people a sign, the rain had stopped suddenly, and the sun had appeared, resembling a disc of silver. Those gathered had been able to stare straight into the sun without discomfort. Then the sun had trembled and danced in the sky and appeared to be hurtling toward earth. The word *miracle* had rung out among the crowd. The newspaper article included photographs of the sun in that strange condition, which the reporter described as a miracle.

Father Carrera read the article with great joy and was satisfied that the children were safe. *After all, if the Virgin Mary appeared to them, how could they not be safe? Imagine that. Jesus's mother coming to earth in my lifetime. She must have an important message for the world.*

Having made a full report to the bishop about the apparitions and the message the children had told him of Mary's request to have the pope and all the bishops consecrate Russia publicly to her Immaculate Heart, he was convinced the Vatican would get involved to see to the children's well-being and fulfill the Blessed Mother's request. He put the newspaper down and began his workday, wondering if he would ever see the children again.

BOOK 2

THE TEACHER AND THE BOY

RUSSIAN REVOLUTION

Four-year-old Dmitri Volgonov woke to the sounds of angry crowds shouting in the streets. He crawled from under the covers to look out the second-floor window of his family's apartment to see thousands of people marching with signs and shouting loudly. Just then, his father and mother came into his room. His mother swept the boy up in her arms while his father closed the curtains, and they quickly retreated to the small kitchen, where the old stove and some weak coffee would keep them warm. It was early March 1917, and Moscow was still bitterly cold—and bitterly divided. The czar was still in power, but the people had been cold and hungry for too long now. Even the czar's own soldiers were now marching with the crowds demanding food and change.

The Industrial Revolution had finally come to Russia at the beginning of the century, many decades after it had transformed most of the countries of Europe. Most of Russia's hundred million or so inhabitants were still illiterate farmers barely eking out an existence in rural feudal farms. Now many were flocking to cities, such as Dmitri's Moscow, to work in factories owned by the fortunate few of the educated Russian middle class. Dmitri's father, Yuri, was fortunate to have been educated, and although he was not wealthy, he worked as a manager in a steel factory for an owner who, unlike many other factory owners of the day, valued his employees, paid them decent wages, and provided food and medical care. The Volgonovs had a better life than most, but they knew their livelihood and comforts were at risk as malcontent gripped the nation and the city. Many Russians wanted the country to become more like the European democracies, but another group, the Bolsheviks, dreamed of a utopian Communist society with no classes. The Bolsheviks were inspired by the writings of a man named Karl Marx.

Led by Vladimir Lenin, Leon Trotsky, and Joseph Stalin, the Bolsheviks first ended the czar's rule on March 13, 1917, and then fought a brutal civil war until 1922, when they finally gained full control of the country and began the transformation into their dream Communist society.

Life for the Volgonov family changed little during that time, as the protests ended, and the factories remained needed to produce all the implements necessary in a fledgling industrial age and a time of war. World War I had finally ended, but now a great civil war was being fought in many Russian cities. Moscow was home to the Bolsheviks—or the Reds, as they were known—and the city was mostly peaceful. People worked long hours in factories, and although food wasn't abundant, stores were open, and cafés were busy. Dmitri's father was still busy at the steel factory, and his mother kept the home and did the shopping and cooking. She also helped Dmitri with his schooling. Dmitri was growing up to be a fine young man and a good student and athlete. The new educational system ushered in by the Communist government was mandatory for all. The government realized the foundation of their new system depended upon complete dedication of the people to the state. This dedication would need to be taught to them from a young age. The Communist ideology would permeate the entire educational system, from primary school to the universities. Religious texts and teachings were forbidden. Many textbooks were full of socialist ideology and propaganda. Classes centering on the life and labor of the family in villages and towns and on scientific organization of labor were taught at twelve and thirteen years of age. The goal of education was to make so-called small comrades, encourage collectivism, and reduce the family and religious influence in a child's upbringing. Students recited oaths of allegiance and pride for their utopian state. Students who excelled at these requirements were held up as examples and became leaders.

Dmitri excelled in his schoolwork and was one of those youth leaders. He joined the new organization called the Young Pioneers, which played a huge role in the education of Russian children. As a Young Pioneer, Dmitri enjoyed many outdoor activities, such as camping, hiking, and fishing—activities a young boy from the city relished. The Young Pioneers partook in many of the same activities the Boy Scouts of America did in the USA, but the organization was also used to reinforce Communist ideology in the youth outside of the classroom. It was effective.

By the time Dmitri entered secondary school at fifteen in 1928, he was at the top of his class in his local neighborhood school near the Moskva River in Moscow. He was taller than most of the boys and had thick black hair. In the summer, the kids would swim in the river, and in winter, they would ice-skate for miles. Dmitri could swim faster and skate farther than any of his friends. He was happy and doing well, but there was a growing tension at home.

Each night at the dinner table, his father would ask him about his day and his schooling. Dmitri, with pride, would recite much of the propaganda he had been taught. His father did not talk about politics, but he was not in favor of the direction his beloved country was going. When the czar had fallen, Dmitri's father and many others had hoped a democracy like many others, including the United States of America, would form. Instead, Communism was being forced on the people, including Dmitri. Yuri tried to speak to Dmitri about it, but Dmitri would become defensive, and he could not afford to have Dmitri say anything at school, for fear of reprisals from the government, which was ever watchful for suspected dissidents. He felt helpless as he watched his son being indoctrinated, and sadly, they grew further and further apart as the years went by.

When it was time for Dmitri to enter university at eighteen, he was sent to the main university in Moscow. Stalin had begun to militarize the educational system via socialist competitions between classrooms, the addition of military classes, and rallies that the students were encouraged to attend. They were taught stories of great battles by brave Russians against enemies of Mother Russia. Schooling also placed emphasis on the child hero. Stories of exemplary children doing the right thing according to the government were propagated throughout the country so children would learn from the actions of these young heroes of the state. There was also formal military training for boys, who learned hand-to-hand combat, were drilled like soldiers with instructors from the military, and even learned fencing. Dmitri excelled at these activities and was seen as a leader by both his instructors and his peers. He was in his element and coming of age. He dreamed of becoming a great soldier hero himself. He grew more and more distant from his parents.

Dmitri loved Moscow and his studies. He enjoyed the cafés near the university and the bustle of the once gloomy city now coming to life with new buildings, factories, and people. He was being groomed to join the Red Army, and after his second year, he was sent to the nearby city of Tula to the Tula Artillery and Engineering Academy, where young officers were trained. Dmitri was elated.

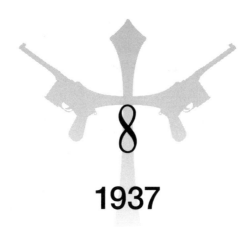

1937

General Slatkin seemed to shrink, as if he knew at once that he was in great danger.

The moment Slatkin had been put in charge of the Great Purge, party officials had warned him about the danger of getting too close to Stalin. The paranoid Stalin had initiated the Great Purge to eliminate any threats to his power. Millions were sent to labor camps or executed, including many high-ranking party officials and Red Army officers. Slatkin didn't want to be one of them.

Officers told him Stalin was pathologically mistrustful of anyone who got close to him. One politburo member said it was because anyone who stood close to Stalin could see that he was not a physically imposing man and had a slightly withered arm, unusually long nostrils, and a thick mustache that couldn't quite cover his curling lip.

Slatkin was old enough to remember Lenin. When in Lenin's presence, Slatkin had always been aware of being near a powerful and imposing man, as opposed to Stalin, who was a wiry Gypsy with volatile emotions. The real Stalin up close in person was never impressive but always fearsome.

General Slatkin faced the impassive general secretary across a long table with sweating palms and all the dignity he could muster.

"Believe me, General Secretary," Slatkin stammered. "We are doing all we can."

"Yes, but tell me of the results," Stalin said softly.

"There are great difficulties."

"Yes," Stalin said. "But what of the results?"

"We have confiscated church property and turned hundreds of churches into community centers. Active Russian Orthodox parishes number in the hundreds, down from more than fifty thousand when we began our work."

"And the priests?"

"More than one hundred thousand executions."

Stalin interrupted. "Have you successfully curtailed the activity of the Roman Catholic Church?"

"Of course we have curtailed them. The people no longer go to the churches in the open, and when we question them, they say they have no trust for the priests. But our spies tell me that they still meet in basements like rats."

Stalin just looked at Slatkin.

A drop of sweat dribbled down Slatkin's forehead, and Stalin began to pace.

"It seems that every time we kill one priest, another takes his place. Yes, they are all like rats," Slatkin spat. "No matter how many priests or worshippers die, it continues."

With a simple jerk of his head, Stalin motioned to the two armed guards.

Slatkin's eyes grew wide, and he froze. "No, please, General Secretary," he begged. "I'm telling you we are making progress. I can do more. Please. No."

"What you have told me is that you have failed," Stalin said, dismissing the guards with a wave of his hand. "And failure is not acceptable."

The big wood door shut with a soft *thunk*. Slatkin's cries echoed down the hallway as the guards led him to the inner courtyard. The general would not survive the afternoon.

The men watching Stalin pace the floor were silent. The only sound was the clicking of Stalin's boots against the tile floor. A distant gunshot announced the fate of Slatkin. Stalin watched the men begin to sweat.

"What can we do about this problem?" Stalin asked. Nobody said a word, so he continued. "The Catholic church is responsible for the only resistance we face. They compete with us for control of the masses. Their indoctrination process is to be both envied and feared. I knew this from the moment my mother forced me to attend the seminary, when she willfully sacrificed me for the priesthood as a tribal Jew might sacrifice a goat on the altar of a God that doesn't exist."

Momentarily overcome, Stalin suddenly and inexplicably stopped speaking. He made some coughing sounds and then went back to the desk. He pounded his fist on it to hide his emotion.

Stalin became too emotional to speak whenever he mentioned his mother. Such observations about Stalin shortened lives when expressed. The leader of the politburo diverted his eyes from Stalin and slowly stepped behind one of the other soldiers.

"That was the Russian Orthodox Church," Stalin said, "but today it is the Roman Catholic Church that threatens us in Poland and elsewhere. I have always known that the Roman Catholic Church has the most potent indoctrination process of any political or religious organization in the world.

"Their method is ingenious. It starts very early in life, you see. The priests and nuns descend on the very young, teaching about the horrors that await the apostate in the afterlife. The chubby little friars and the so-called holy sisters convince the children that they have an eternity of torture to fear from a God who watches every move, monitors each thought, and judges accordingly. These irrational childhood fears form the basis of the adolescent psyche. As the Catholic child matures and learns about the world, he unconsciously filters everything through this prism of terror. By adulthood, the Roman Catholic has become convinced that the only respite from this ingrained fear is the church, the only salvation from this anticipated torture is in the sacraments, and the only way to receive the sacraments is from a priest. It is ingenious. No earthly rational concern penetrates or supersedes this irrational anticipation of an imagined afterlife. No social cause, labor movement, people's revolution, or military victory could separate such a person from this core belief. Whatever happens in this lifetime is temporary. But the afterlife is eternal. This is why weeds continue to grow in the garden: the roots are so very deep. Wherever we free the people of this church, it always springs up again and compels its members to resist the rule of rational government. And because these members have been taught to believe in this afterlife, they do not fear death as much as they fear the church. They believe that dying in defense of their church will lead to an eternal reward. Who can tell me what we can do about this problem?"

After a pause, Stalin said again, "Who can tell me what we can do about this problem?"

None of the men gathered in the room spoke. Stalin began to pace again, and then he stopped suddenly, seemingly possessed with a new idea.

"If we cannot destroy the church, then we must become the church."

Not one person moved. Stalin was watching. The first one who moved was the first one he'd call on.

"Take a look at the Iberian Peninsula," Stalin told his men. "What has happened there? In Spain, there was a revolution, a populist movement that threatened the Catholic dictatorship in that country. It almost worked! They almost threw off the yoke of the plutocratic papist tyrants that has driven that nation backward to the days of feudal barons. The movement is growing; it is very much alive. But next door? In Portugal? Just the opposite is true. Twenty years ago, the Catholics were almost finished in Portugal. The anti-Catholic reformers of that time had been very successful in getting rid of the church's dominance over society. Then, in the same year of our revolution, three children in a field reported a miracle, a sighting of the Virgin Mary. The entire nation grew to worship those children and believe the stories they told about what the Virgin said to them in that field. The result? The number of practicing, believing Catholics in Portugal grew tenfold. The entire society there is now inextricably bound up by the church. No revolution ever occurred in Portugal. Instead, there is a counterrevolutionary movement, spearheaded by the extremely reactionary President Salazar. Six years ago, the bishops of Portugal consecrated their nation to the Immaculate Heart of Mary. They want to consecrate our nation to this so-called Mother of God as well, because three children in a field told them that the Virgin Mary said they must consecrate Russia, or we will harm the world. They believe all this in Portugal, according to my informants. And why? Because of three children. Three children. Do any of you see the significance of that?"

"What do you mean, Secretary General?" the politburo leader finally asked. He was a small bald man who never appeared without a military uniform of some sort.

"It all begins in early childhood. Don't you see?" Stalin asked. "Surely you have the intelligence and foresight to share this new vision?"

Again, he was answered by silence. Stalin felt too inspired to become irritated. The thoughts were filling his mind quickly. He hoped he could say it all before one detail got lost in the flood of ideas.

"We will train all of our youth, starting at a very young age, to despise the church and believe in the party and the state. And we will send our agents to the seminaries, and they will become priests and then bishops and cardinals. We will mold the Roman Catholic Church from within to make it a tool for the state. And then we will systematically destroy it. It could take years, but the church would be infiltrated at the highest levels. We will train young children as agents to be priests and teach them to commit heinous acts that would repulse the masses, discredit the church, and destroy it. I will destroy the church from within.

"These agents must be specially chosen and trained from childhood. Because childhood is the key to this, and by *childhood*, I mean specifically the fears of childhood. These agents should be trained from very early in their lives to fear and despise the Catholics. And they must be equipped with the will and the means to act upon that fear, to willingly annihilate in the name of that fear."

"How would we place these agents within the Catholic priesthood?" asked the politburo leader after a moment of hesitation. He was the bold one, it seemed.

"That is the beauty of this plan." Stalin beamed. "They would present themselves to the local clerics as young men who are ready to dedicate their lives to the priesthood. They would be ready to pass any test of scriptural knowledge and make any pledge of faith necessary. They would convince the bishops and the church at large of their faith and their holy calling to be priests. They would attend the seminary and excel. They would keep their vows as priests and seem to serve God and the church, but all the while, they would secretly serve the state."

He smiled and looked to the others for agreement. Their heads began to nod, slowly at first, and several of the men smiled as they nodded to show their agreement. Someone had to speak, and the responsibility fell to the leader of the politburo.

"What sort of child would you select for this project, Secretary General?"

Stalin took a long time to seriously consider the question.

9

1939

On August 23, 1939, the Germans and the Russians signed the Nazi-Soviet Nonaggression Pact. Adolf Hitler would use the pact to clear the way for his invasion of Poland.

Only one week later, on the night of August 31, a group of German agents dressed in Polish military uniforms staged an attack on and takeover of a German radio station in Gleiwitz. From that station, they broadcasted a brief anti-German statement in Polish. A well-known Polish sympathizer was murdered with a lethal injection, dressed in a Polish military uniform, riddled with bullets, and left at the radio station as proof of the attack.

Less than six hours later, on the first day of September, explosions rocked the Polish people in the early morning hours, signaling the beginning of not just a second world war but also decades of foreign oppression. Hitler, claiming he was responding to Polish attacks, called it the 1939 Defensive War, and he sent in his armies. The Polish people were not in any way prepared to defend their nation or even their homes. In the ensuing battle, it was not unusual to find Polish soldiers armed with swords on horseback, facing oncoming German tanks.

The Nazi forces poured into Poland and proceeded to devour the nation.

Bombs took out entire buildings. Everybody ran for cover all over Warsaw. Black smoke and deafening noises filled the air. Not far behind came tanks and orderly rows of marching soldiers.

A six-year-old boy fixed a steady gaze upon the crucifix that hung over the fireplace. His mother knelt beside him, praying the rosary.

"Rolf, stare at the crucifix, and repeat the Hail Mary," his father told him.

"I just did," the boy said.

The whole house shook from the bombs. The fighting in the street was frighteningly close.

"Keep praying, Rolf."

Rolf's family huddled together in the front room. Rolf's mother, father, and two older sisters were praying.

"I don't want to die," one of his sisters said.

"Hush," his mother said, stroking her hair. She turned to the other sister, who was covering her face as she sobbed against her mother's shoulder.

Rolf didn't know which was worse—the din from their sobbing or the loud booms from the bombs.

"Look on the cross, and say your prayers," his father told them.

That was what Rolf did. In between Hail Marys, he concentrated on the cross so hard that he could see the individual thorns on the crown worn by Jesus. He could count them one by one.

"One. Two. Three ..."

The cross on the wall began to tremble. Then the walls started to shake, and a deafening noise louder than thunder took away the cross, the fireplace, and that entire side of the house.

Rolf was blinded by the dust and could not move. He tried to catch his breath. Through the dust, Rolf saw a black boot in the stone. Then soldiers with powerful guns came through the hole where the fireplace had once stood, kicking aside huge pieces of rubble that used to be the living room wall.

Rolf saw his mother and sisters running for the back door, and then his father grabbed him and threw him over his shoulder. Rolf was confused and crying, but he could still see his mother and sisters up ahead as his father ran for the fence.

Once Rolf was over the fence, his feet hit the ground running with his entire family, along with many of his neighbors, all running toward the church on the corner. Rolf saw his best friend, Boris, crying loudly, still being carried by his father, and he could hear Father Perum yelling for them to come to the side of the church.

"You will be safe here," he said. "They won't dare come into the house of God."

Rolf tried to keep up, but as his parents and sisters ran past the priest into the stairwell leading to the church basement, he tripped and fell to the floor. When he heard the heavy boots of the soldiers behind him, he scrambled to the corner to hide behind the door to the parish entry.

Suddenly, two storm troopers arrived at the top of the steps, where Father Perum blocked their entry.

"Get out of our way," one of them said to the priest.

"I don't stand alone in your way," Father Perum said to the German soldiers. "Christ stands with me. You will not bring your destruction into the house of the Lord."

The first soldier shot the priest without hesitation. The priest fell to the floor right in front of where Rolf was curled behind the door. The priest's blood ran onto the floor as Father Perum stared into Rolf's eyes. As the priest started to reach for Rolf, he died. The storm troopers stomped over his body in their shiny black boots.

Rolf trembled but did not make a sound. He curled into a tighter ball behind the door and covered his ears as agonized screams and gunshots came from the basement. Then, suddenly, quiet came. Soon the boots tromped past where he lay hidden and out the door.

Rolf lay as still as he could to be sure the Germans were gone. Then he scooted around the body of his priest, rose from the cold stone floor, and stumbled down the dimly lit stone stairs to the basement. As his eyes adjusted to the dust and darkness of the room, he saw the bodies of his mother, father, sisters, and neighbors, as well as many of the people from weekly Mass. Some of the dead were staring in frozen astonishment at the horror that had ended their lives. Others had fallen facedown into pools of their own blood.

His mother still clutched a crucifix in her hand. Her face was angelic, and her eyes were open. Rolf was certain she was still full of life. He scrambled over the body of his friend's father, and when he reached his mother, she lifted the crucifix toward Rolf for a brief moment and then slumped to the floor. He knelt to kiss her cheek and put his arms around her. For hours, he held her and sobbed and shivered. She never moved again.

Everyone Rolf had ever loved was dead.

10

1941: THE NEW YOUNG PIONEERS

Returning from a predawn reconnaissance of the surrounding hills, a Soviet *starshina*, or sergeant major, tilted his head to the early morning October sky. The low roar of the planes announced the Luftwaffe flying over the Soviet army camp outside of Leningrad.

Hitler had issued Directive Number 1601, ordering that Leningrad be erased from the face of the earth. The lives of civilians were not to be spared. The great Russian city had been bombarded and completely cut off from food, supplies, and any potential help. Starvation competed with Luftwaffe bombings to be the main cause of death among civilians. Unable to help in any way, Stalin had issued a statement calling the situation hopeless.

Dmitri Volgonov ran back toward the camp to assemble his men. He quickly scaled the small hill and took a shortcut through the undergrowth. When he reached the top, near the trail, he ran along nearly flat ground. However, his left foot became entangled in a root, causing him to tumble down a bank. He managed to roll over to a protective rock outcropping just as the air attack started and the German bombs made a direct hit on the encampment. Although he was still a half mile away from the camp, he could see the tents on fire and hear the screams of his men engulfed in flames.

Dmitri knew from his training that it would be his responsibility to execute the surviving men to ensure they did not fall into the hands of the Germans. Protecting the secrets of their mission was the foremost imperative that every noncommissioned officer was taught at the military academy in Tula. He'd been an excellent student.

By the time Dmitri reached the camp, the sounds of the wounded had quieted but for one young soldier whom he knew as Lestak. Lestak had been gored by shrapnel, and although he was still able to weakly grip Dmitri's coat as Dmitri checked the young man's pulse, his gurgled breath signaled that he was close to death. Dmitri stepped back, pulled his weapon, and, without hesitation, shot the boy between the eyes.

One by one, Dmitri checked the other soldiers, and after ascertaining that they were all dead, he started collecting provisions and weapons that had made it through the bombing.

His hands shook as he dumped his kit bag onto the ground. He would leave behind anything that didn't contribute to survival. He filled a large backpack with as many tins of food, canteens, and blankets as he could find. Then he took up the mission on his own, marching along the path that the NKVD, the Russian security agency, had charted.

The mission of the unit became the mission of its sole surviving Russian officer that day. It involved finding a remote Soviet weapons depot and guarding it against the encroaching forces of the Wehrmacht. Dmitri did not once doubt that he alone could fortify an ammunition depot against the German army. He simply moved forward, ever alert to any discovery along the way that could enhance his chances.

For three days, he doggedly followed the course, surviving on drops of water, small portions of canned food, and inner discipline. Then he saw something that would change the course of his mission.

The fire was low, but it was a fire nonetheless. A small girl tended to it, squatting down in the dirt. She was with another girl and six other boys. They appeared to be from ages eight to fourteen.

Dmitri hadn't moved, but the youngest girl saw him. As if they were one unit, all the children rose and ran to him.

"Please help," the smallest one said.

"We don't know where the others are," one boy said.

"Please. They bombed us. We have no food!"

They spoke all at once.

"Stop talking," Dmitri said. At the sound of Dmitri's low and firm voice, the young children stopped speaking and stood quietly. "If you follow me and do what I tell you, you will be saved and make a great contribution." He bent down to speak to the oldest boy. "How would you all like to be part of a great adventure?"

The children nodded hesitantly. He then reached into his backpack and offered them each a morsel of food and a sip of water just to seal the deal.

The oldest boy stole a glance inside Dmitri's kit and could not resist trying to steal more food. Dmitri caught him and quickly punished the boy with a fast, powerful blow to the head. The boy fell to the ground and didn't move.

"We'll have to leave him behind. Let's go," Dmitri said as he gathered his backpack and started to march on. The remaining children were scared but in need of this adult's help, so they followed Dmitri single file without a backward glance at the fallen boy.

A short time later, Dmitri heard fast footsteps behind him. He tried not to smile before he turned around.

"I'll do whatever you say," the boy said, catching his breath. "I can help with the others. I'm the oldest."

Dmitri looked at the earnest face of the boy. "I accept," he said. "What's your name?"

"Soren," the boy replied.

"Soren, follow me," Dmitri said, nodding.

Dmitri and his army of children covered as much ground as was humanly possible. Dmitri doled out miniscule portions of food and water and issued each child a blanket. Each night, they slept on the ground. On the third day, Dmitri shot a rabbit and taught the children how to skin it, start a fire, and cook it. The portions were small, but Dmitri made certain each child got an equal portion.

By the fifth day, the children were acting, marching, and thinking like soldiers without arms. Soren used military drill jargon to keep them in line. Dmitri saw to it that they maintained the necessary pace to enable them to arrive at their destination.

The ammunition depot was dug into the side of a hill, just as Dmitri had been instructed in his orders. There was no evidence that the Germans had found the depot, but there was also no evidence of the Russian army. Dmitri didn't know why, but he knew he had to follow orders.

The padlock on the door was rusted shut. Dmitri shot the lock with his rifle and exposed to the children a storage vault full of rifles, grenades, automatics, antiaircraft cannon rounds, handguns, bayonets, other assorted ammunition, and much-needed rations. Dmitri noticed large containers labeled "Gas" in the back of the vault and wondered what use he could make of the gasoline without a vehicle.

Then he sat them down on the ground in a circle and explained the importance of the weapons and the mission they were there to complete.

"These weapons belong to Mother Russia," he told them. "They do not belong to us. Even though I will soon issue each of you one or two of these weapons and teach you to use them and care for them, they must eventually be returned to our government. We are here to guard these weapons with our lives. German soldiers will soon be coming for them. Our job is to kill those soldiers before they can get these weapons. It is our job to stay alive and protect them. I will show you how that is done. If the Germans get their hands on these weapons, it will be because every last one of us is dead. Do you understand?"

He waited a moment for the children to nod, and soon they all did.

"Do you also understand that if any of you allows a German soldier to touch any of these weapons, I will kill you myself?"

After a long stillness, Soren led the other children in nodding.

Almost as if to reward the children for their grim-faced understanding, Dmitri chose that moment to dole out a small but equal share of food and water to each one of them.

Dmitri took as much advantage as he could of the short time left before the dreaded arrival of winter. He kept them active during the days with target practice and exercises, campfire building, scavenging for food and water, gun-cleaning drills, and war games. They spent their nights around the campfire, with the children listening to Dmitri tell inspirational stories of the heroes of the revolution. Dmitri and the children took turns keeping night watch.

As soon as the first flock of geese flew over and Dmitri shot one, the children became more interested in learning to shoot so they could share fresh meat instead of the tasteless rations. The cooked goose served as an incentive against their fear and their hunger. Once Soren shot and killed a lone deer, the interest in shooting and caring for the guns rose to new levels. Target practice took on a new importance, and Dmitri helped all the children become excellent marksmen.

However, the threat of winter was no small thing. Dmitri knew the brutal Russian winter would eliminate most of the wild game, curtail most of their activities, seriously challenge the strained food and water supplies, and most likely kill some of the children. His hope was that they would be engaged in combat of some sort sooner rather than later.

Their first encounter occurred at the end of their second month at the depot. While on lookout, Soren spotted a lost patrol of ten German soldiers. Dmitri quickly gathered the children, and they all took their weapons to the high rocks. As the German soldiers came close to the camouflaged weapons depot, they expressed an unhealthy curiosity about it and moved in to check it out.

"Fire," Dmitri said in a calm, quiet tone of voice. Immediately, Dmitri and the children opened fire on the Germans below. Before the unwary soldiers could even raise their guns, they were all down.

"I don't know of any unit of grown soldiers who could have done better," Dmitri said to the children, filling them with immense pride. "Let me go down first. Then, when I signal, you follow at a distance."

One of the boys, Ivan, said, "Let's see what the soldiers brought us today!" He bolted down the rocks toward the soldiers.

The sharp report of a gunshot told them what happened next. Dmitri watched Ivan's body jerk once. One of the soldiers was still alive and had shot the boy. Dmitri walked down the slope. He killed the man instantly and made certain the other soldiers were dead.

He nodded. The children searched the Germans' pockets while Dmitri went through the kit bags.

As he rolled over one of the Germans, they found a generator strapped into a satchel carried on the back of the soldier.

Dmitri smiled at this find, as now they could put the storage of gas in the vault to use without signaling that they were there. This generator would be a great help against the oncoming cold. Except for the loss of Ivan, the arrival of the invaders was a blessing. Dmitri surveyed the pile, looking for food, weapons, tools, warm clothes, blankets, and any other personal effects that could be of any use whatsoever.

Dmitri saw that several of the younger children were sobbing, and all of them stared silently at Ivan's body. He knew they were horrified at having seen death so intimately for the first time, and he was prepared for the possibility that some of the children might try to desert or simply give up hope within their camp. He needed all of them to stay focused on their mission.

"Soldiers!" Dmitri yelled. "We must gather to honor our fallen friend's courage." Dmitri bellowed assertively to shift the kids' attention from Ivan's body to his voice. "Soren and Oleg, you will dig a grave three feet deep for our fallen friend, and the rest of you must go gather large stones to mark his grave. Go now!" Dmitri barked, pointing to the rocky hill they had just scrambled down. "If each of you has not provided at least two stones in the next thirty minutes, all of you will be denied dinner."

Dmitri knew that all the children but Mariska would have the strength to climb back up the hill to retrieve the stones. He knew by the sound of her cough, which had worsened over the last three days, she was weakening.

"Mariska, you stay with me so we can prepare the funeral," Dmitri said soothingly as he put his hand out to her. "Come. We will ready the food and open that dead German's vodka so we can all toast our comrade."

Dmitri saw Mariska look back up the hill at the others. She rubbed her eyes with the back of her arm and then stepped forward to take his hand.

"Mariska," Dmitri whispered, "I know you are scared, but soldiers must confront their fears, and you will feel better when you have completed your next task."

"What may I do to prove that I am brave, sir?" Mariska whispered back. "I know I am not as strong as the others, but I've learned to shoot like you taught, and I am a good lookout."

"Go retrieve one of the blankets from inside, and we will wrap Ivan's body. We will drag Ivan's body with the blanket and place him in the hole when they are done." Dmitri turned abruptly and yelled, "Soren! Oleg! You are digging too slowly! You must finish before the others return with the rocks. We are bringing the body very soon."

Mariska brought a blanket to Dmitri, and he took her hand to walk her to Ivan's body. Just as Mariska started to tremble, Dmitri jerked her down toward Ivan's body, placing both their hands on his wound.

"Mariska, you must feel the blood of your fallen comrade. You must rub his blood on your face as a symbol of a soldier and to show the others you are brave," Dmitri said as he rubbed the blood between his palms and then rubbed Ivan's blood on his own face.

Slowly, Mariska rubbed her palms together, mimicking Dmitri, and then she placed both hands on her face as she took a deep breath. "I honor you, my dear friend, and I'll show the others that I am brave to wear the blood of our friend who shed it." Mariska looked up at Dmitri as if in a trance.

Dmitri stretched the blanket out next to Ivan's body. Mariska immediately bent to pick up Ivan's feet as Dmitri lifted him under the arms. The two dragged him onto the blanket and then rolled his body to the left until the blanket covered him like a cocoon. Then they carried his body to the hole being dug by Soren and Oleg.

"Mariska, it will be your job to instruct the others on the placement of the stones in the grave. It will be your decision who goes first, then second, and so on until all the stones are placed. You must be the first to speak about the bravery of our fallen friend, and you will make sure each of the others honors him with the placement of each stone," Dmitri said as he walked to the edge of the pit.

"Sir, we have the hole at three feet," Soren said as he breathed hard from the constant digging. He wiped his forehead with his right hand, and Dmitri noticed the blood left by the boy's bleeding palm.

"Three feet is fine, Soren," Dmitri said. "You and Oleg have done well. Now help Mariska and me bring the body to your hole."

Soren and Oleg jumped out of the hole, and seeing Mariska's face covered in blood, they both froze in place at the edge. They looked at Dmitri and then back at Mariska, not able to speak but frightened that she had been hurt by Dmitri.

"Comrades, do not be afraid of the blood Mariska wears. She has shown her bravery and honor by wearing the blood of our fallen comrade." Dmitri stood erect and then bowed toward Mariska, who dropped her end of Ivan's body and walked directly to where Soren and Oleg stood.

"I have proven my bravery now, Soren. I know you think I am weaker than you, and you did not think I was brave, but I touched Ivan's wound and put his blood on my face for strength," Mariska said as she pulled her hair back to show her face. "The two of you must come help me with Ivan's body to put it in your hole. The others are coming down the hill now with their stones, and I must instruct them on the order of placement."

As Soren, Oleg, and Mariska were pulling Ivan's body into the hole, Dmitri went to meet several of the children who were rolling larger rocks down the hill.

"You have figured out a very clever way to get these rocks down. Now you must work together to carry them over to the grave. Take your rocks to Mariska, and wait for her instructions." Dmitri pointed toward the hole that the body had already been rolled into.

One by one, the children came down the hill, bringing their rocks. Some dragged the rocks behind them wrapped in their jackets, and others rolled them down, as the other two had done. Dmitri instructed them to get the stones to the hole and await Mariska's direction. It was just getting to be dusk as the last of the children walked to the hole. None of the children spoke as they awaited Mariska's instructions, but they stared at the hole where the wrapped body lay. One of Ivan's shoes had fallen off as he had been rolled into the hole, and seeing the shoe reminded them that it was their friend who had been shot.

"We are all gathered here to talk about our courageous comrade." Mariska's voice was strong and fluid as she addressed them. "We must each tell a story about our brave comrade Ivan, who gave his life for Mother Russia, and when I tell you it is your turn, you must first roll your stones onto his body and then throw dirt on top of him. You are not to cry, and we will all cheer and clap after each person speaks."

Dmitri was impressed; Mariska firmly instructed the children, and she had created an entire ritual for each one to participate. He could see they were confused by her newfound authority as well as the blood on her face, but they seemed too exhausted to challenge her. They simply followed her instructions as she called on each one by name and insisted he or she tell a hero's story about Ivan.

That night at the campfire, Dmitri saw to it that they all took turns retelling the story of the Ivan's death. Each child added new details to the story, and each new detail became accepted as cherished fact. Each time the story was elaborated, the notion of a heroic and patriotic martyrdom became more pronounced. It was then, by the campfire, that Dmitri saw the children really come to life. Their eyes glowed in the firelight at the thought that one who had been among them had now become a hero. One among them had disappeared into legendary mythology.

Dmitri knew for certain he had trained a loyal fighting unit, and he wondered when the Russian army would arrive to retrieve the weapons and rescue his young band of soldiers.

But none came. They were tied up in battles elsewhere with the Germans.

OCCUPATION

Rolf, now ten years old, saw the German soldiers as he hid behind the garbage pile at the side of the public house. The half-eaten apple he saw at the edge of the trash pile behind the public house was tempting enough for him to get close enough to a group of soldiers that he could hear their conversation.

Jews were hunted down, lined up, and executed in the streets. In 1943, the remaining Jews in Warsaw fought back against the Germans in the Warsaw Ghetto Uprising, the first mass rebellion against the German occupation of Europe. After that, the Germans demolished the Warsaw ghetto block by block with fire and bombs, killing fifty-six thousand people in a matter of a few days.

The Germans were confident they had the run of the city, and anything they wanted, they took. Those who stood in their way were killed.

On that night, four German storm troopers drank beer on the back porch of a Warsaw public house. Rolf watched as a frightened waitress brought them four fresh mugs of frothy beer. One of the storm troopers pointed his gun at her.

"Just keep it coming," the German soldier said.

The waitress shook so much she almost dropped the tray of beers, but she awkwardly recovered herself. With trembling hands, she served the beer. As she did, each storm trooper touched her body with his hands. She quickly ran back inside. The soldiers all roared with the loud, raucous laughter of wild young men who'd had too much to drink.

One German soldier suddenly stiffened, and Rolf froze.

"Did you hear something?" the soldier asked the man next to him.

"Just relax," the other man said with a wave of his hand.

"Something moved over there," the nervous soldier said, pointing into the darkness behind them. "I heard somebody go through that." He pointed to the crack in the wall of the public house. The other soldiers laughed at him.

"I said relax," the other man said. "This entire country is ours to enjoy. This is the safest place a German could be. What are you afraid of? Polish waitresses?"

All the soldiers had a good laugh at that.

After quietly retrieving the apple, Rolf stuffed it into the pocket of the gray coat he had stolen from a drunken soldier the night before, and then he crawled through the crack in the wall and made his way to a tunnel that connected the public house to the old public library.

By the light of a stolen military flashlight, the boy grabbed a thick book off the shelf, scrambled up the remaining stairs to the top floor, and climbed a bookcase to reach the rafters. The book, one he often chose to take with him to the rafters, was like one his mother had once read to him. She had originally told him about the Knights of the Round Table. He had memorized all the stories when his mother read them to him. When he'd found that book in the library, he'd recognized the pictures. Rolf read every night up in the rafters, and that book had helped him learn to read at a higher level. He had now read it hundreds of times. He dozed off, soothed by the story.

The sound of a nearby machine gun jerked Rolf awake. The sudden noise almost made him fall and drop his book, so he gripped the rafter with both legs. He steadied himself as he saw the back door kicked in by two of the storm troopers he had seen drinking beer in the public house the night before.

Rolf knew his secret hiding place of three years had been found and would no longer be safe.

Rolf slowly moved off the rafter to the top of the bookcase and then to the floor. He peered through a knothole to the ground floor below him. The two storm troopers had dragged the Polish waitress into the deserted library. He watched as they savagely tore off her clothes and shouted vile-sounding German words at her.

Rolf squeezed his eyes shut, but the sounds of the troopers beating the waitress were only eclipsed by the sounds of them taking turns raping her. The screams of the waitress drowned out any thoughts Rolf had of moving, and he knew if he tried to do anything to stop the Germans, they'd kill him. Over the previous three years, he had stayed still and quiet through many such moments, and he had seen other German soldiers do unspeakable things to anyone they wanted. Rolf knew the assault would eventually end, perhaps with the death of the waitress, and they would eventually go away.

Once the laughter and grunting of the soldiers stopped, Rolf heard them ask her demanding questions in German. He understood enough German by now to know that the waitress would not be able to satisfy their questions. Rolf looked down. The waitress would not look at or speak to the soldiers; she just huddled in the corner and wept. Rolf closed his eyes when he heard the loud echo of a gunshot, and then he looked down as the soldiers dragged the waitress's body outside. He could see the face of the woman, now completely at peace, and he remembered the face of his mother in the basement the night his family died.

Rolf muffled a sob and gripped the book he had taken with him to the rafters. After taking a deep breath and wiping the tears from his eyes, he opened the book in the middle, where the colored pictures of the knights were still clear enough for him to read the titles with his stolen flashlight. Through his tears, he read a caption under a picture of a knight named King Arthur: "Knights, brothers in arms, your courage has been tested beyond limits."

Rolf repeated that sentence over and over until the image of his dead mother faded, and the sound of his father's voice telling him to pray faded away as the storybook took him to another world, a world where the strong protected the weak. Rolf wished the German soldiers were part of his book so they would be killed by one of the knights. While the boy identified with the brave knights in the book, he knew he could never be one of them. He'd been too afraid of the soldiers to help the waitress.

That night, hunger made Rolf brave enough to emerge from hiding again. He swung down from the rafters and landed on the highest bookshelf, balancing for a moment to adjust to the darkness. This time, he could leave through the front door since the soldiers had blown it down with their gunshots. Rolf listened for the sound of soldiers when he reached the opening, and he wondered if his hiding place would be safe when he returned.

12

RUSSIAN WINTERS

Dmitri and his young soldiers took turns keeping watch outside, looking for intruders.

He heard a quick, high whistle like that of a bird.

Dmitri looked at Mariska, who was gesturing frantically. He quietly took the binoculars and crept toward the end of the depot. Raising his glasses, he could see four German soldiers slogging through the ravine single file.

"*Poydem*," he said through the door. "Take your positions."

He didn't have to tell them twice. He watched with pride as the boys and girls grabbed weapons and fanned out into the woods around the depot.

They had drilled for this exact scenario. The four German soldiers didn't stand a chance and were killed with a minimum of gunfire. Dmitri and the children stripped them and pushed the bodies farther down into the ravine.

They took the loot back with them to the weapons depot, where they were camping for the winter. They were warmed by the heat given off by the gas generator retrieved from the dead Germans, as well as their own body heat. They fed on the food they had hunted, gathered, and foraged and rationed supplies. The depot was reinforced, so they were also safe from the bombing runs that terrorized Leningrad. They were better off than those in Leningrad; the Nazis had cut off all supplies, and people were starving.

The Soviets finally broke the Leningrad blockade in January 1943 with Operation Iskra. It would be another full year before the nine-hundred-day Siege of Leningrad would end after a joint effort by the Soviet army and the Baltic Fleet.

By January, Dmitri, Soren, Anton, and Viktor were the only survivors left. Mariska had died a painful, lingering death from pneumonia, and Yeva had followed shortly after. Dmitri had consoled the children by offering them extra rations.

One day in mid-January, Anton rushed into the depot. "New unicorns!" he said.

Dmitri stood up. "What? Make sense, boy!" He had little patience for Anton's inability to find the right word when he needed it most.

Anton took a breath. "New uniforms!" he said. He frantically pulled at his knees, making it look as if the pants ballooned out.

"This is good," Dmitri said, recognizing the description. "The others are finally here, and we can show them how well we guarded the depot." He called the children, and they went outside to greet the NKVD.

Every single weapon, item of artillery, and piece of ammunition in the inventory was present, freshly cleaned, and in excellent working order, less what they'd needed to defend the depot. Not one German soldier had touched any of those weapons. Children had given their lives defending the Soviet arsenal.

However, Dmitri didn't get the reward he expected. The NKVD officials made the three children wards of the state and enrolled them in a prestigious school in Moscow.

They arrested Dmitri.

Dmitri was brought before a tribunal that pronounced him an enemy of the Soviet state. He stood before his judges: four men and a woman. The portly woman with short gray hair sat at the front of the room behind a wooden table. She led the questioning as the head of the tribunal.

"Do you have anything to say?" she asked. "Any apology to make for your crimes?"

"Name the crime against the state of which I stand accused," Dmitri said.

"Insubordination. You were ordered to report to duty elsewhere, and you stayed with the depot."

"I couldn't let it fall into enemy hands," he said. "Surely that—"

"Your question was answered; the time for you to speak has passed," she said.

Dmitri was sentenced to twenty years in the Vorkuta gulag.

Shortly after beginning his prison sentence, Dmitri discovered he was not the only casualty of the Leningrad Siege sentenced to the Vorkuta gulag, just one of hundreds of similar labor camps. Many other soldiers and adult civilians who had survived during the brutal siege suffered the same fate. Stalin made it clear that no outward display of self-sufficiency would go unpunished in his Soviet Union. Collectivism, not individualism, was the ideal and expected behavior of the Russian citizen.

<hr />

Dmitri watched impassively as two women fought against the brown stone of the unheated barracks. The smaller one had an advantage in that she was more savage, pulling the hair of the larger one out in clumps and pushing her head into the wall. Dmitri glanced up at the guards in the tower. They were watching the fight, doing nothing. The women were fighting over a single sock.

Dmitri walked around the edge of the barracks, away from the women and toward a bench. He was constantly watching his back—never knowing who was true friend or true foe—but Dmitri nevertheless began to build a small but effective group of allies. He did so with a sneaked piece of bread here and a small favor there—nothing big, but his method was effective. Dmitri had every reason to believe he was there for the rest of his life.

Just one year into his sentence, he was digging a piece of frozen ground with a pickax on one of his work details. It was brutal work, and Dmitri hated it. Two men in suits approached the site. Dmitri saw them but did not stop working. They'd beat him if he did. He was not that upset when they suddenly grabbed his arms and dragged him to a waiting car.

They threw him into the back seat and rolled down the windows.

"Where are we going?" he asked.

"Moscow," his driver said.

"Why?"

"You'll see," the driver said.

Skinny now and exhausted, Dmitri decided to enjoy the warmth of the car. He figured anywhere was better than the gulag.

Moscow was Dmitri's birthplace and where he had grown up as a young man. He had not expected to ever see Moscow again. When he first saw the city lights, he knew the war was over—the Germans had been defeated, the spoils had been collected, and Moscow now ruled half the world. Even though he was handcuffed, was escorted by guards, and had no idea what was ahead for him, he smiled. His war was won.

The five-hour trip by car from Kurvuta led to a military base, where his head was shaved, as was his beard. A man washed him down, clothes and all, with a high-powered hose, and then Dmitri was sent into a shower with soap. New clothing awaited him, and after two hours of sleep, he was put back in the car. The NKVD touring car delivered Dmitri and the guards to the Kremlin.

He was pushed into a holding cell and told to wait. Before long, Dmitri heard a man coming down the hallway. A baton clanged across the bars as the man stopped in front of the cell.

Secretary General Stalin himself stared at him from the other side. "Do you understand your mistake?" Stalin asked.

Dmitri didn't quite meet Stalin's eyes. "I understand, Secretary General." That answer, Dmitri had learned, would enable him to continue to live.

After a significant pause, Stalin asked him, "Do you understand the need for the precautions we must take?"

"Counterrevolutionary infiltrators," Dmitri answered. He saw Stalin's lip curl into a smile under the cover of his mustache. Dmitri felt as if his life hung in the balance, so he waited.

"How did you get those children to behave like trained soldiers?"

Dmitri took a deep breath and stifled a smile of his own, enormously proud that his wartime accomplishment had not gone unnoticed. "My training at the academy in Moscow and my experience teaching physical education and coaching teenagers in wrestling gave me the control I needed. Then, as a starshina, in the Red Army, I trained many young soldiers." The first part was true. He had trained at the academy. The rest were lies, but Dmitri hoped Stalin wouldn't know.

"Wrestling," Stalin said. "Amazing."

"I've always worked well with young people," Dmitri said frankly.

"How did you develop this ability?" Stalin asked. "At the academy?"

"As a child in Moscow. I excelled at team sports and track events."

"But many who excel do not have the ability to instruct children."

"I suppose I developed that particular talent in my childhood."

"How?" Stalin leaned forward on the bars.

"At age nine, I was the biggest boy in my age group."

"And you were put in charge of the other children?"

"Yes, Secretary General."

"So their progress and behavior became your responsibility."

"Yes. Exactly."

"If the other children misbehaved, you were punished. You learned how to make children behave."

"Very quickly."

"When did you become a soldier?"

"In 1940."

"What were your duties?"

"I was put in charge of supply and inventory."

"A waste of talent," Stalin said.

Dmitri didn't reply.

"When your regiment was wiped out, you proceeded with your orders on your own?" Stalin said.

"Yes."

"Where did you find the children?"

"They were stranded—part of an evacuation from Leningrad."

"And you became their commander?"

"As soon as I saw a group of children, I knew I could make them a platoon."

"I wonder if you know what you've just committed yourself to."

"I live to serve," Dmitri said.

"What are your feelings about the Catholic church?" Stalin asked.

"I have no use for it, Secretary General."

"You harbor no secret longing for the sacraments?"

"None whatsoever."

"Why not? After all, many Russians believe in God and the church." Stalin said.

"Foolish fairy tales for sheep. Where was this God during the Siege of Leningrad?" answered Dmitri.

Stalin stepped forward and pushed his right hand through the bars toward Dmitri. Unsure what that meant, Dmitri stepped slightly forward as well. When it became apparent that Dmitri was quite a bit taller than Stalin, he tried to stand in a slouching position to lessen the visual impact of their contrasting heights.

What is this? Dmitri wondered. After a moment, he clasped Stalin's hand in his with as much dignity as the cuffs would allow.

"You will go right to work," Stalin promised him.

Dmitri hoped his work wouldn't be at the gulag. "What are my duties, Secretary General?"

"You will train undercover agents for the NKVD," Stalin informed him.

Dmitri nodded, anxious to hear more. He didn't have to wait. Stalin told him more of his grand plan.

"I too, Dmitri, have no use for the church. They fill people's heads with fear of some God that doesn't exist, all the while growing rich and powerful while the people suffer. Now, Dmitri, the state and Mother Russia will change that for the benefit of all the people. We sit, you and I, on the precipice of a new world order. We must win the acceptance of the masses for our great new society, which will benefit the workers, not the proletariat and the church! Now that we have the Germans in retreat, the only real threat to us in Europe is the Catholic church. In twenty years of attempting to purge our world of the church, I have learned one thing: unless you pluck the priests from the ground by their very roots, they will grow back every time. Burn any church, and watch another one spring up from its ashes. The church has survived armies and conquerors throughout history. The only way we can truly eliminate the church is to destroy it from within."

Dmitri took note of a sudden glow in Stalin's eyes that reflected a determination so fierce as to make his words sound like the truth, not just a threat.

"I want you to train an army of loyal Russians to enter the priesthood. On my orders, they will work to change the church and make it a tool for the state and then commit other insidious acts that will crumble their followers' faith. The church will lose all credibility and be seen as the enemy of the people, and Mother Russia will become the savior."

13

1944

Shifting in his chair to pat the pockets of his cassock, Father Carrera wondered for the umpteenth time where his glasses were.

The knock on the door startled him just a little, and his cane clattered to the floor. "Come in."

"Father Carrera, you have a letter from the bishop," Sister Elena said from the doorway. "It says it's important and confidential."

"Just a moment, Sister. I do not move so quickly anymore." Father Carrera chuckled as he retrieved his cane and, with some difficulty, hobbled to the door. "Please come in, and help me find my glasses."

Thank God for Sister Elena's assistance, Father Carrera thought. She had taken over his daily duties at the orphanage seven years ago, after he had taken a serious and almost fatal fall while riding Quieto at the Festival National. He had broken both legs and ruptured a disc in his back. Although the broken legs had healed, his back would never be the same, and arthritis had set in after the trauma. He now walked with a cane.

Sister Elena looked at the tidy desk and then back to Father Carrera. "Here they are!" Sister Elena smiled.

Father Carrera turned to her. "Where? I couldn't find—"

She smiled and pointed to the top of her head. When Father Carrera touched his head, he found his glasses.

"I just don't know what I would do without your help these days." Father Carrera sighed. "I do know the Lord protects and keeps us, but sometimes I long for my youth."

"Don't we all?" Sister Elena smiled.

Carrera shuffled to his chair and put his cane to the side as he motioned Sister Elena to his desk. "Please read the post for me. The bishop usually seals his posts with wax, so you will need the letter opener in the top drawer."

She retrieved the letter opener. "Are you sure it is all right for me to read a confidential message from the bishop?" Sister Elena fumbled with the letter opener, carefully slicing the top of the envelope. She looked serious. "I do not desire to intrude on a private message of such importance."

And this is why you shall read it to me, Father Carrera thought. *I could not hope for a more trustworthy assistant.* "Sister, what possibly could the bishop have to say? Please read, as my curiosity is beginning to make my nose itch."

He was happy to see her laugh, and he settled back into his chair as she unfolded the letter.

"'My dear friend and faithful servant, Father Carrera.'" Sister Elena cleared her throat. "'You are needed for a private meeting in Spain at the convent of the Sisters of Saint Dorothy. I know you have not traveled for some time, but this is very important, and you must leave immediately.'" Sister Elena pulled another document from the envelope, looked up, and handed the find to Father Carrera. "Father, it is a train ticket to Tuy. Tuy is on the northern border of Spain. Such a long journey for you."

Spain? Why would he send me to Spain? I don't travel the way I used to, but if someone is in trouble, I want to help, Father Carrera thought. "Bishop da Silva would not summon me to travel so far without serious consideration. What else does he say in the letter, Sister?"

"'Do not be concerned about your daily duties. I am sending Father Alphonso to assist at the orphanage, and Sister Elena will make sure he follows your protocols.'" Sister Elena blushed when she read her own name in the bishop's post. "'You will receive further instructions once you arrive at Saint Dorothy's. May God bless your journey.'"

"That's it? No mention of what I am to do once I arrive in Spain but to go to a convent?" Father Carrera lifted himself slowly from his chair and motioned to Sister Elena to bring him the letter. She handed it to him.

Reading the letter himself, Father Carrera wondered why Bishop da Silva of Leiria had suddenly and mysteriously relieved him of his duties at the orphanage and ordered him to travel to an obscure Spanish convent. "Well, I must admit that it's been too long since I had a good adventure, so let's get me packed for the train trip." He laughed, handing the letter back to Sister Elena.

MYSTERIES

The four-day train journey was difficult for Father Carrera, and although the bishop had provided a private berth in which he could sleep, sleeping on the hard bed, which was no more than a cot, magnified the pain of his arthritis. He asked the conductor for assistance to traverse the stairs from the train car to the platform when they arrived in Tuy.

"Thank you, young man, for your help," Father Carrera said as he handed the engineer forty lire.

"Father, I do not require money for my help to you. I ask only that you pray for my wife and our baby that will be here soon—by the grace of God."

"Well then, young man, may God bless you with the gift of a perfectly healthy child, and through you, may your child be led in the ways of our faith." Father Carrera placed his hand on the young man's head and looked directly in his eyes before he made the sign of the cross. "Now, point me in the direction of the Sisters of Saint Dorothy convent. I have work to do, and you need to get back on the train to get the conductor to his next stop." Father Carrera chuckled despite his aches, and the young man crossed himself and jumped back on the train.

As he shuffled toward the train station, a nun approached and reached for his satchel. "Father Carrera? Excuse me. Father Carrera? I am Sister Angelia from Saint Dorothy's. Come with me, please. I have a wagon waiting."

It was a short but bumpy ride to the convent, and Father Carrera was grateful he did not have to walk. As if she had seen them approach, the prioress opened the heavy wooden door and stared at him. She was dressed in black, her veil a long black scarf with a strip of white around her face, covering her ears and neck. Without a word, she motioned him to follow her, tucking her hands in the huge sleeves of her tunic.

He walked slowly down an immaculately clean hallway with wooden floors. He was led to a small sitting room, where a dark-skinned nun dressed like the mother superior awaited him.

Father Carrera recognized her immediately. "Lucia!"

"You remember me. I am honored."

"How could anyone forget you? You changed the face of Portugal."

"Not I," she said. "It was Our Lady and her prophecies. Please sit down."

Though the mother superior had moved toward the doorway, Father Carrera could see she was still nearby with a watchful eye on Lucia. He sat down on the chair and smiled at Lucia. "Were it not for your courage, what would anyone know of these prophecies?"

"Were it not for your courage, what would anyone know of me?"

They sat in silent reflection for a moment.

"How much do you know of the three prophecies Our Lady gave me?" she asked him.

"They are secrets, no?"

"Yes," Lucia said. "The first two I wrote down."

"Yes, I heard something about that. Bishop da Silva insisted."

"I had pleurisy. He was afraid Our Lady's prophecies would die with me."

"Thank God you recovered."

"I still haven't written the third one."

"The first prophecy was the vision of hell you told me about the day we visited the Cova de Iria all those years ago?"

"Yes. In the vision, I saw a sea of fire and horrifying demons in human form. The vision lasted only a moment, but it was unforgettable."

"The second prophecy contained instructions for avoiding hell?"

"In the second prophecy, Our Lady predicted the current war. She also said that unless Russia is publicly consecrated to her Immaculate Heart by the pope and all the bishops of the world, the country will spread its evil across the world, annihilate nations, and persecute the church."

"I remember. I don't know why the Holy Father has not done this yet. And what of the third prophecy?"

Lucia's face showed slight consternation. "The third I have never been able to share with anyone in any way until now. It is simply too horrible. I cannot bring myself to say the words. Last year, Bishop da Silva made a special journey here to give me a formal order to write down the third secret. Still, I could not bring myself to do it. Then, last January, the Blessed Virgin appeared to me. She told me it was God's will that I reveal the third secret by the year 1960 at the very latest." She handed him a sealed envelope from inside her sleeve, and Father Carrera's hand trembled as he took it. "I forced myself to write down the entire terrifying prophecy. Bishop da Silva told me I can entrust you with it."

"Me?" Father Carrera was surprised and suddenly dropped the envelope onto the stone floor.

She calmly picked it up and handed it back to him. "When I was in danger, you were the only one with the single-minded courage to stand up for me," she said. "I was caught in the middle of a battle between nonbelievers and those desperate for miracles. Even my own father would not stand up for me. The people in the town started to protect me only because they thought I would bring glory to Fátima through these miracles."

"Which indeed you did," Father Carrera said.

"But you," she said. "You cared nothing about the opposing force of the mayor of Ourém. You only cared about the safety of the three children at risk, me and my two little cousins."

"What is it that you are entrusting me to do?"

"Take this envelope to the Vatican. Make sure the current pope and all succeeding popes read it and know of it. Guard it against all other eyes. Then, in the year 1960, Our Lady wishes for the pope to tell the world of these secret prophecies."

Father Carrera shook his head as she spoke, and his eyes opened wide. "I know of no one at the Vatican, and I am not fluent in the language of Italy."

"The language of the Vatican is Latin. You speak Latin."

Father Carrera shook his head. "But why would the bishop remove me from a position where I can help children to give me this courier service for which I am ill suited?"

"I will tell you something of the third secret, one of the most difficult parts for me to speak of. I am emboldened to do it because I know that once you have heard it, you will stop at nothing to protect the church and her children. That will allow you to accept my request." Lucia paused to fix her habit. "One of Our Lady's predictions in the third secret is that unless the proper steps are taken, Russia will spread her evil secretly into the church in the form of priests who answer not to God but to the Russian government. These so-called priests will be teaching our children and will commit unspeakable acts against them. The Holy Father will have much to suffer, and it will shake the very foundation of the church."

"Priests will harm children deliberately?" Father Carrera said, shaking his head slowly. Then, realizing what Lucia had described, he painfully whispered, "It cannot be true."

"Our Lady told me that unless certain precautions are taken by the Vatican and by the church hierarchy, many Catholic priests will attempt to subvert the true teachings of the church and make the church a tool of the Evil One."

"This cannot be so," said Father Carrera.

"Everything else Our Lady predicted has come true."

Father Carrera was silent for a moment as he tried to internalize this repugnant thought and hold his temper.

"Say it does come true," Father Carrera finally muttered. "What could I possibly do about it?"

"Carry this envelope to the Vatican. Show it to the pope and each succeeding pope and no one else. It contains specific instructions for avoiding this dreaded result. In 1960, Our Lady tells me, the world will be ready to understand her instructions, and there will still be time to act to avoid this ruinous outcome. You must make sure that in 1960, the pope makes a public pronouncement of this entire prophecy so that the necessary steps may be taken to save the children and the holy church."

"What if I die before 1960?"

"Use your judgment and your faith to lead you to another whom you can trust to carry on the work."

As Father Carrera blessed Sister Lucia and left with the envelope safely tucked away, he knew that his life would be forever changed by this meeting and that both his belief in the prophecies of Our Lady of Fátima and his dedication to helping children would be tested for at least the next sixteen years.

15

1945

Rolf had recorded each day he had hidden in the library by dog-earing one page of a book. He had started with the top of the page, and then he had continued with the lower edge. He now had seven of his favorite books lined up on the top shelf of the highest bookcase. He had practiced his math over and over, and his daily ritual was to count the books and multiply the number of pages by two. Today he counted 2,132 dog-ears. He pulled out another book to start a fresh count but traced his finger to the start of the stack to the first book he had dog-eared. The book was a children's book about farm animals that was mostly pictures, with some words describing their sounds and funny names for the animals. Rolf remembered staring at the pictures over and over to block the sounds in the street. He had gone back to that picture book at the end of every day when he felt safe, despite finding more challenging books to read. He'd taught himself to make use of dictionaries, encyclopedias, and foreign-language texts. In those six years, he'd read books on agriculture, geography, and philosophy and many of the great works of world literature. His favorite books were cookbooks that described ingredients he did not understand; oddly, reading them helped stave off his hunger.

Rolf left the safety of the library at night, when he would scavenge for food. A couple of months after the Germans had raped the waitress in the library, Rolf had decided he needed to find out if anyone from his parish was still alive. He couldn't remember all of the people in the basement the night his mother died. He had been terrified sneaking into his old neighborhood at dusk, not knowing whether he could move undetected, and he'd feared being captured by the Nazis if he wandered too far from his hiding place.

Rolf had seen nothing but destruction when he had slipped quietly through the city's blocks from the library to his old neighborhood. Many of the landmarks he remembered had been destroyed or damaged beyond repair. When he'd reached his family's block, he'd realized that although his own home had been bombed and was nothing but rubble, the shell of his uncle's house down the street still stood. Cautiously, he'd crawled to the open door and then through the house. He'd found no one there, nor had he seen or heard anyone else from his parish. No life was to be found anywhere in the neighborhood, so he'd returned to the library as the sun was rising and the Nazi soldiers were slowly waking from their prior night's drunken stupor.

It was winter of the sixth year when Rolf heard gunshots and bombs again. A new army had arrived, and they, like the Germans, had tanks, wore shiny black boots, and seemed horrifying.

After eight days, the loud booms of the gunfire stopped, and exhausted after keeping watch the whole time, Rolf crawled to the corner of the library and fell asleep. It was so cold in the library that his soft breath formed wisps of smoke as he slept.

Rolf's sleep was fitful, and he dreamed about the day when the parish priest's hands had reached for him at the top of the basement stairs. He woke himself with a scream, remembering the pool of blood that had oozed from the priest's head.

"Over there. Hurry. There's a boy over there."

Rolf jumped awake. Soldiers had come into the library, his hiding place for years. They had caught him by surprise—he had fallen asleep down on the floor, near a bookcase. He scrambled to the book stack with three soldiers running after him.

Rolf pushed hard on one of the tall book shelves, causing a row of the shelves to fall. The loud clatter of metal and books falling was deafening, and Rolf noted with satisfaction that a falling shelf knocked down one of the soldiers and pinned him underneath it. The other two soldiers tried to help their comrade by lifting the shelf, but the books fell everywhere, causing them to tumble as well.

Rolf made a run for the back door, but the remaining two soldiers heard his footsteps, found their footing, and came after him.

As Rolf looked back at the soldiers, he lost his footing as a pile of books shifted below him. This night would not end like the night in the church. These soldiers, he thought, would not take him so easily. He scrambled up, grabbing a broken chair leg, ready to defend himself.

The soldiers stopped in their tracks when they saw him. They saw a twelve-year-old gnome with long, stringy, matted hair and the eyes of an animal. He had survived for years by scavenging for food at night and hiding in various places, his favorite being the library, where he'd read books, starting with the easy ones and working his way up to more complicated texts. He wore layers of discarded German uniforms.

The soldiers started toward him, and Rolf threw the broken chair leg at them. He dropped to the floor and crawled like a lizard, scrambling around the corner of a book shelf, out of sight. He tried to slow his breathing. He hoped they would give up and leave, and he closed his eyes tightly.

When he dared to open them, he could see only the pressed uniform pants of the infantrymen.

"Is it human?" one of the soldiers asked.

"Not judging from the smell," the other one replied.

Rolf stood, looking quickly to the left and then the right. Both escape routes were blocked. What to do? He could not fall into their hands. He leaned back and then ran straight into one infantryman, who grabbed him. The boy bit his wrist.

The soldier screamed as Rolf drew blood.

The other soldier grabbed Rolf by the hair. "Little beast!"

Rolf whirled around, flashed his teeth, twisted away from the soldier, and ran in the other direction. The second infantryman tried to grab him, but Rolf twisted, grabbing a book from the shelf and throwing it at him.

Rolf started to run toward the door, but the sight of the soldier and the rifle made him freeze.

"Stop!"

The Russian soldier lowered his gun and approached him. Once he was close enough, Rolf ran into the soldier, springing up suddenly and ramming his head into the soldier's face. The soldier fell backward, and Rolf scrambled over him.

However, the other two were ready. With their combined strength, they brought Rolf down to the floor with a flying tackle. Rolf kicked, bit, scratched, and struggled furiously against the hold of the two soldiers.

"We are here to liberate you!" one of the soldiers said. "Not to hurt you!"

One of them put a wet rag over Rolf's nose. The sickly-sweet smell was the last thing he remembered as he lost consciousness.

16

STALIN'S BOY

The man in the white coat watched as the boy regained consciousness. Shackles held the boy's wrists and ankles, and he was lying on the floor of a padded room with one mirrored wall.

The boy struggled with all his remaining strength and screamed as loudly as his lungs would allow, but nothing changed.

Long after the boy had exhausted his voice and his strength, the man put on a surgical mask and opened the door.

"Can you understand what I'm saying?" the man asked. "Are you hungry?"

The boy nodded.

"Then you had better use words to tell me, or you may never eat again. What is your name?"

The boy turned his head away from the man and said nothing.

"You look, act, and smell like an animal. If I decide there is something wrong with you, you will be killed like an animal. And no one will know. I think under the circumstances that should encourage you to talk to me."

After a moment, the boy began to scream and yanked against the trusses with fury. The man just stood there and waited as the boy struggled to exhaustion.

"Nobody can hear you. And no one will come for you." With that, the man left.

He watched the boy fall asleep after trying to turn so that he could avoid the bright light on the ceiling. The boy finally rolled over onto his side so that at least one eye was shielded from the glare.

75

"That will not do," the man said.

Another man in a white lab coat put on a surgical mask and walked into the cell. He nudged Rolf with the toe of his boot. "Boy, wake up."

Rolf squinted in the light.

"If you lie down, it has to be faceup."

The man kicked him in the rib cage repeatedly until he rolled over onto his back to face the glaring light. Rolf opened his mouth and began to scream.

———◇———

On the other side of the glass, the team of Soviet psychiatrists in the vast, darkened subterranean workshop turned off the speakers. There were endless rows of padded rooms like the one the boy lay in. Each housed patients for observation. Groups of government physicians in suits watched, talking softly among themselves and making notes.

A supervising doctor entered the observation tank to hear the latest report on the boy.

"Where did he come from?" the supervisor asked, reviewing the notes.

"He is an orphan from Warsaw. He was brought here by the Third Infantry after they liberated the city."

"Have you tried feeding him?"

"We can't get close to him. We haven't even been able to wash him. He smells putrid, like a rotting animal."

"Try tempting him with food," the supervisor suggested.

A short time later, a third man entered Rolf's cell, this time with a tray of food. The boy knelt, closing his eyes and sniffing the air.

The man put the tray of food on the floor, far away from Rolf. Rolf started to inch toward the tray of food, but the man stood in his way.

"I brought food for you," the man said. "Would you be interested in this food?"

The boy looked up.

"Aren't you getting hungry?"

The boy nodded.

"But before you can have anything to eat, you must tell me one thing about yourself."

The boy said nothing. He just stared longingly at the food and looked away from the man.

"Tell me one thing. It could be one word, really."

"Hungry," Rolf said in a hoarse voice. The man smiled. The observers made note of the time and continued writing on their clipboards.

"That's very good."

Rolf nodded and then eyed the food tray again.

"What's your name?"

"Rolf."

"Rolf. We have a name. Very good. I believe this is wonderful progress. Just to show you how wonderful, I'd like to take the restraints from your wrists so you can feed yourself. Rolf, do you think you could behave yourself if I were to do that?"

Rolf nodded.

"Can you use your words?"

"Yes," the boy finally croaked.

The man took out a small key and unlocked the shackles from Rolf's wrists. Fueled by one last rush of adrenaline, Rolf leaped at him.

Rolf got his hands around the man's neck and started choking him.

Two large men in white came running into the padded cell. One had a hypodermic needle and tried to quickly inject it into the boy's shoulder, but Rolf lunged and knocked the syringe out of his hand.

———◇———

A door opened in the observation tank, and a uniformed official stuck his head in.

"Look busy," the official said to the observers.

"Why?" one observer asked, irritated at the untimely intrusion.

"Surprise inspection," the intruder answered.

All the observers knew what that meant and immediately snapped to attention. Even their pencils stood straight up.

Two Russian soldiers bustled into the room, and then, in his gray uniform with the large buttons and black boots, Soviet Premier Josef Stalin strode confidently into the room. Leading the way was a highly placed Soviet doctor who was giving Stalin a private tour of the facility.

"This is the new Pavlovian wing of the People's Psychiatric Center," the doctor told the Soviet premier. "The observation tanks—"

"Don't let me interrupt your schedule," Stalin said as he walked directly to the observation window. "Keep working."

Stalin watched the wild boy fight the three medical aids who were trying to get him back into the manacles and jam a hypodermic needle into his arm. The boy was winning the struggle against the exasperated men.

"Who is this boy?" Stalin said.

"Polish refugee picked up in Warsaw," the supervising doctor quickly answered.

"This is the kind of boy," Stalin said, turning to his personal assistant, who stood at his elbow. "This!"

"What kind of boy is that, Secretary General?" the assistant asked.

"Get this boy to Dmitri," Stalin ordered.

17

DMITRI

Rolf slowly began to wake up, this time finding himself in yet another room. He noticed that this room was more like the one he'd slept in as a child. It was simply furnished with a single cot in the corner and a small table next to the door. He was lying on the floor, when a tall man entered the room.

Rolf had never seen a bright blue uniform like the one the man wore. It was nothing like the uniforms worn by the Nazis, the Russian soldiers, or the laboratory technicians. This was a one-of-a-kind uniform, one that looked as if it would never be worn by anyone else. The uniform also had red epaulets and many medals and decorations. This man seemed happy, yet Rolf could also feel his strength and control.

"You must be hungry, Rolf," the man said in a cheerful voice, setting a tray down on the small table.

Oh, the food! He immediately wanted to get to it, but Rolf just sat up on the floor, watching the man, who moved in front of the tray. He couldn't be trusted, Rolf decided.

"You may call me Comrade General. Once you have addressed me properly, you may have some food."

Rolf looked around and then quickly stood on his toes. He tried to lunge past the man for the tray of food but found himself slammed into the wall.

"That hurt," Rolf growled. Then he lunged, teeth bared, heading for the man's wrist, but before he could make contact, the man had him by the ankle and was swinging him through the air. Rolf's shoulder hit the wall first, creating an intense pain, and then he slid down to the floor. His shoulder felt as if it were already swelling.

Angry now, Rolf sprang from the floor, but a quick jab to his chest stopped him and, in an instant, took all his wind away. He folded and fell again to the floor, panting.

"You may call me Comrade General."

After a moment, the man reached down, took his hand, pulled him to his feet, and led him to the chair by the food.

Rolf stared at him, angry and terrified. *Why didn't the man hit me again?* Rolf wondered.

"You may call me Comrade General," the man said, waiting.

Rolf forced himself to say it. "Comrade General."

"Sit and eat," Dmitri said as he smiled, pointing to the food on the tray.

Never taking his eyes off the man, Rolf moved next to the tray. He grabbed a handful of food and shoved it into his mouth without sitting.

"Sit in the chair, and eat the food properly. There's more when you're finished," the man said.

Rolf froze, staring at the man like a terrified animal. Something was wrong. No one in a uniform could be trusted.

"Sit in the chair, Rolf." The man's voice was not loud, but there was no mistaking his seriousness.

Rolf didn't move.

"I would be happy to place you in the chair."

After a tense minute, Rolf sat in the chair and looked at the man with distrust. He grabbed the fork like a weapon, his hand trembling but threatening. The man towered above him. The steely look in his eyes told Rolf he wasn't going to tolerate anything less than what he had commanded. After a moment, Rolf dropped the fork to the table. This man was ready for anything, and Rolf would rather eat than fight, so Rolf sat and ate.

"I understand you are a very good fighter. Would you like to learn more about boxing, wrestling, and hand-to-hand combat?"

Rolf looked up at the man as he ate, not answering.

"The way I handled you just now had nothing to do with the fact that I am more than twice your size," the man said.

Rolf looked more and more puzzled.

"It had a lot more to do with what was going on in my mind. Combat skills I learned in the Red Army. There are things I could teach you."

Rolf found himself nodding. He was interested in what the man was saying, and he wondered why this man seemed friendly but firm.

"Would you like to learn to fight and win every time?"

Rolf nodded and even smiled for the first time in many years at the thought that this man might be of help to him.

"I can arrange for that."

Rolf went back to eating.

"Who are your parents, Rolf? What is your last name?"

It had been so long since Rolf had spoken the name. While he had been in hiding, he'd had no one to talk to, and he had been very young when they'd died.

"Wozzak."

"Are your parents alive?"

"No."

"What happened to them?"

"Shot."

"When?"

"Long time ago."

"Germans?"

Rolf nodded.

"I'm sorry."

Rolf looked up at the tall man and sensed that he felt sympathy for him. Rolf had not known sympathy since before the death of his mother.

"Our house blew up. They chased us. We ran to the church. The priest said he would protect us."

"And did he?"

"They came in anyway, and they killed them."

"Your parents?"

"And my sisters. And the others. Everybody."

"Where were you?"

"I was hiding."

"You survived."

"I hid with the dead people. Then they changed."

Rolf lost all interest in eating. The memories of that day flooded his thoughts. He could smell the stench of the dead again as he remembered the piles of bodies in the basement. He dropped his fork. One tear fell from his eye and then another. Unable to stop the flow, Rolf broke down crying.

"Don't cry," Dmitri said forcefully. It was an order. "You have no reason to be afraid. Not anymore."

Rolf sniffled, wiping his tears on his sleeve. He looked up at Dmitri.

"That priest didn't do you much good, did he? He said he'd protect you. He was weak and a liar. Listen, Rolf, the Nazis came into your country, and the church did absolutely nothing to stop them. It took the Soviets to stop them, and I should know. I was on the eastern front of the war, and that's where it was won. Those Nazis are still out there, and they're as bad as ever, and the church does nothing and is as evil as the Nazis. But you couldn't be safer than right here."

18

DISCIPLINE

Rolf put his head back on the chair, listening to his tutor drone on and on. Dmitri had arranged for this tutor at the academy he had formed. Because Rolf knew how to read so well, the tutor was trying to teach him additional languages. Rolf began to tap his fingers on the desk, his mind going to the book about knights as he wondered if he would be able to read it again.

"Sit still!" the tutor barked.

Rolf responded with a kick under the desk, hitting the tutor's knee—again.

The small man could not move far enough back to avoid Rolf's kicks, and he stood up. "I've had it," he said. "When you can sit properly, you can learn properly." He left.

Rolf took the opportunity to climb out the window and hide from view in a tall tree. From that vantage point, he could see the entire compound. He waited in the tree for a while and then went to the garbage area and began rifling through the garbage bin, just as he had done daily for six years in Warsaw.

That was where Dmitri found him.

As soon as Rolf saw the look on Dmitri's face, he knew he had made a mistake. Dmitri did not say anything. He silently signaled for the boy to come back inside.

Rolf returned obediently to the room he had escaped, and soon a new tutor, someone of a larger size, replaced the old one and started on the boy's education where the previous one had stopped.

That night at dinner, Rolf listened to Dmitri tell him colorful and inspirational stories about famous athletes and war stories until Rolf became tired, and Dmitri sent him to bed.

Rolf had just fallen into a deep sleep, when the door to his room slammed shut, and the bright ceiling light over his bed was suddenly switched on. Rolf jumped up from the bed, ready for the intruder, just as Dmitri swung his leg in a kick that knocked Rolf back onto his mattress.

"What is it?" Rolf said in shock. Why had Dmitri burst into his room?

"Silence!" Dmitri yelled as he punched Rolf in the face and then roughly stripped him of his bedclothes.

Rolf was dazed after the punch and weakly struggled against Dmitri, but he gave up when Dmitri pinned him down, pushing his knee down hard across Rolf's chest.

Rolf stared up as Dmitri lashed his wrists to the headboard and then swiftly lashed his ankles to the bedposts. Then he felt an excruciating electrical pain in his ribs.

Rolf could see that Dmitri had a long metal object in his hand, and he poked it into Rolf's ribs a second time.

"Please stop. It hurts. Why are you doing this?" Rolf said.

"This is for this afternoon!" Dmitri yelled. "When you don't do as you are told and forget to succeed at the tasks you are given, this is how I will remind you."

"I am sorry, Comrade. Please stop. I beg you." Rolf sobbed as Dmitri prodded him for the third time.

"Do you understand that you are nothing to me unless you obey me and do as you're told?" Dmitri yelled.

"But, Comrade, I—"

Dmitri threw the prod to the ground and gripped Rolf's throat with both hands, hovering over him.

Rolf, terrified, looked into Dmitri's eyes as he struggled for breath.

"Do you understand your mistake?" Dmitri demanded as he tightened his grip on Rolf's neck.

"Yes," Rolf said weakly. He began to feel nauseated. "Yes, I ... will ... obey," he said just before he lost consciousness.

Rolf woke up slowly. He was in a hospital, lying on white sheets not unlike the ones he'd had in his room. Dmitri was sitting next to him.

Rolf struggled to speak but realized he could not open his mouth, as it was wired shut.

"As long as you continue to learn and remain obedient, this will not happen again," Dmitri assured him. "I have full confidence that you will excel at your studies and, when your body has mended, your athletics as well." It was a lie, of course. It would happen whenever Dmitri felt it was needed. One couldn't learn to control fear if one didn't also inflict it.

Dmitri looked deeply into Rolf's swollen eyes. He seemed satisfied that the boy was in some way comprehending his words.

"You have many talents, Rolf. Perhaps more than some of the others. But you need to learn other things too," Dmitri said.

Rolf saw Dmitri as the one adult he knew he could depend on. His mother and father had loved him, but they'd pointed to the cross on the wall when they should have protected him from the German soldiers. The priest had promised protection and shelter and delivered neither. Dmitri had promised Rolf he would protect him from the Germans and said the Catholic church was as bad as the Nazis and the enemy of their state. Dmitri would punish him if he didn't behave, but Rolf would grow up to become fearless like his teacher.

19

247

"That's it," Dmitri said. "Just pull a little to the left."

Rolf made the adjustment and hit the target but not in the center.

"Remember the men who killed your family," Dmitri said. "Focus."

Rolf took a deep breath, closing his eyes. He had been trained to tune out external stimuli and create a singular focus: the soldiers. He saw their black boots and heard their shouts, all burned in his memory. When he opened his eyes, his hand was perfectly steady, and his gaze was sure as he lined up the gun with the target. When he fired, he hit the center. Enemy eliminated.

It was five years later, and Rolf had grown into a young man the soldiers who'd trapped him at the library would have failed to recognize. With Dmitri as his role model and Dmitri's approval as his goal, Rolf excelled at all forms of athletic and combat endeavors, though the artillery range was his favorite. At fourteen, he'd become highly skilled in Combat Sambo, the Russian version of martial arts developed by the Red Army in the 1930s. His skill at fencing was unmatched among the other boys in the same training program. He'd become a master swordsman.

The years he'd spent hiding and reading in the Warsaw library served him well in the classroom. He had read the classics and had moved on to works of abstract math, physics, and Marxist economic theory. Dmitri also ensured that Rolf took a course called Theology. It taught that the Catholic church was the source of all problems, its priests especially. Rolf needed little convincing. His priest had failed to protect him or his parents.

Dmitri stopped and reset the targets. Rolf held his gun and stood proudly at attention as Dmitri prepared a series of four moving targets, all shaped like men.

"The one on the left is American Communist hater Senator Joseph McCarthy," Dmitri explained. He often treated the targets as if they were real people. "Next to him is Cardinal Mindszenty."

"Who is Cardinal Mindszenty?" Rolf asked.

"He is a Hungarian priest who tried to stop the party from turning church property over to the people of Hungary."

"A priest?" Rolf asked.

"Yes," Dmitri said. "He is the worst kind. He keeps the property of the church from falling into the hands of the state, where it rightfully belongs."

"A priest," Rolf said. His lip curled in disgust.

Dmitri went on with his descriptions of the other targets. "Next to Cardinal Mindszenty are Chinese chairman Mao and fascist dictator Generalissimo Francisco Franco on the right. They are all enemies of Russia. You'll only get one shot. I want you to use it wisely, shooting the one who is the most dangerous."

Rolf took a shooting stance, focused on the targets.

Dmitri pulled a lever. All four targets came flying at Rolf, and without hesitation, he quickly raised his revolver and shot the second target from the left.

Dmitri took down that target. Rolf had put a bullet right through the center of the heart, the bull's-eye.

"Cardinal Mindszenty," Dmitri said proudly. "You're quite correct, Rolf. He's the most dangerous of the four." Dmitri put a congratulatory hand on Rolf's shoulder. "I think you are ready for your first 247."

Rolf looked at Dmitri curiously. "I remember that you told me I would learn about a 247, but you did not say what that meant."

"A 247 is an order to execute an enemy of Mother Russia," Dmitri said. "It is of the highest importance and is the supreme opportunity to prove your loyalty. Properly responding to a 247 order means you risk everything to do it correctly, because there is no second chance—no questions asked. Come with me."

"Yes, Comrade General," Rolf said.

They both donned their coats and walked out of the shooting range into a snowy white courtyard. Two uniformed guards held a middle-aged man who was desperately struggling to get away.

"Rolf, this man is a Nazi," Dmitri said, gesturing to the man. "We caught him in Berlin. He is one of the storm troopers who destroyed your home and killed your parents. We have brought him to you because your training has taught you what to do. This is a 247 order."

The guards let go of the man, who immediately started screaming, "No! I didn't! I wasn't there!"

Rolf held his hand out in front of Dmitri without saying a word. Dmitri reached into his holster and handed him his gun. Rolf looked down at the gun and then looked at Dmitri.

"Yes," he said as he walked forward and stood in front of the German. "My loyalty is without question."

Rolf aimed and pulled the trigger once, hitting the German between the eyes and stopping his denial midsentence. The man slumped to the ground, a pool of blood forming. Rolf nodded, looking at Dmitri. The guards stepped forward to grab the man by the ankles and started to drag him away.

"Very good, Rolf," Dmitri said proudly. "You knew exactly what to do. Your first 247. There will be more."

20

NATASHA

Sometimes in the dark privacy of his room at night, Rolf would think of Natasha, one of the girls at the academy. She had dark hair and sat near him in his economic theory class. When he looked at her or thought of her, he would feel a strange loneliness and a physical sensation he could not identify.

One day Natasha caught Rolf staring at her and smiled back at him. After class, she walked with him. He had no idea how to act or what to say. He had no experience with peers and no idea how to socialize or even how to carry on a simple conversation. It wasn't that he was shy. He simply didn't know where to start. He was an outsider, and he felt more comfortable being an outsider than trying to learn to interact with people. He only had room in his heart for one person: Dmitri. His entire life was about pleasing Dmitri, honoring Dmitri's high expectations of him, and becoming as much like Dmitri as he possibly could.

But Natasha had been on his mind, and now there she was, not really caring about his silence, taking his hand and leading him.

"Shhh. Come with me, Rolf," Natasha whispered as they went to the side door of the library.

"Where are we going?" Rolf felt his face flush and avoided eye contact with Natasha.

"I have a special place where we can be private." Natasha opened a second door that led to a corridor in the back of the library. "I've watched you, Rolf. You are strong and handsome, but you don't flirt with me like the other boys. Why is that?"

"Well, I have to focus on our instruction. Dmitri has high expectations for my work, and well, I don't know. I think you are pretty." Rolf stuttered nervously as he pulled away from Natasha, and she skipped to another door in the hallway.

"Here we are, Rolf. I've brought you here so you can show me what kind of man you are." Natasha giggled as she opened the door to a maintenance closet marked "Staff Only."

"Come on. Follow me." She disappeared into the room.

Rolf looked back and forth down the hall to make sure no one had seen them sneaking to this place. He wasn't sure how he was supposed to act and certainly didn't know how he was supposed to show her what kind of man he was. He hesitated for a moment and then opened the door, finding Natasha naked from the waist up.

Rolf froze as he stared at Natasha's breasts and the pointed nipples. He could not look away, and as he stared, he felt an unusual tightening in his britches that was uncomfortable but also pleasurable.

"Do you want to touch them, Rolf? Have you ever touched a girl's breasts? I'd like for you to rub them." Natasha walked toward Rolf, grabbed both of his hands, and pressed them hard to her breasts.

Rolf could not speak.

"I have been told by many of our comrades that I am the most beautiful and desirable girl here at the academy. But I've chosen you to be with me," Natasha purred as she pressed her body against Rolf and kissed him hard on the mouth.

Rolf's mind was suddenly flooded with images of the naked women who had been beaten and raped in the library by the storm troopers. Memories of the brutal rape and murder of the Polish waitress came rushing back.

His breathing ragged, he pushed Natasha away. "Stop. Don't touch me. Get away from me."

She fell to the floor. "So that's it, Rolf. That's why you haven't flirted with me. You are one of those boys. You are not a strong man after all!" Natasha laughed and then sneered at him as she gathered her clothes and pushed past him to the door.

"Wait, Natasha. Wait," Rolf said, leaning against the wall.

"We have a saying for boys like you: *petushila!*" Natasha spat at him as she slammed the door behind her.

Rolf knew enough Russian to understand that she had just called him a fag and in the most derisive way—the way the prisoners used the word in the gulags.

Rolf tried to avoid Natasha after the encounter in the maintenance closet, but several times after that, when he saw her in the hallway, she whispered insults that she knew he would hear. He never spoke to her directly again, and he did his best to avoid looking at her after that.

He was humiliated by the memory of that experience. It stood in his mind as an experience he never wanted to have again. He used it to help him stay focused on his studies and his training.

THE ASSIGNMENT

The gold leaf on the crown molding and the silk-brocade-upholstered chairs lining the walls gave the ballroom a sophisticated feel. While the others were socializing and celebrating their graduation from the academy, Rolf sat alone, reflecting on his accomplishments. He felt true pride for the first time. The finest caviar had been served on eighteenth-century china, and Rolf didn't want to leave any of it uneaten.

The Budapest String Quartet played in the background.

Suddenly, he looked up to see Dmitri sitting next to him, smiling broadly.

"I must congratulate you on your achievement, Rolf." Dmitri beamed.

Rolf was speechless, proud to hear words of praise from his demanding teacher.

"I have much to tell you," Dmitri said in a tone that Rolf knew well, a tone that said, "Put away all that is superfluous, and listen."

Rolf put down his fork and pushed back the plate.

"No, no. Please. Keep eating."

Rolf obediently went back to eating.

"In fact, I'll join you in celebration." Dmitri picked up a table bottle of vodka and poured some into a glass. He made a silent toast to Rolf and then took a drink, which impressed Rolf. He'd never seen Dmitri take a drink.

"Your classmates will all be going on to the next level of training, Rolf. But you will not be joining them," Dmitri said.

Rolf put his fork down again and looked up at Dmitri, expecting disappointment in Dmitri's eyes, fearful of his future. "But I have done everything you asked of me," Rolf said with a slight quiver in his voice. "What else must I do?"

Dmitri smiled broadly as he poured another glass of vodka for himself and then a glass for Rolf. "You have excelled, Rolf, so much that it is only you who is ready for an assignment. The others are not."

Rolf sighed deeply in relief that he had not failed Dmitri. He was proud that instead, he had been singled out from the others. "I am ready, Comrade General. What would you have me do, and when do I get started?"

"You will enter the priesthood."

Rolf waited to hear more, but that was all Dmitri said. He assumed he had misunderstood his teacher's words. "The priesthood?" Rolf asked to make certain.

"For almost twenty years—"

"The Catholic priesthood?" Rolf interrupted him without meaning to, as he was so certain he had misunderstood the assignment. "Everything I've learned from you about the Catholic church has told me that it is the enemy."

"That's right."

"But I thought—"

"You thought?" Dmitri asked. It was more a challenge than a question and more a reprimand than a challenge.

Rolf closed his eyes. He knew that tone. "Please continue, Comrade General."

"Thank you," Dmitri said with a tight smile. "For almost twenty years, long before there was a NKVD, back when we were known as the Cheka, there was a plan to infiltrate the Catholic church to undermine it at its very core. You see, the church indoctrinates the masses to follow it aimlessly while it grows rich and powerful. All the while, the church's propaganda calls our great society, which cares for the well-being of the workers, an evil regime. The Catholic church is our greatest enemy. This plan to infiltrate the church and destroy it from within was Stalin's own idea, and it became one of his most important projects. It might interest you to know that Stalin himself handpicked you to become a part of this plan of his."

"I never met Stalin."

"You only think you never met Stalin. He saw you from an observation room and chose you himself."

"He chose me to be one of the priests?"

"Yes."

"But the priests turned my parents over to the Nazis." Rolf couldn't help but interject. These were, in fact, words Dmitri had taught him.

"Exactly," Dmitri agreed.

"And you want me to be one of them?"

"You will be more than just one of them. As a priest, of course, you will help lead them and follow our orders as we execute Comrade General Stalin's plan."

"How would I lead them?"

"Earn the right to wear the collar and carry the cross. They will follow you blindly."

Rolf was quiet for a moment as he considered what the man he trusted with his life was telling him. None of the words made the slightest bit of sense. "This is not the type of assignment I was expecting."

"It was selected for you long ago. Is this a problem? If it is, I should know now. The state has already invested quite a lot in your training," Dmitri said.

Rolf knew what his job was now: to assure the teacher that he understood perfectly, even though he didn't understand at all. That was the way to survive with Dmitri.

"I shall become a priest," Rolf assured his teacher.

"But first, can you?" Dmitri demanded. "Can you keep to the vows of a priest? They must commit to a life of celibacy. It's very important that you do, and there are men—" Dmitri stopped himself for a moment, watching Rolf. "Can you abstain from sexual relations with women?" Dmitri said plainly.

Rolf was relieved he could give his teacher the assurances he wanted. One quick thought of his experience with Natasha was enough to make those assurances easy to give.

"Yes," Rolf said. "Of course. Is that all you're worried about?"

"Well, there are other vows, but that's the hardest."

"I have no sexual interest in women or men," Rolf said to reassure Dmitri. "Ever."

"It is absolutely necessary that you keep your cover. Once you're in the priesthood, you must stay in if you are to be of any real use. You will have to deceive everyone."

Rolf knew now that he had to convince Dmitri. He had learned that convincing Dmitri was everything. "You have chosen well, Comrade General," he assured his teacher.

"In the future, your contacts will present you with one of these to identify themselves," Dmitri said, reaching into his pocket. Dmitri smiled and nodded at the waitress who came to fill the vodka bottle. When the waitress had finished, he handed a strange-looking crucifix to Rolf. "Our great leader, Stalin, used his own mother's Russian Orthodox cross as inspiration when he had these crosses made for our agents. Did you know that Stalin was forced by his mother to attend the seminary in Tiflis?"

"Are you saying that Stalin himself became a priest?" Rolf asked as he traced the rough gold edges of the three bars of the crucifix down to an odd-looking raised skull covered in rubies.

"Of course not." Dmitri laughed as he grabbed the crucifix from Rolf's hands. "That seminary was where he learned that the church indoctrinated and demanded reverence for the czar and God in equal measure, and it was where he saw that religion shackled the masses. He joined the revolution while there, and socialism became his religion. Look at this cross." Dmitri handed it back to Rolf. "There is no Christ figure nailed to the cross. He doesn't exist. Stalin's cross is blank but for the skull. Stalin called it the Judas cross. Your contacts and all of our agents in the church will have one."

"So there are already others like me?" Rolf asked. "In the priesthood?"

"There are now more than a hundred the world over. And there will be more. These are Russia's unseen heroes."

"How can they be heroes if they are priests?"

"These undercover priests have won many battles for us across Eastern Europe. We haven't held on to those countries with just our military. Those brave men in black have played a major role with their intelligence gathering, their service as couriers, their secret skills in weaponry and combat, and the missions they have carried out purging certain priests and even bishops from the church. They have followed their training and know that when a 247 is issued, they must kill their targets without being detected or suspected. Their courageous sacrifice for the state is the very definition of the word *heroic*. I am asking you, Rolf, to be one of these heroes."

Rolf was suddenly filled with pride and determination. The idea that Dmitri might come to view him as a hero was exhilarating. He was now anxious to proceed. "How does one become a priest?" Rolf asked.

"It is necessary that you are recommended by a priest, are accepted into the seminary, and perform well in your studies there. You are to return to Warsaw."

Rolf remembered the ugly setting of his childhood, the place where the world had become hell and stayed that way for a long time. That memory and the thought of being away from Dmitri were enough to make him feel sick.

Years of training kicked in as he realized his moment had come. Nothing could stop Rolf from doing what Dmitri wanted him to do. He would go to Warsaw and become a priest, or he would die in the effort.

"Whatever is called for," Rolf replied bravely.

Dmitri stood and gave him a salute, and that salute was all the reward Rolf thought he would ever need.

BOOK 3

THE PRIEST

22

HOMECOMING 1951

Rolf stood in his old hiding place. The old library's walls and roof had been shoddily repaired. They kept the snow out, but the building was not worth looking at, and it wasn't open to the public or even really a library anymore. It was a place where boxes of paper records were kept, records of things no one would ever remember or care about. Rolf thought about looking for the book about knights, the book he'd loved all those nights, but the rafters where he'd hidden it were not accessible.

It was cold. Rolf walked out of the library and into the street. The Soviet army had an unmistakable presence in the whole town. *What would the city of Warsaw be without foreign uniforms everywhere?* Rolf wondered as he shivered. The coat he was wearing was tattered and threadbare. He was supposed to look like a returning refugee who had been living off the Sisters of Mercy. He had little money in his pocket, so he had to walk. He vaguely remembered his way around.

The best that could be said about postwar Warsaw was that it was clean. During the German occupation, the streets, parks, and courtyards had become junk yards cluttered with the rubble of bombed and fallen walls. The Soviets had removed the debris of war and replaced it with the sterility of utilitarian concerns. The Polish architecture was still there but buried under the coverings and signs of collectivism. The old marketplace had become a setting for endless breadlines. The public house was now a Communist Party substation. The train station was neat, clean, and covered with Communist iconography and signs. The trains ran on time, but nobody rode them, because few had the fare.

As he walked the familiar but different streets, he kept reminding himself that he would be a hero in Dmitri's eyes. He had to remember that he was no longer a homeless, friendless boy scrambling through garbage cans. He was a grown man with academic and athletic accomplishments, a man with a mission and a connection to a powerful nation. Those thoughts kept the anxiety at bay.

He made it to his old neighborhood, and when he saw it, he was disgusted. He was surprised many of the homes were still standing, as they looked so dilapidated. He'd thought they had all been destroyed by the Nazis the way his house had been destroyed. He'd thought everyone he knew had been killed, but Dmitri's intelligence force had discovered Rolf's uncle and cousins had come to Warsaw after its liberation and were living in the old neighborhood. He remembered that as a small child, he and his friends would play games on the sidewalk and even in the street. It was clear nobody did that now. People stayed huddled indoors, hoping for the state to send some heat through their old radiators.

He knocked on the door of a house that he remembered as the home of his uncle, his father's brother. Nothing happened, so he knocked again.

Finally, the door opened, and an old man appeared, neither beckoning nor pushing away, just looking out at a world that had already claimed too much from him. Rolf didn't particularly recognize the face as that of his uncle, but he knew he had come to the right place.

Rolf pointed down the street at the building that stood where his old house once had been. An ugly government building—low, square, and brown—now stood in its place.

"Did you know the man who lived there before the war?" Rolf asked the man at the door.

"He was my brother," the man said simply.

"I am his son," Rolf said just as simply. They looked at each other in silence. The man didn't believe him, of course. That was to be expected.

"The Nazis killed him," the man said, near tears.

"I was there," Rolf said.

"Killed his whole family." The man went on, heedless of Rolf's words, lost in the memories of his brother.

"Uncle Josef?' Rolf asked after a respectful silence.

"Could it really be you, Rolf?" the man asked after gazing at Rolf for a long time.

Rolf simply nodded, and the old man came out and threw his arms around Rolf. Rolf stood there, hoping he could seem as emotional as the old man was now willing to be. Rolf felt the man's tears against his cheek and wondered how long this old man was going to let him stand shivering on the porch.

"Praise God, Rolf, that you are alive. We were told that all of you died the day the Germans invaded."

Rolf could see that his uncle's cheeks were streaked with tears.

"Marta, come quickly! It's a miracle! Rolf—he is alive, and he has made it home!"

Rolf's uncle dragged him into the small home, and Rolf saw four women emerge from the back room, as if they had been hiding.

"Rolf, this is your aunt Marta, and these are your cousins Anya, Gita, and Justyna. You might not remember them, as you were only two when we left Warsaw. I begged your mother and father to come with us."

"Hello, cousins. I'm very happy to see you again," Rolf said softly as he opened his arms in welcome to the women.

Rolf could see that his cousins were surprised at his visit, and no one spoke for a few minutes, until Aunt Marta stepped forward and crossed herself.

"Glory be to the Father, the Son, and the Holy Spirit," Marta prayed. "You are the unexpected blessing sent back to us, Rolf." Marta wrapped her arms around Rolf, and the cousins followed.

"Come, Rolf. Let's get you next to the fire, and I will bring you some tea to warm you up. We need to hear where you have been all this time," Marta said as she went to the woodstove to warm water for the tea.

For the next two hours, Rolf carefully told them the story he had rehearsed for Dmitri and in front of a mirror. He knew it well. Some of it was even true. It began with the Nazis, the murder of his parents, and the six years of hiding and scrounging, including the monstrous brutality he had observed daily, the ever-present terror of getting caught, and the gnawing hunger that had driven him to regularly emerge from hiding and risk his life.

"I managed to stay alive by basically becoming an animal," Rolf said.

"I lived like a rat that trembles in the darkness and feeds on garbage." He paused and looked at their faces. They were entranced. "But tell me, Uncle—how did you escape before the invasion? I was young and don't remember when you left," Rolf said to get the attention off him and have them remember the difficult time they all had shared before the war.

Rolf's uncle came to his side at the fireplace. "We left for England just before the Nazis came. I begged your father to come with us, but he was very proud and difficult. He said that it was his country, and he would not run like a coward."

"Yes, but we missed Warsaw, and as soon as we knew the city had been liberated, we started saving our money to come back home. We've been back for three years, and slowly, we have repaired the damage to the house, and your uncle started his shoe-repair business again," Marta said proudly as she poured another cup of tea.

"But, Rolf, how did you make it all that time alone in Warsaw, and where have you been?" his cousin Justyna blurted out.

Rolf realized she was the only one of the cousins who had spoken the whole time he had been in their house. She looked to be the oldest and not as shy as her sisters. Rolf vaguely remembered that Justyna had helped teach the scriptures to him and his friends at church. He remembered her as a teenager then, so he thought she must be at least ten years older than he was.

"I was rescued by an order of the Carmelite Sisters," Rolf said. "The sisters took me to Switzerland, where I was educated in a parochial school, shoulder to shoulder with the sons and daughters of the Polish resistance. When I think of what might have become of me if not for those sisters and their courage, generosity, and unswerving faith …" He left the rest to their imaginations. "I made my mind up then and have never told a soul until now. I have nursed a beautiful secret. I have come home to find you, the only family I have left, to confess it. I have decided to enter the priesthood."

"Praise God!" shouted Josef, jumping out of his chair to embrace Rolf once again. His uncle and aunt were both crying. Soon two of his cousins were trying to get their arms around Rolf.

"A priest in the family!" exclaimed Marta.

"I have to be recommended by a parish priest," Rolf said, managing to avoid being suffocated by the women's affection.

"I'll take you to Father Novak," said Josef, already putting on his coat. "The old church was badly damaged, but we have been working to repair it, and Father Novak is rebuilding our faith as well."

Rolf realized as he walked down the block with his uncle Josef that he now had to tell his story with as much conviction as he could muster. However, he was feeling uneasy, and memories of the bombed-out buildings and dirty streets where he had crawled at night were tugging at nerves that were much harder to calm.

Rolf followed Uncle Josef to the side of the church and down steps leading to the basement, where Josef knocked on the door. A figure moved in front of the peephole before the big wooden door opened.

Rolf could see that Father Novak was so thin that his clavicle was partially visible behind his collar.

"Father," said Josef, putting his hand on the priest's shoulder, so excited that he didn't wait for the priest to greet him. "I want you to meet this young man. He is my nephew."

"I didn't know you had a nephew," said Father Novak in a faint, easygoing voice.

"He has an amazing story to tell you," Josef told the priest. "His name is Rolf."

Rolf felt the priest's small, bony hand in his. He looked into Father Novak's eyes and saw a gentleness he had never seen in a man's eyes.

"Rolf, I am Father Novak."

Rolf was speechless for a moment. His mind flashed back to the day of the bombing, the look in the priest's eyes as he lay dying on the floor, and the days he'd spent with the decomposing bodies of his parents.

"He doesn't mean to be rude, Father," Josef said. "It was right here in Warsaw, at this old church, where his parents and sisters were brutally murdered by the Nazis."

Father Novak put his other hand on Rolf's shoulder and said, "Let us mark this day as a special blessing from God that you have returned to us."

Rolf relaxed a little. The priest didn't seem to be a threat to him just yet. How could a man this caring possibly say no to him?

The priest led Rolf and his uncle to the rectory, a small building attached to the church. They sat around a simple wooden table. "Rolf has something to tell you," said Josef, unable to contain his enthusiasm. "He wishes to become a priest."

Suddenly, Father Novak's eyes changed. They were just as gentle as before but less receptive and immediately suspicious. "Indeed?" was all the priest said, still pleasantly enough.

"I was hoping you would recommend him for the priesthood," said Josef.

"I must hear it from him, Josef," said Father Novak.

"It is true what he says," said Rolf, suddenly speaking up. "I want to dedicate my life to God and the service of His church."

"There are many ways to do that," said Father Novak. "The priesthood is a special calling."

"It is my calling," Rolf boldly asserted.

After a moment of studied silence, the priest motioned to Rolf. "Step into my office. Could your nephew and I speak privately, Josef?"

Josef nodded and backed away anxiously.

The thin priest led Rolf to a small room in the basement with two chairs, a shelf full of books, and a cross on the wall.

They each took a seat. Father Novak said nothing. He looked earnestly into Rolf's eyes, as if he could read his thoughts.

"Please, Rolf, tell me about your experience and your calling to the priesthood," Father Novak said firmly. He leaned back in his chair and waited for Rolf to speak.

"After my parents were killed, I spent six years hiding from the Nazis. There was nowhere to go and no one to trust, so I lived in the library and lived off what I could scavenge from the trash piles." Rolf raised his voice and made sure to mimic a tremor of fear. The priest did not seem to react. "The brutality of the soldiers and the things they did—I almost gave up, until the city was liberated by the Russians. That's when the Carmelite nuns rescued me and took me to Switzerland." Rolf knew from his training that he needed to say as little as possible, but he didn't think Father Novak believed him. "When I think of what might have become of me if not for those sisters and their courage, generosity, and unswerving faith in me … I was no more than an animal when they found me. It was through their example I decided to devote my life to God and become a priest."

Rolf could see that Father Novak had no problem with staying quiet as they sat there for a long time before Father Novak spoke.

"Describe it to me."

"Describe what, Father?"

"Your call experience."

"Well, as I said, it was the inspiration of the Carmelite Sisters and their courage and generosity—"

"Yes. You said 'their unswerving faith.' But what of the call experience itself?"

"I'm not sure I understand."

"Describe to me the moment you knew you were called by God to become a priest," Father Novak said.

"Describe it?"

"Have you been called by God, Rolf?"

"Yes. I believe I have."

"You *believe* you have?"

"Yes."

"What makes you believe a thing like that?"

"I wake up every day grateful for the generosity of the nuns who are led by the church. There wasn't only one moment when I thought that. I want to give that same blessing to others." Rolf did not know what he had to say to make Father Novak believe him.

"Any man who has been truly called by God can never forget the moment, Rolf. Look at St. Paul. He was blinded by his call so that he could never forget. I know that when I was called, I was having pastry and coffee in a small kitchen on a very cold morning. The moment was more prosaic perhaps than Paul on his way to Damascus but very specific and clear and more unforgettable a memory than the invasion of Poland in 1939." Father Novak let out a patient sigh and put his hands together.

"Father, would you recommend me for the priesthood?"

"No."

"I don't understand, Father. I sincerely wish to become a priest. Is there any way I can change your mind?"

"I honestly do not know. If you are truly dedicated to God and can prove that to me over time, perhaps. But I can make no promises. You may study with me. If you study hard over a period of time, perhaps God will guide you toward your calling."

Rolf felt a warm tingling feeling crawl up the back of his neck. This priest was in his way, and he would disappoint Dmitri. With a single blow, Rolf could kill him.

To avoid the temptation of violence, Rolf removed himself from the office without a word. He needed advice on what to do next and how to handle the mission. He headed for the side exit to avoid Josef. Next to the door was a simple wooden box with some coins in it, marked for the poor. He reached in his hand and helped himself.

Rolf was unfamiliar with the streets of Warsaw after so many years, and he went on a search for a public phone. Most of the phones did not work, and he lost most of his coins attempting to make one of the most important calls of his new life. He finally found a phone that worked near the train station as he dropped his last coins in and dialed Dmitri.

23

THE PATH

"La' Breithe shona dhuit, la' breithe, la' briethe, la' briethe shona dhuit!" Gregan bellowed the traditional Gaelic happy-birthday tune, his nose a bit red from his second Irish whiskey. He beamed with pride as Sister Blandine carried out the three-tier birthday cake decorated in green and white icing and topped with a mariposa good-luck clover.

"Gregan, come here, and help me with this cake," said Sister Blandine as Gregan grabbed Shannon's hand and twirled her as if he intended to start an Irish jig.

"Today is our Shannon's eighteenth birthday, and what a fine young woman she has become!

Shannon blushed, as usual, her freckles turning a bit redder, and she stopped in the middle of the twirl, planting her hands on her hips to feign surprise that Gregan wanted to dance. She laughed loudly, curtsied to Gregan, and then pulled her unruly swirl of long auburn curls back into a ponytail as she escaped to the table. Gregan was always loud and fun and made life feel lighter. Shannon loved it when he spoke Gaelic, and his Irish tune made her laugh as well.

"Now, Uncle Gregan, you are embarrassing me again—and in front of all my friends!" Shannon said as Gregan followed her and pulled out the chair for her to sit at the front of the celebration table.

Gathered around the long wooden table in the kitchen of the St. Joachim convent were the people most important in Shannon's life, people who had nurtured and believed in her since her arrival seven years ago as a penniless orphan: Sister Blandine; Gregan; the parish priest, Father

Murphy; and the Nolans, Peggy and Jack, the main benefactors who had paid for her schooling and provided a stipend to help Sister Blandine with the necessities Shannon needed. More importantly, Mrs. Nolan had helped her understand the mysteries of being a young woman and taught her etiquette and social manners. Peggy Nolan had grown up in the French Quarter in New Orleans and had yearned to converse in her native tongue. She'd found Shannon an eager student and tutored her in French, which Shannon had picked up immediately.

Sister Blandine had been the mother she had never known, as Shannon had been raised only by a father after her mother's death at her birth. Shannon's father had tried to show his love for her, but he had been aloof and, as a simple laborer, had not known how to care for a little girl. Her education had suffered when she quit school after her father was diagnosed with cancer.

Sister Blandine had immediately focused on getting Shannon back in school at St. Joachim and enlisted the Nolans' help with the expenses of raising a young girl. Although Shannon had been shy at first and uncomfortable with other kids her age, she'd felt grateful to be back in school and soon begun to excel in her studies. Sister Blandine spent her afternoons helping Shannon with her homework and, most importantly, tutoring Shannon about their Catholic faith so she could prepare for her first communion.

"Shannon, my dear, blow out the candles, make a wish, and then tell us what your heart's desire is for your birthday," said Father Murphy, St. Joachim's parish priest, who had baptized Shannon on her twelfth birthday.

Shannon blew out the candles with one breath, squeezed her eyes shut tightly, and crossed her fingers as she made her wish. "Father Murphy, my heart's desire is to make all of you proud of me as I keep working to become a teacher. You have all been so generous with your guidance and love. I want to help other young girls realize their dreams, like you all did for me."

"Well then, Shannon, tell us old folks about being accepted at Boston College and all the adventures you are planning. And even though it's bad luck, I want to know about that wish you made!" Mrs. Nolan said as she started cutting the green-and-white birthday cake into thick slices for the guests.

Shannon laughed and passed out the cake slices, kissing the forehead of each person as she set a plate in front of him or her. "As you all know, I am not the adventurous type, so I'm not sure how to answer that part of your question, Mrs. Nolan, but I am excited about the teaching program at Boston College and am happy I will still be able to live with Sister Blandine and continue to work at the rectory while I go to college. It may take me awhile, but I will get my teaching degree!"

"You know you are welcome to stay with me forever, Shannon, but it's time for you to explore the world outside of our walls at St. Joachim," Sister Blandine said as she pulled an envelope from the pocket of her apron. "We have a birthday surprise for you, Shannon. The parishioners have set up a college fund for you that will pay for you to live on campus so that you can do nothing else but focus on your studies and be with others your age. We want you to enjoy the full experience of college life."

Tears welled up in Shannon's eyes as she took the envelope from Sister Blandine. In the envelope was a bank account statement in Shannon's name. The account held $10,000, more money than she could have imagined in one bank account. Along with her scholarship, this money would allow her to study full-time and not have to work.

Shannon's birthday wish had been answered.

24

LAST CHANCE

Rolf made it to the vacant building on the outskirts of eastern Warsaw just in time to see a Soviet government touring car pull off the road toward an abandoned park that still had old, large oaks standing despite the park being abandoned after years of neglect. He pulled his hat's sheep's wool earflaps down over his ears and pulled up the collar of his coat to keep the snow off his skin. It had started snowing heavily.

Rolf saw Dmitri get out of the touring car with his hands shoved in his pockets. He could see even from that distance that Dmitri was not pleased. Rolf was afraid to face him. He swallowed hard and walked forward.

"He said no," Rolf said as he crossed the street toward Dmitri.

"Don't give him that option," Dmitri snapped. "Make him say yes."

"I tried everything."

"Not everything! This has happened a few times before, but in each case, our agent found a way to change the mind of the shallow priest. Are you not as capable as the others, Rolf?"

"He won't budge."

"Budge him."

"How?"

"Any way that you can. This outcome is unacceptable."

"Isn't there another priest I could go to?"

"This is your family's church, and you have a history that can be traced. Maintain your cover, one that won't be suspected, and you will convince this priest. Do you understand?"

Rolf had desperately hoped his teacher would come up with some ideas to help him. Now, standing face-to-face with him in the falling snow, he realized he needed to work harder to convince Father Novak and prove to Dmitri that he could complete his assignment.

"He said he'd take me on as a student," Rolf said desperately.

"That's good." Dmitri almost smiled.

"But he said it will take time."

"You're an excellent student. Time is not an issue. You will have the opportunity to change his view."

"But he said—"

Dmitri cut Rolf off with a stinging slap to his face. The cold air and the emotion that accompanied the slap accentuated the physical pain. Rolf's hands curled into fists, and he kept them deep in his pockets so he would not touch his face—or Dmitri. After a moment of silence, Dmitri spoke.

"Did you mention the fact that you saw your parents murdered by Nazis in his church?"

"My uncle did."

"Talk about it in detail. Rub his nose in it."

"I will do my best, Comrade General."

"You will. I agree. You have no choice."

Dmitri turned abruptly to walk to the car but then turned back to Rolf and said, "You will not see me again. You are someone else's responsibility now. It would be wise never to even attempt to contact me again. But make no mistake: I will be watching."

Rolf stood in the falling snow, feeling the sting of the slap, and watched the touring car's taillights disappear. He knew two things: first, he would never again see Dmitri, and second, if he failed to get Father Novak to change his mind about recommending him for the priesthood, Dmitri would most likely order his death, since failure was never an option for Dmitri.

Rolf wandered around Warsaw for another hour before he returned to his uncle's house at six o'clock in the evening. His aunt and uncle were clearly upset when he walked in, as they had been worried when he disappeared for so long after talking with Father Novak. When Rolf told them Father Novak refused to recommend him despite his profession of faith and calling, Josef reacted by grabbing his coat and Rolf's arm and dragging Rolf back to the church to convince Father Novak of his mistake.

"You're breaking his heart," Josef said. "And mine, Father."

"I do not like breaking a young man's heart," Father Novak insisted. "And certainly not an old friend's." Father Novak again looked deeply into Rolf's eyes. "Do you believe in God?"

"Of course," Rolf said quickly.

"Why do you say 'of course' and not simply 'yes'?" Father Novak asked. "It's not a given." Father Novak again looked deeply into Rolf's eyes. "I look in your eyes, and I see a young man who is troubled inside."

Rolf hesitated and then blurted out, "My mother and father were murdered by the Nazis, along with a priest and members of the Polish resistance, right in front of me at this church. I have witnessed unspeakable evil from the Nazis and have seen the love of God from the nuns. I want to join them in sharing God's love."

"I believe that much," the priest said, "and I offer a prayer of thanksgiving for your deliverance and a prayer for their souls."

Josef put his hand on the priest's shoulder and spoke sincerely and firmly. "Let me put this to you another way, Father. My family has supported this parish for more than two centuries. You would deny us the opportunity to give the world a priest?"

Father Novak stepped away. He looked at Josef with compassion and said, "Josef, I will grant him another interview since it means so much to you and your family. But the final decision is mine, and I won't be bullied. First, I will give him a course of study on the catechism, and I will give him two months to complete the studies I have assigned him. Then I shall question him again. And, Rolf, honesty, please."

Josef bowed gratefully before the priest. "Thank you, Father. I can ask no more than that."

———◇———

Rolf took the books that Father Novak gave him and returned to his uncle's house. He studied them around the clock, staying up until all hours in his uncle's kitchen. He took occasional naps on the couch, but mostly, he worked on the books night and day. He was familiar with the material, of course. He had learned some of it at the academy, but it was in a different context now. He was studying for his life.

Once, in the middle of the night, he was aware that his aunt and uncle were standing on the stairway in their bathrobes, watching him pore over the books.

"If that stubborn priest doesn't change his mind," Rolf heard his uncle say, "I'm going to the bishop."

Sure enough, when the day of the all-important second interview arrived, Rolf walked into Father Novak's small office and saw a bulky gentleman with a large, round face in full bishop's regalia: black robe with red buttons, small skullcap, scarlet sash, and scarlet cape.

"Hello, Rolf," Father Novak said. "We are honored today with a visit from the bishop."

"An honor indeed," Rolf said. He breathed deeply, trying to control his nerves, just as he'd been taught.

"This is Bishop Pavnik," Father Novak said.

An awkward pause followed. Father Novak and the bishop looked at each other. Rolf sensed immediately that something was wrong. They seemed to be waiting for him to do something, but he could not figure out what. He knew he would not get a third chance. Then he saw the gigantic ring the bishop wore, and he knew.

His move was clumsy, but he made it. He bent over and kissed the bishop's ring. The bishop and Father Novak looked a little embarrassed for him, but they both smiled to allow the discomfort to pass.

"Your Excellency," Rolf said.

"Bless you, my son," said the bishop.

"The bishop will sit in on our meeting today," Father Novak said. "I have told him of your wish to enter the priesthood."

The questioning began. Father Novak queried Rolf about the catechism. Rolf fell back on his training from the academy, remembering to settle his breathing, calm his heart rate, and speak clearly, if a bit quietly. Then, when it came time to describe his calling, Rolf was ready. He had concocted a story about a time at Mass with the nuns who had taken him in. They'd been singing beautifully, and suddenly, the light from the sun had pierced through the stained-glass windows, and he'd known at that moment God was calling him to the priesthood.

Several awkward moments passed. Father Novak shook his head. "I have no choice but to deny your request again," Father Novak said.

"Are you serious?" the bishop asked.

"Yes," Father Novak said.

"This is a fine young man," the bishop said.

"I agree," Father Novak said. "He just isn't a sincere young man."

"I tell you I am," Rolf insisted.

"To stand before God is to stand naked," Father Novak said. "And to be fully exposed. God knows and sees all. That is a wonderful story, Rolf, but you never mentioned it before. When you bear false witness, you insult God's intelligence. Why lie about your life? What could it matter what you've done? Confess it in full to God. You will be forgiven."

"I have. And I always will."

Father Novak looked apologetically at the bishop and said, "I can't recommend him for the priesthood."

"I beg you to reconsider," said Rolf, more desperate than ever.

"I'm sorry," Father Novak said.

Suddenly, out from the bishop's flowing sleeve came an ice pick. In a swift motion, the bishop put the ice pick in Father Novak's neck, just behind the ear. It was the move of an expert assassin. Father Novak fell to the floor with the ice pick's handle sticking out the back of his neck. He bled little. He died in that instant.

Rolf's mouth dropped open, and he backed away from the bishop. Then he grabbed the bishop in a choke hold on instinct. The bishop, though choking, managed to reach into the pocket of his robe and pull out a strange-looking cross.

Rolf saw it and went inert, letting go of the bishop. The bishop gathered himself and then calmly pulled the bloody ice pick out of the dead man's neck. To Rolf's unspoken question, he said, "Yes. I had to kill him. It's all because of your blundering. The comrade general warned me you might not convince him, but I had no idea you were this pathetic. In another moment, you'd have told him everything. It would be a good thing for you if I made an incomplete report of this to the comrade general. Wouldn't you agree?"

"We will be executed for this!" Rolf gasped.

"The NKVD has a lot to say about who gets executed around here," the bishop said. "It will be found to be a natural death; I have done this many times. He passed out right in front of us. You tried to revive him, but it was too late. You will go tell your uncle that Father Novak has died quite suddenly of what will be termed a fatal heart attack. A state physician will provide the necessary autopsy. We will have a wonderful funeral. I will preside."

Rolf was gasping and trembling, not convinced someone wouldn't blame him for the priest's death. "What will happen?" Rolf stammered. "What will happen to me?"

"I will recommend you for the priesthood. After all, I am the bishop. It would have been better for both of us if your family priest had recommended you. We would both be less exposed that way. But of course, your incompetence made that impossible." The broad-faced bishop laughed sardonically. "You're my problem now. Help me with the body."

Rolf looked down at the dead priest.

25

FREEDOM

After the burial of Father Novak, the bishop accompanied Rolf to Belgium, where he would recommend Rolf for the priesthood. Rolf said little during the long journey. He realized that he would now have to become like this bishop and that Dmitri's training at the academy was not a game but to be practiced in the real world. From time to time, the bishop mentioned that Rolf should study hard and make the best of his preparations for the priesthood. For now, that was all that would be expected of him. The bishop reminded Rolf that he couldn't afford to make any more mistakes. Should there be a next time, it could prove to be fatal.

The bishop introduced Rolf to the presiding professor at St. Joseph's Seminary in Brussels, Father LaBeau. He was a rail-thin middle-aged man with a narrow face and badly receding hairline. The bishop told Rolf he was soon to be a bishop himself. Bishop Pavnik and Father LaBeau had long been friends, since their days in the seminary together. The bishop did not tell Rolf whether or not Father LaBeau had a Judas cross.

"I recommend this very dedicated and spiritually gifted young man from my diocese in Warsaw to the priesthood," the bishop informed his old friend.

"Your recommendation in this matter is enough alone to get him enrolled here at the seminary and taken under care," LaBeau said, smiling at Rolf. "Welcome."

When their visit concluded, before the bishop embarked on his journey back to Warsaw, he leaned close to Rolf and whispered, "No more mistakes.

Study hard, and work to get ordained. I will contact you when you are needed."

Rolf was relieved when the broad face of the bishop was out of his sight. He moved into his dormitory room in an old stone building built hundreds of years ago by a nobleman. The room was simply furnished, with a wooden desk, clean wooden floors, a dresser, and a bed. He stayed there at all times except when going to meals, vespers, or classes in the few other buildings across the manicured lawn and gardens. He lived as he had lived at Dmitri's academy in Moscow, speaking to no one unless spoken to and studying around the clock. He gave the appearance of praying and pretended piety when observed by others. He found the pretense of piety to his liking, for it was a way to shut everything out and focus. The priest's murder had brought up unpleasant memories—memories of his family's murder, the murders he'd seen the Nazis commit, the man he had killed under Dmitri's training—that interfered with his ability to think. Even with his training, he had a hard time reining in the panic that threatened to engulf him.

However, every day that separated him from the events of his past was a good day. Memories became more manageable with time. He was well fed, and as long as he preoccupied himself with learning, people left him alone.

Because Rolf was an advanced student, he did well in his studies. On his way to becoming a priest at the seminary, he became the youngest teacher at a Jesuit secondary school in Brussels. He taught Spanish and French. There, Rolf became a master of languages, becoming almost thankful for his boring language tutor at the academy. He enjoyed teaching young people.

Those were good years for Rolf. During that time, he found he could keep his mind focused, and the thoughts of Dmitri's threats and disappointment faded. Rolf, for the first time in his life, experienced happiness, as teaching came naturally to him.

All of that ended one day when a visiting Spanish Jesuit priest with a film can tucked under his arm walked into the school assembly hall, where all the students and teachers had gathered. While threading the sixteen-millimeter film projector, the Spanish priest told the high school students and their teachers that they were about to hear about something miraculous, something they might not believe.

"And yet," the Spanish priest assured them, "it really happened. And seventy thousand people saw it. The film of this miracle was made in 1952."

The lights went out, and the film began. It started with black-and-white images of Fátima, Portugal, and the field known as Cova da Iria. Portuguese shepherds and townspeople from all over Portugal gathered and watched three small children converse with the Virgin Mary in a series of apparitions, a deep-voiced narrator explained over a soundtrack of angelic music.

"They were watching a miracle," the narrator explained. He went on to relate that the mayor of Ourém kidnapped the children and threatened to kill them if they did not renounce the miracle.

Even though he did not believe in miracles, Rolf found himself drawn into the film because it was about children who were, to some extent, in danger. He could relate to that, having once been a child in danger himself.

Against the cloudy sky on the film screen, the image of the Blessed Virgin appeared. A narrator with a woman's voice spoke her words, accompanied by an angelic choir, calling out the first secret, a vision of hell.

"Plunged into a great sea of fire are demons and human souls together, glowing like embers, shrieking with pain and despair, and burning from within."

Rolf watched as his students covered their eyes when the visions of hell were shown on the screen. He was not particularly bothered by the visions, since he didn't believe in hell, but he marveled that the children squirmed and seemed to be afraid.

The second secret revealed in the film caught his attention, and he was caught off guard when the female narrator's voice was amplified: "Russia will spread her errors throughout the world, starting wars and persecuting the church. The virtuous will be martyred. Nations will be annihilated."

Rolf's mental and emotional agonies began. He knew full well that the Russian government had trained him to subvert the church because the church was the enemy, but he now began to wonder if he was a part of something evil. Even though he believed in neither God nor hell, he did find that he could not only believe in evil but also experience it as inescapable. Images of the man he'd murdered in cold blood and the murdered Father Novak flooded his mind, and he suddenly could not sit in the school auditorium while the film and lecture were presented.

He bolted out of the assembly hall and took to his room for several days, experiencing blinding headaches. Every night, he experienced nightmares that combined the worst of his childhood memories with his suppressed recollection of a man he himself had murdered at point-blank range. The nightmares marked the first spell of dark depression that he would struggle with in the coming months. He passed his depressive episodes off to his instructors as delicate health and was quite debilitated until he found ways to escape the mental torment and physical anguish.

"Liars, the whole lot of them," he mumbled in a feverish sweat. "Bullies too." An image of Dmitri and others in the NKVD flashed before him. "Get out! Away with you!" Rolf yelled, holding his head. He paced the small area between his dresser and bed, running his hands through his hair. Hadn't Dmitri been the loving father figure worth pleasing? Nothing could have been further from the truth. *The beatings.* Rolf touched his cheek where Dmitri had slapped it. *The manipulation. The carrot and stick.* Rolf shook his head. His only consolation was that Dmitri had said he would never see Rolf again.

The night bled to dawn, as did many after that, without sleep. Sleep brought horrifying images from his childhood, and waking brought agonizing fears of when the NKVD might show up and what they might order him to do. Ever present were the twin memories he wanted to submerge forever: the man he'd shot at point-blank range as a teenager and the murder of Father Novak.

However, when no one contacted him, he began to get a handle on the anxiety. He could manage to stay outside his room, going about his daily tasks, and he found if he stayed busy and came home tired, the nights were much easier to manage.

He wondered whether Stalin's undercover priest program had long ago been scrapped and forgotten, along with hundreds of other insane policies.

After all, Rolf had not heard from the bishop or anyone from the state since he'd entered the seminary. As time went by, he started to hope they had somehow forgotten about him.

26

1958

Father Carrera had spent thirteen years in Rome since Lucia dispatched him on his mission. Following his arrival, he was able to arrange an audience with Pope Pius XII and shared with him Lucia's story of the apparitions and her handwritten letter describing Mary's prophecies. He explained that the Blessed Virgin wished to have the secrets made known to each pope and that the letter's contents were to be shared with the world in 1960, as things would be clearer then. Until then, Father Carrera was to guard the secret. The pope then assigned him a post at the Vatican Secret Archives, where thousands of texts of sensitive documents were kept as part of the greater Vatican library. Many items, such as King Henry VIII of England's request for a marriage annulment, a handwritten transcript of Galileo's trial for heresy, and letters from Michelangelo complaining he had not been paid for work on the Sistine Chapel, were kept safely out of the public eye.

Now, all these years later, Father Carrera was sick. He had tried to call the pope and was on hold again. He knew he would soon be dead. However, he'd outlived Pope Pius, who'd died in October. It fell to Father Carrera to share the third prophecy of Fátima with the new pope. This job was important, because the new pope, John XXIII, would likely still be pope by 1960, only fourteen months away. He would have the responsibility to share the third secret of Our Lady of Fátima with the world at large.

Father Carrera hung up the phone, frustrated. John XXIII had again not taken his call, even when he'd used the words *Our Lady of Fátima*.

Those words had opened the door with the previous pope thirteen years earlier.

He still had the envelope, and he knew he had to get it to the pope. He thought about what to do. He remembered Sister Lucia's advice. He would use his own judgment and faith to pick a successor, someone who could safeguard the secret after his death. After hours of prayer, Father Carrera decided upon a young Brazilian archbishop named Octavio.

Octavio, who was slender and handsome, with jet-black hair and olive skin, was part of a new breed of archbishops at the Vatican, who often argued in favor of such ideas as the recognition of world religions and promotion of social welfare as important to the papal agenda. Father Carrera had first met Octavio in the Vatican library, where Father Carrera worked. Octavio, being Brazilian, spoke Portuguese. Father Carrera, in thirteen years, never had gotten over his homesickness for Lisbon. It gave him great joy to speak in his own language with Octavio. He and the young archbishop often engaged in lengthy conversations about world events and matters of faith. They disagreed about ecumenism, but they were closer in agreement on matters of social welfare because of Carrera's decades-long fight for the enforcement of child labor laws and the treatment of orphans.

He's perfect, Father Carrera thought excitedly. Octavio's youth was an advantage, and more importantly, he seemed to enjoy a certain cachet with the new pope. Most of the meetings the pope attended had to do with plans for a Second Vatican Council. Octavio was an active part of planning those proceedings, and that assured him the ear of the pope. However, the main reason he decided to trust Octavio was the friendship Carrera had found with him, the only such friendship he had formed during his time at the Vatican.

He called Archbishop Octavio from the hospital. Octavio came to talk to him there, bringing several newspapers. It was their custom to discuss newspaper articles when meeting for coffee.

After they had discussed the news for a while, Father Carrera leaned forward. "I have to entrust an important secret to you," he told his Brazilian friend. "It has to do with the prophecies of Our Lady of Fátima. Are you familiar with the story?"

"Yes, of course." Octavio smiled. "There's a Hollywood movie about it, starring Gilbert Roland."

"I know her, the older girl who received the messages from the Virgin Mary. Her name is Lucia. I visited her and the two other children in Fátima at the time of the apparitions. Thirteen years ago, I was summoned to a meeting with Sister Lucia, when she was cloistered at a convent in Tuy. She entrusted me with an envelope that she said contained the third prophecy of Our Lady. It has never been revealed in public. It is very important to the church, the world, and the welfare of children everywhere that Pope John know of this prophecy and make it known to the public. If I die before I can bring it to his attention, I want you to carry on this work for me. Would you?"

"Of course," Octavio said, a bit surprised by the request. "You pay me a great honor."

"Can you get me into the Vatican on Thursday? There's not much more they can do for me here. I'm sure I will be released by then. I may not have many days left, and I would like to show you where Sister Lucia's letter describing the third prophecy is kept under lock and key."

"Of course," Octavio said with great concern. "We shall do it."

Later that week, they did. Father Carrera could not walk well, and his breathing was labored. Octavio had to help him in and out of the cab, and as they walked toward the Swiss Guard at the private entrance gates, Octavio had to hold Father Carrera steady. When they entered the Belvedere Courtyard, Father Carrera directed Octavio to the Vatican library, a massive building filled with books and artwork from all over the world. They entered through the grand doors, past the statue of Hippolytus. Off on the side, not part of the library itself, was a suite of small offices, one of which he had used for many years. He locked the office door to ensure privacy. He removed a painting of Mary from the wall to expose a small recessed safe. He took a key from his pocket and unlocked the safe, exposing a compartment with an envelope in it. Father Carrera pulled out the envelope.

"This is it," he told Octavio. "I will leave a key for you in a safety-deposit box at the Vatican Bank so you may easily retrieve it when I die. This envelope written in Sister Lucia's own hand, the only account of the third prophecy, will then be entrusted to you and you alone."

"Have you read it?" Octavio asked.

"No. The only person who has read it was Pope Pius."

"What about the one who wrote it? Sister Lucia?"

"She is now a Discalced Carmelite at a convent in Coimbra. She speaks to no one."

Octavio moved so quickly that Father Carrera never saw him coming. He shoved Father Carrera to the floor and tightly held his hand over the sick priest's nose and mouth. Father Carrera gasped for breath, but none would come. He grabbed Octavio's hands, trying to get them to release, but they would not. He stared into the cold, hard black eyes of his friend until life left him, and his body went slack.

Octavio rolled him over, took the envelope and the keys, and then closed the safe and the compartment door, positioning the painting carefully. He wiped the keys and put them in Father Carrera's cassock. Then he put the body on a chair and pushed him forward, making it look as if he'd died at the desk. After a quick look around, Octavio left the office.

27

THE PRIESTHOOD

Rolf put on the white robe as he prepared to be ordained as a priest at twenty-five years of age after just more than six years at the seminary. A ceremony would be held at the Cathedral of St. Michael and St. Gudula in Brussels. Rolf had been told that more than two hundred priests and bishops would be in attendance. It was a ceremony Rolf had dreaded for months.

Rolf had participated in three other ordinations, assisting in each as the thurifer, holding the incense censer to his breast for hours as each of the priests and bishops welcomed the newly ordained priests. Rolf remembered his discomfort as the sweet-smelling smoke rose to the ceiling each time he swung the censer to signal for the next priest to come forward to welcome the newly ordained at the altar. Each priest would walk up the stairs toward the altar, kneel as he made the sign of the cross, and then approach the newly ordained to use oil to make the mark of a cross with his thumb on the man's forehead. Afterward, the priest would kiss him on both cheeks.

Rolf dreaded that part of the ordination ceremony for himself. He preferred to avoid intimate physical contact of any kind since it always reminded him of the day at the academy when Natasha had pressed her naked breasts against him in the maintenance closet. So far, he had managed to avoid any further humiliation from a woman, and although he had periodic sexual stirrings, he had remained celibate, as he had promised Dmitri. He had simply put a wall around himself, and although he was always respectful in his interactions with his fellow students and instructors, he remained distant and did not share anything personal with them.

He knew that as a priest, he would now have to come to terms with this issue, as he would be expected to comfort his parishioners as they dealt with the traumas of everyday life and death.

Rolf made his way to where he would process in with the other priests. He was uneasy. The ordination would finally fulfill an important part of the charge he'd been given by Dmitri. He wondered if Dmitri might be there or if other Soviet comrades would be there with his next orders. The ordination itself was a relief in that no Judas cross made itself known there. However, nothing had prepared Rolf for the intensity of the ceremony.

With the glow of the sun shining through the large, round stained-glass window, striping the back of his white robe with bright flashes of blue and red, Rolf lay facedown before the altar. The French-speaking Bishop LaBeau sang out the name of each saint individually, and after each, the congregants responded, "Pray for us."

"Guide and protect your holy church," sang Bishop LaBeau.

"Lord, hear our prayer," the others responded.

"Keep the pope and all your clergy in faithful service to your church," sang Bishop LaBeau.

"Lord, hear our prayer."

"Bless this chosen man," sang LaBeau.

"Lord, hear our prayer."

With his face buried in his folded arms, Rolf felt the power of two hundred holy men calling down God's blessing upon him. Even though he didn't believe in God, he found the moment awe-inspiring and was deeply moved by the majesty of the church. Rolf began to contemplate the idea of sacred duties and whether burying himself in those rituals might protect him against the forces of his past. The mysterious power of this sacred gathering and the ritual of his ordination seemed inspired by something beyond the earthly.

"Bless this man, and make him holy, and consecrate him for his sacred duties."

"Lord, hear our prayer."

Near the end of the mass, Rolf knelt before Bishop LaBeau, who invoked the spirit of God upon Rolf by the laying on of hands, and then the bishop lifted Rolf and turned him to face the line of almost two hundred priests and bishops who were there to welcome him into the priesthood. Rolf knelt again on the hard marble, but this time, he faced away from the altar and crucifix above. He knew from assisting at other ordinations that he must now bend in a bow from the waist to rest his forehead on the velvet cushion in front of him. The thurifer emerged from the side chapel and walked to stand at Rolf's right side. Each time the thurifer would swing the censor twice, it signaled that another priest was to step forward. Rolf would raise his forehead from the cushion to present it to his fellow priest for the blessing of oil and the kisses on each check, and then he would recline his upper body once again so the cushion would absorb the oil, clearing his forehead for the next blessing.

By the end of that part of the ceremony, Rolf was exhausted, but he knew he must maintain his calm demeanor for the final physical ritual once he was formerly ordained.

Bishop LaBeau enjoined Rolf to conform his life to the mystery of the Lord's cross and spoke the final blessing, which signaled that the formal ordination had been complete.

After that, more than two hundred priests and bishops spontaneously lined up to embrace Rolf and welcome him to the diocese. That part was human and heartfelt, not part of the ordination ritual. It was overwhelming, one man after another calling him brother. Rolf was in tears by the end of it.

After the long afternoon of celebration following the ordination, Rolf returned to him room, but he was unable to sleep. He sat at the foot of his bed, reflecting on the strange intimacy and acceptance he had experienced that day. That night, he resolved to immerse himself in religious life, and although he still did not believe in God, he realized for the first time that he might be in a place where he could begin believing in people, not having to be cautious and distant all the time. He also hoped he could free himself from the dread of a Soviet handler's return.

Rolf decided he would do so by committing to these sacred duties in one of the far corners of the earth.

28
ANOTHER SECRET

Octavio had dressed in a gray business suit for his flight from Rome to Geneva. He decided to take a taxi from the airport directly to the Hotel De La Paix instead of taking the train, as he was cautious he not been seen by too many people.

"*Grazie e buona giornata*," Octavio said as he paid the taxi fare and stepped out of the cab. He had decided to pose as an Italian businessman for this trip, and he was accustomed to switching between his native language of Spanish and Italian or even French. Language, for him, was a question of his mood, and he smiled in anticipation of his stay.

Octavio paused at the bottom of the marble steps that led to the lobby as a bellhop approached to retrieve his suitcase. Octavio thought for a moment about whether he should allow the bellhop to take his bag, but he decided it was all right to do so. This was Switzerland, the safest place in the world. It was a place for making watches and decadent chocolate and, of course, hiding secrets.

Octavio followed the bellhop to the front desk, reflecting on his luck at the Fiumicino Airport. He had gotten on the flight as a standby passenger for an immediate departure to Geneva, and he was positive he had not been followed. He let the bellhop take his bags to his room and stopped off at the bar for a drink.

Octavio ordered a glass of kirsch cherry vodka at the bar and walked out to the balcony overlooking Geneva Lake. He considered his situation and ran through all his options in his mind once again. He had always been a careful planner, mapping out every possible course of action for as long as possible. He had been given an assignment a year ago to affect the outcome of the Second Vatican Council in a specific way, but he had not been able to influence the debate sufficiently as the aide to Cardinal Gabrielle Gianfranco, the president of the Pontifical Council for Culture. He knew his Russian handlers would not be happy, so he had planned his escape quickly when a coded telegram from Moscow had arrived in his office. If the escape proved faulty, he still had a secret he believed could save his life. He had devised a contingency plan years earlier.

After his second vodka, Octavio decided to go to his room to change for dinner. He had heard about a restaurant set in the hills along the lake called La Pinte des Mossettes, where one could view Mont Blanc in the distance, and he would need to leave soon to make the reservation he had made when he'd checked in.

He opened the door to his room and froze. The suitcase was on the bed, but it was open. He quickly went to the bed, looking frantically inside the suitcase. He pulled out all the shirts and pants so neatly folded. Finally, he tipped the case upside down, scattering the remaining clothing on the bed. The gun case holding his revolver was gone.

A mistake. The bellhop and the drink. All a mistake. Octavio nervously ran his hand through his hair.

The door suddenly opened, and a tall man strode forward, holding a silenced gun pointed at Octavio's heart.

"Dmitri," Octavio said, betraying no fear. "It has been a long time."

"What did you not accomplish of your assignment during the Vatican Council?" Dmitri asked in a low tone that assumed total knowledge of the upcoming answer.

"Let's sit down, Dmitri, and let's talk about what I did accomplish."

"You were given two direct orders," Dmitri said as he waved the gun toward the sofa, summoning Octavio to sit. "Tell me why you are now in Geneva."

Octavio smiled, put his hands down, and sat on the sofa. He knew he could not betray fear. His temperament was perfect for just this sort of situation.

"The Metz Pact," boasted Octavio. "That move was all mine."

"We don't talk about that," Dmitri said simply. "Do not bring it up again."

"Oh, calm yourself, Dmitri," Octavio said, as if he were talking to a friend. "There's nobody here but us, is there? What is wrong with saying things that both you and I know are true? There was a meeting in Metz, France, between Cardinal Tisserant and a certain KGB operative whose name you damn well know. And at that meeting, it was decided that there would be no condemnation of Soviet Communism issued from the Vatican during the entire three-year Vatican II conference. You know all about that."

"Then why are you telling me?"

"I made that meeting happen. I was the one who lobbied Cardinal Tisserant to go to Metz. That meeting would not have taken place without me."

"Who cares what a pope says about Soviet Communism?" Dmitri snapped. "I want you to tell me why you left before you completed your assignment. Two things: celibacy and infallibility."

"They are not ready," Octavio said quickly, trying another tack. "They want the clergy to be celibate, so they can control the religious. It is simply who they are. They are proud of their high standards for clergy."

Octavio did not see Dmitri react to anything he told him as Dmitri stood with the gun pointed at him.

"It never would have passed, Dmitri. I suggest you look at what did pass. The possibility of a vernacular Mass. Alternate penances instead of the obligatory no meat on Friday. Ecumenism. The recognition of other religions. They came a long way."

"Who cares what they want? Your assignment was twofold: pass a resolution relaxing the celibacy vow for priests and nuns and pass a resolution redefining papal infallibility."

"Next time."

"There won't be a next time for you, Octavio."

"Before you kill me, please understand that I have something you will want. Something I've held back just in case I might find myself at this very juncture with you. If you kill me, you will not get it."

"There is nothing out there that I need that badly."

"How about the third prophecy of Our Lady of Fátima?"

Dmitri was quiet and still. Octavio waited a moment to see if that meant anything to him. Dmitri betrayed nothing, but he didn't shoot.

"You have heard of it?" Octavio asked.

Dmitri nodded.

"The Portuguese nun who claimed to have heard the prophecy from the Blessed Virgin wrote it down only once. There is a legend that says her bishop has it, but I have it. And no one living has seen it except me and Sister Lucia, who has taken a vow of total silence on the subject. The Portuguese priest she entrusted it to entrusted it to me. He showed me where it was hidden. I killed him and replaced it with a forgery. In this forgery, I excised many things she had written down, especially any instructions alluding to the Soviet infiltration of the Catholic priesthood. Had this original prophecy ever been made public, you and I and our entire project would have been exposed to the world. By stealing it, I have, in a sense, saved us from that fate. We may now, thanks to my efforts, continue our path. I left in the forgery one part of the original prophecy, a mention of a bishop clad in white stumbling across a field of strewn corpses. I left that in because it seemed obscure enough, and on the off chance a papal emissary might have a conversation with Sister Lucia on the subject, she might hear that reference and believe the entire prophecy was intact. I gave that to the pope. But the real prophecy—it is amazing, Dmitri. It tells how the church will self-destruct in the most publicly humiliating way you could possibly imagine. It is uncanny, the things she predicted. She knew about us, Dmitri. She predicted our activities back before even the revolution. Because I have it and it can never be made public, there is no way they can heed her warnings. You must see this prophecy, Dmitri. And if you kill me, you never will. I'm the only one who knows where it is."

Dmitri shot Octavio twice between the eyes.

"To hell with you and your secret prophecy," Dmitri said to Octavio as Octavio crumpled to the floor.

29

AFRICA

After ordination, Rolf volunteered for a pastorate in Kampala, Uganda. Africa was about as far as he could be from the watchful eye of the KGB. The small church on the outskirts of the city had a lot of potential, and Rolf was working in the office. *The heat and humidity will take some getting used to*, he thought, wiping his brow. *No snow here.*

Rolf was working with a local deacon, Kintu. Kintu was a tall, thin man with very dark skin and a very bright smile.

"The cases of water are in the shed," he told Rolf.

"Any trouble with the landing?" Rolf asked. He had learned to fly a small plane, and Kintu and Rolf took turns using it to get supplies that would otherwise have been hard to get, if they could get them at all.

"None at all."

"Good, good. That will help many, to have clean water."

"It certainly will."

Later that afternoon, Rolf was walking to a local market. As he rounded a corner, he heard a slap. It was an unmistakable sound.

Just like that, he was no longer in Uganda; his mind had transported him back to Russia. He was in a room with Dmitri, where the beatings continued, and then again on the streets of Warsaw.

Rolf leaned against the wall, both hands touching the wall. His breathing was ragged as he struggled to maintain calm.

"Father? Father?" A familiar voice broke through. Kintu reached out to touch Rolf's sleeve, but Rolf recoiled a little.

"Father?" Kintu tried again softly. "It's all right," he said. He began to hum a lullaby.

Slowly, Rolf's breathing seemed to normalize. He felt bewildered. Kintu reached out again and took his sleeve.

"Let us go for a little walk," Kintu said, guiding Rolf away from the crowd beginning to gather.

Kintu took Rolf home and helped him to bed. It wasn't the first time. Occasionally, something would remind Rolf of his time hiding from the Nazis or one of his beatings from Dmitri. These moments would hurl his mood to unspeakable depths and send him to bed for days. He would feign poor health, but his physical health was fine. His mental agonies were unbearable.

Clutched in his palm at those times was a small book called *The Spiritual Exercises of St. Ignatius of Loyola*. He would choose those moments to meditate on the pains Jesus had felt on the cross. It was just what the book said: an exercise. He used it to vainly cover the memories of pain and deprivation in a murderous world.

The spiritual exercises did not give Rolf a spiritual life, but they gave him something to think about. He still struggled with his belief in God, and the more he suffered, the more he worried the agony would never cease.

To keep from thinking painful thoughts, he stayed active. Anytime he could think about someone else's troubles, he found peace from his own.

⟨———◇———⟩

When war broke out between Nigeria and Biafra, Rolf learned that from eight to twelve thousand Biafrans were dying of starvation every day. The Nigerian army had Biafra blocked off from any help and was executing a successful campaign of genocide. The Red Cross flew illegal airlifts of several hundred tons of food for Biafra at night, when Nigerian fighters were unable to shoot down the planes. From his position as pastor of St. Joseph's in Kampala, Rolf wrote letters and made speeches, raising contributions for the Biafrans from all over the world.

When he contacted the Red Cross, he discovered that the airlifts to Biafra had stopped because a Nigerian fighter had shot down a relief plane.

An American diplomat had informed the Red Cross that the Nigerian Air Force now had night fighting capability.

Rolf volunteered to make the nightly airlifts himself, flying a plane provided by Joint Church Aid, an umbrella organization for thirty-three church relief agencies. Every night, he braved the dark and the threat of the Nigerian Air Force to airlift food and supplies into Biafra.

One overcast night, as Rolf flew over Biafra, he encountered strong winds and rains. The visibility was so poor that Rolf experienced vertigo, a condition Rolf knew could rob him of the ability to judge distances. His pilot trainer had taught him that when a flier experienced vertigo, the only thing to do was watch the control panel and believe the instruments. Just as Rolf glued his tired eyes to the instruments, a deafening blast sounded. Rolf looked around, but all his instruments indicated the plane was still flying. He looked down and realized he was under fire from Nigerian ground forces with antiaircraft weapons. Even with the bad weather, poor visibility, vertigo, and hostile fire, he had to smile. He knew he was more at peace in that plane than he would have been lying safely in bed while haunted by his nightmares about the Nazis and the Soviets.

Rolf visited other countries, even at one point meeting Mother Teresa, who encouraged him to find the love of God. When a sudden death robbed the archdiocese of a bishop, the pope quickly appointed Rolf as bishop. Rolf served for three years, but he was not happy in a position that took him away from the work that kept him sane. He wrote letters to the pope and was finally relieved of the position and replaced by a more suitable priest who was a native of the diocese. Rolf was then appointed to serve as an executive board member of both Catholic Charities International and the Center of Concern. He spearheaded humanitarian projects in India, Africa, and South and Central America. He lectured on hunger throughout the world. He wrote three books on the subject, one of which netted him a coveted French literary award.

On good days, he thought of himself as indestructible and unreachable by the KGB. However, the fear always lurked just beneath the surface.

30
1976

Shannon helped her fourth graders put on their coats and gloves, led them out to the playground, and watched them instinctively run and jab at each other. From time to time, she glanced at the fence, where a tall, handsome man in a suit and topcoat watched her for the third day in a row. This time, aware that he had been caught staring, he smiled and waved. She walked over to the fence.

"Can I help you?"

"I didn't mean to stare," the man said. "Do you teach these kids?"

"I do. Fourth grade."

"You don't seem old enough to be a teacher."

"I got my teaching degree from Boston College four years ago."

"Well, that makes it official." The man laughed. "Are you from this neighborhood originally?"

"Grew up right there," said Shannon, pointing at the St. Joachim rectory next to the school. "I was raised by the sisters."

"I'm Phil," the man said.

"Shannon."

"Shannon," he repeated, as if it were now a special word. "I've been trying a case over at the courthouse, and it seems to break for lunch every day at the same time, so I walk over here to watch you and the kids."

"You're a lawyer?"

"Yes, a trial lawyer."

"Is it an exciting case?"

Phil laughed. "No. My excitement is walking a few blocks to see you and the kids on the playground. Would you care to meet for coffee later?"

He said it so casually and with such charm and innocence that Shannon found herself accepting his invitation without her usual circumspection.

After school that day, Shannon met Phil at the café around the corner from St. Joachim's. They talked of simple things, such as movies, childhood memories, music, and the recent Boston mayoral election. It wasn't what they talked about that interested Shannon; it was the way they talked. Phil seemed attentive and amused by whatever she said, hanging on her every word. This was a new experience for Shannon. She had not dated any of the boys in college, as she'd found them crass and immature, and once she had returned to live with Sister Blandine, she had thrown herself back into life at the parish, where most of the men were either priests or married. She was attracted to this man, however, and couldn't help imagining him as the hero on horseback from an old story Sister Blandine used to read her.

Phil and Shannon regularly met after that, either at the café or, in nicer weather, at the Boston Public Garden in the center of the city, where they would go on long walks around the waterfront neighborhood or pedal around the lake in the swan boats like tourists. She was deeply attracted to him, not only by the look in his eyes when he saw her each time but also by the lightness in his voice as he willingly discussed whatever topic she chose. The outright friendliness of his affection for her began to fill a void she had felt but had not understood until now. While she was growing up an orphan raised by the sisters, Shannon's only real companion had been Sister Blandine. In both high school and college, Shannon had kept to herself simply because her peers did not share her deep religious convictions and tended to behave in ways that made her uncomfortable. She had not made lasting friendships, and despite her beauty, she had never even been asked out on a date. She had virtually no experience with men. Phil's gentle, undemanding attentiveness intoxicated Shannon. Soon she found herself daydreaming about becoming his wife.

On a blustery day near the end of winter, Shannon and Phil walked out to the harbor to watch the ships. It was there where he first kissed her. It was her first kiss, and it meant more to her than anything that had ever happened in her life. Phil's tenderness and the way he held her face in his hands stirred a warm sensation inside her that she had never felt.

The following Sunday, Shannon sat down for lunch with Sister Blandine after Mass, as was her weekly ritual.

"I've fallen in love," Shannon shyly admitted as she dabbed the corner of her mouth with her napkin.

"My goodness, Shannon," Sister Blandine said as she jumped up to hug Shannon. "I don't know whether to cheer or to cry! Who is he? Tell me!"

"Oh, Sister, please, sit. Finish your lunch, and I'll tell you all about him."

"Shannon, this is such a surprise. We didn't know there was a special boy! Why haven't you brought him to Mass?"

Shannon cleared her dish from the table, and as she walked to the sink, she said, "He is not a boy, Sister. He is a man. His name is Phil."

Shannon looked back at Sister Blandine in time to see her cross herself and kiss her rosary. She knew it was going to be hard for Sister to accept that she had fallen in love with a man fifteen years older than she.

"His name is Phil Roth, and I met him in September. He would walk every day during his lunch break in the park across the street from school, and he always enjoyed watching the children play at recess." Shannon took a deep breath and brushed away the red lock of hair that had fallen past her ear from her long ponytail. "He is an attorney and has been trying a case at the district court for months, but he doesn't live in Boston. He commutes here from Hartford, Connecticut, and stays with family friends over in Framingham when he is here."

"Well, my goodness, he sounds like a very successful man, Shannon," Sister Blandine said as she took her own plate to the sink. Without looking at Shannon, she asked, "How old is he, Shannon?"

"Sister, he is a thoughtful, respectful person. He treats me with such kindness, and he is actually interested in what I have to say," Shannon said without answering Sister Blandine's question about Phil's age. "And he makes me laugh."

"But, Shannon, what do you really know about him? Have you met his family? Is he Catholic? Does he have siblings? How old is he?" Sister Blandine asked in rapid fire.

"No, Sister, I have not met his family, so I do not know if he has siblings." Shannon untied the apron she had put on earlier to prepare lunch. "Yes, he is Catholic, and he is thirty-seven."

"And he's never been married?" Sister Blandine asked as Shannon left through the back door of the kitchen.

◇————◇————◇

The following Friday, Blandine caught up with her old friend Police Lieutenant Gregan, now a plainclothes detective with the Boston Police, as he was on his way to confession at St. Joachim's.

"Our girl says she has fallen in love," Blandine said bluntly.

Gregan was immediately concerned. "You know the boy? Good Catholic?"

"I have no earthly idea. Shannon told me in no uncertain terms that he is a man, not a boy, and the only real things I learned before she stormed out of the parish on Sunday after lunch were his profession and where he lives." Sister Blandine's tone reflected her weeks' worth of worry.

"Sister, you sound worried." Gregan patted Sister Blandine on the back. "Is it his profession that has you so worried or something else?"

"Shannon said he is a lawyer and has been in Boston trying a case."

"What kind of lawyer?" Gregan asked, trying to withhold a judgmental tone. "Some lawyers do good work, but most of 'em I've seen are as crooked as the criminals they help return to the streets."

"I don't know. Shannon said something about him trying a case at the district court. But that's not what has me worried, Gregan." Sister Blandine sat down abruptly on the pew closest to the confessionary. "I'm worried about his age. She is not experienced enough in worldly matters to be dating a thirty-seven-year-old man."

"Give me his name, and I'll see what I can find out," Gregan said worriedly.

"You'll be discreet?"

"I am a professional."

◇————◇————◇

It had been two weeks since Phil had seen Shannon, and since his court case had been recessed for the day, he called Shannon at school and asked if she would meet him for an early dinner.

As Phil walked down the courthouse steps on his way to meet Shannon, he saw a large man waiting for him at the bottom of the steps, displaying a detective shield raised in his left hand.

"I'm Detective Gregan. I'd like a few words with you, Mr. Roth."

"I really have very little time," Phil responded curtly as he tried to walk quickly past Gregan.

"It's about the young woman you're on your way to meet right now," Gregan said, stepping in front of him. He had gotten Phil's attention. "Does Shannon know that you have a wife and two children?"

Phil said nothing.

"I suppose it hasn't come up in your conversations together." Gregan pointed at the wedding ring on Phil's finger. "Do you wear that when you're with Shannon?"

After a long silence, Phil finally said, "No. I take it off."

"I don't suppose you're preparing to leave your wife for her."

Phil shook his head.

"There are some very important people," Gregan said softly but firmly, "myself included, who take an abiding interest in Shannon's welfare. If you see her again, I'll know. And I'll see that your wife knows. Do we understand each other?"

Phil nodded.

Shannon arrived at the Union Oyster House about fifteen minutes before she was to meet Phil. He had invited her there for an early dinner, and she was a bit overwhelmed that he was taking her to such a legendary Boston landmark.

Shannon saw the famous sign as she approached the restaurant's entrance, and she crossed the street. "Ye Olde Union Oyster House, established 1826," she said out loud.

She smiled in anticipation as she opened the centuries-old door to the restaurant's vestibule.

"Welcome, madam, to the oldest restaurant on the Freedom Trail. May

I take your overcoat?" the hostess said as she reached out to take Shannon's coat. "Under what name is your reservation?"

"Thank you. The reservation is under Mr. Roth. I'm a bit early, but do you think you could seat me now?" Shannon said shyly as she took off her coat and gloves and handed them to the hostess.

"Of course. Let me see where you are seated." After flipping to the night's reservations in the handwritten reservation book, the hostess looked up and smiled. "Well, this must be a very special evening, as Mr. Roth reserved the Kennedy booth. Come this way."

Shannon had read that when President Kennedy was a senator, he would come to the restaurant every Sunday afternoon and stay for hours, always requesting the same booth. The story was that he would often bring about five newspapers and read for the whole afternoon as he nursed one order of lobster stew. The restaurant had formally dedicated the booth to President Kennedy the year before and had labeled it with a plaque and an engraved image of Kennedy.

"I will bring Mr. Roth up when he arrives. In the meantime, I will ask Maurice, your waiter, to stop by." The hostess smiled as she unfolded a napkin and placed it across Shannon's lap.

Shannon rubbed her hands across the solid oak tabletop and then placed a palm on the image of President Kennedy. "Great men are few and far between," she said. Then she crossed herself and whispered a soft prayer. "Heavenly Father, please guide me as this love I have for Phil grows. Please help me know the right things to do and—" Shannon stopped mid-prayer as she heard the voice of Sister Blandine.

"Shannon, my dear child, Father Yeagar and I are here to talk to you about something very important."

"Sister, how did you know I was here? Did you follow me?" Shannon said as she slid out of the booth and stood to confront Sister Blandine. "Phil is meeting me here for a special evening, and I think he may ask me to marry him. Why do you not trust my judgment?"

"Shannon, please sit down. I am so sorry to surprise you, and I'm sorry you are upset with us being here. But when we tell you what we have learned, you will understand. I just don't know how to, well—Father Yeagar, can you start?"

"Shannon, we have learned that Mr. Roth is not the man he portrays himself to be. Yes, he is an attorney, and yes, he is from Connecticut. But he is already married, Shannon, and he has a family there."

Shannon looked angrily at Father Yeagar and then at Sister Blandine. "I don't mean to be disrespectful, Father, but I don't believe you. And I don't understand why the two of you would try to hurt me by saying such awful lies about Phil. I thought you loved me and wanted me to be happy."

"Shannon, we are sorry to cause you hurt, but Detective Gregan checked out Mr. Roth's background and confronted him this afternoon. He admitted everything, and that's how we knew you were here." Sister Blandine reached out to take Shannon's hand. "Come. Let us take you home."

"No, I just can't believe what you are saying is true. He told me he loved me. I loved him." Shannon started to sob. "I can't … No, I need to talk … No, I can't live without him. No. Please. What is happening?" Shannon broke down as Sister Blandine wrapped her arms around her, and she buried her face in Sister's chest.

31

THE HOLY PLACE

Father Rolf Wozzak held a suitcase in each hand, standing in Italy. In the pocket of his robe was a receipt for several boxes of books that would be delivered one day soon.

He was overwhelmed by the power of the Vatican. It was a collection of breathtaking art and architecture. It was the smallest sovereign nation in the world, yet its power and beauty could be felt all over creation.

The word *impenetrable* came into his mind as he looked at the gates. The gates where he stood had been designed to repel invading armies. Few people ever got to see beyond St. Peter's Square and its massive cathedral.

He walked to the gate and presented his orders to the officer of the Swiss Guard who was there to secure the gate. One glance at the sealed document Rolf presented made the guardsman open the door to the private entrance to the residential and administrative areas.

Waiting on the other side of the private entrance doors with an outstretched hand was a cardinal at least ten years older than Rolf. He was tall and slender and had a certain zeal about him. He had a round face, thin dark hair, and a gleeful smile. Although a cardinal, he greeted the newcomer as a brother, a peer, an equal. Rolf soon realized why. The tie was one of national origin.

The cardinal extended the kiss of peace to Rolf, who responded in kind.

"Father Wozzak, I am Cardinal Wojtyla," the cardinal said in a language Rolf hadn't spoken in many years, "but please call me Karol."

"And it's Rolf. My pleasure."

"I am here to greet you because we are both Polish. Don't get used to it. You'll be up to your neck in Italians soon enough."

Both men laughed.

"I have long admired your work all over the world," said Karol.

"Thank you," said Rolf, self-conscious because he knew nothing of this Polish cardinal. "My eyes are wide—is it obvious? I'm like a tourist."

"This is your first time here?"

"I have visited a few times. But I always forget the true grandeur. I am always new to it. Absolute beauty everywhere you look. The books don't do it justice."

"In that case, you'll love what comes next. A certain audience with someone?"

◇

"Your Imminence, may I present soon-to-be Archbishop Wozzak," said Karol.

"Your Imminence," Rolf managed to say, although he was dumbstruck.

Sitting in a large, ornate chair with red cushions, the pope wore his typical white vestments with the white zucchetto skullcap, and his beautiful gold long-chained pectoral cross hung around his neck.

"Father Wozzak," said Pope Paul, "we meet again."

"I am honored that you remember," Rolf said.

"When a Catholic priest flies a humanitarian airlift against hostile fire anywhere in the world, that is a memorable day at the Vatican. How could I forget you? Besides, I have Mother Teresa to help me remember you."

Rolf smiled at the thought of the little nun. "How is Mother Teresa?"

"I worry for her health," the pope admitted. "Sainthood awaits her no doubt, but I'd rather wait until her work here on earth is done."

"We need her," Rolf said.

The pope shifted in his chair. "But I am sure you are wondering why I have called you here. It's not only to consecrate you as archbishop but also to offer you a full-time position with the Secretariat of State."

Rolf had heard as much, which was why he'd come with his belongings, but it was wonderful to hear it from the Holy Father.

"But why make me archbishop if I'm not returning to my diocese?"

"Because I want you near me," the pope said. "Help us guide our policies toward third-world countries with your knowledge of Africa, India, Central and South America, and the Far East. Help us help them. Lecture us about your experiences. And congratulations—your book on world hunger has made quite an impression on all of us. When a priest wins a literary award for nonfiction, that is also a good day at the Vatican. You have given us many such good days."

All three laughed. Rolf was immensely proud. Somewhere in his mind were the words "If I die now, it was all worth it." But he didn't want to die at all. For all intents and purposes, it looked as if the best part of his life was just beginning.

The Secretariat of State, the government of the Roman Catholic Church, performed all political and diplomatic functions of Vatican City and the Holy See. It was divided into two sections: the section for general affairs and the section for relations with states, known as the First Section and Second Section, respectively.

Rolf was quickly drawn into a whirlwind of meetings at the Secretariat of State, interviews on radio and television talk shows all over Europe, book signings, magazine and newspaper interviews, and a schedule of world hunger lectures that kept his suitcases packed and made his face a familiar one to the Swiss Guard at the great bronze door long before the ordination was to take place.

Rolf went to work for the Second Section as personal attaché to the Vatican's foreign minister. It was an important job but one that enabled Rolf the freedom to continue his successful lecture tours. He was especially busy lecturing on world hunger at various conventions all over Western Europe and North America, but despite the frenzy of travel and constant engagements, he continued to worry that a contact from the past would interrupt his new life.

When he was asked to speak about hunger, he would look out at rows and rows of earnest faces, saying, "You can't really understand the impact of starvation until you see the children." His eyes fell upon each face, making certain that the one face he never wanted to see again, a face he hadn't seen in twenty years except in his nightmares, was nowhere in the vicinity. His old fears would not die.

Rolf walked in the procession through the elliptical colonnade and the two pairs of Doric columns of St. Peter's Square due east of the basilica and then into the basilica itself, past the masterpiece known as the *Pietà*, and under the dome Michelangelo had designed in the sixteenth century. Rolf could not help but be amazed.

This was to be an age-old ceremony involving weeks of preparation spearheaded by the minister of liturgical ceremonies, including the timing of the procession, the careful laying out of vestments, preparations for thousands of guests, and the assembling of a score of angelic-voiced children's choirs.

It took place within St. Peter's Basilica, a monument to Peter the Rock. After St. Peter was martyred on an inverted cross, he was buried in a small-roofed grave on the side of Vatican Hill. Three centuries later, the first Christian emperor, Constantine, built the basilica on the site of St. Peter's grave, although it was on a hillside.

Dressed in his purple vestments with thirty-three buttons representing Christ's thirty-three years on earth, the tall white miter, and the customary shepherd's crook symbolizing a bishop's role as caretaker of the flock, Rolf came forward for the papal laying on of hands.

As was his habit, he scanned the people in the audience. He saw many of his fellow teachers and grown students from the Jesuit high school in Brussels where he'd taught a decade and a half earlier. Even a few priests and parishioners from his church in Uganda had made the journey to celebrate the consecration. Also present were representatives of the major international world relief organizations, all of whom had benefited from Rolf's good works. It was Rolf's most joyous moment.

Then he saw a familiar face in the third row in the front of the cathedral. He recognized the broad face with wide cheekbones and full, sagging cheeks. He recognized the Polish bishop who had murdered Father Novak so long ago in Warsaw. In a way, it was a relief: he could stop worrying when they would appear again, as there sat the evil that had haunted him.

For the first time in many years, he realized that once again, he would be in the grips of his Russian controller, unable to implement his own plans.

32

THE NEXT ASSIGNMENT

After the ceremony, Rolf hurried to his quarters and locked the door behind him. However, the bishop was already there waiting for him. Angry at the intrusion, Rolf also felt a calm, an absence of fear.

The bishop stood, holding out the Judas cross. Although Rolf said nothing, the bishop read his thoughts.

"You remember me then," the bishop said.

"Some faces you don't forget," Rolf said.

"I'm flattered."

"Don't be."

"It's been many, many years since we last spoke," the bishop said, sitting next to him.

"Yes, it has."

"After what I considered to be a rough start, you've done very well for us."

"I've done nothing for you," said Rolf. He wanted to tell this man that he and the KGB had no hold on him.

"You have completed your first and, may I say, most difficult assignment," the bishop said proudly. "To make a name for yourself in the priesthood was the underlying mission. Now you're archbishop. This is an area in which many of our most promising operatives have failed. It is not every man who has the personal qualities that make for a successful and influential priest. Those of our agents who have succeeded in climbing the Catholic ladder, so to speak, have done so in very much the same way that it is done in party politics: through equal doses of intimidation and obsequiousness. They go from throttling a neck to the most elevated kind of flattery and then back again. It works for a few, but most fail to get any control. If one becomes too disagreeable, he is judged as godless. A priest who seems godless goes nowhere. But you." The bishop started to laugh so uncontrollably that he lost the thread of his words.

Rolf looked upon this man, a gross reminder of his past, as the man convulsed with laughter, and he thought the bishop's behavior was oddly grotesque.

"You," the bishop said, recovering, "made an ingenious choice about how to do it. I have to admit that I misjudged you. I thought you were Stalin's one mistake. I should have known. That man was a genius visionary to have seen in you those qualities when you were nothing but a young child alley rat. And of course, Dmitri gave you excellent training. You may be our finest operative ever."

"I assure you," Rolf said, gritting his teeth as an intense dread engulfed his entire body, "I am no operative whatsoever."

"You can drop the act," the bishop said.

"It's not an act," Rolf said. "I know who you are."

"Yes, I know you do," the bishop said. "I admit I misjudged you, but I've now studied you for many, many years." He almost looked as if he would pat Rolf's arm and shake his hand, but instead, he said, "You chose the hardest path toward gaining influence within the priesthood. You chose the saintly path. You became known all over the world as the priest who feeds the hungry. The pope wants to wear you like a medal." The bishop suppressed another laugh. "Your credentials are beyond question. Brilliant. You've done very well for us, for here you are at their most holy place on earth, at a time and place in which you can render most invaluable service to us."

"But it's been so many years," Rolf said.

"Yes," the bishop said. "We've established that."

"I never heard from you," Rolf said. "Or from anybody even remotely connected to—"

"Oh, we've been around, working on our plans. There has been no need to contact you until now. You've done everything perfectly. You had excellent training. We didn't have any immediate need for you. It was better for establishing your cover to keep you free of any contact with us for as long as possible."

"That was another life," Rolf said.

"Your life is ours," the bishop told him.

"I don't believe that anymore," Rolf said bravely. "You see, I have been all around the world—"

"I know all about it," the bishop said, interrupting.

"I've seen amazing things," Rolf said. "I've been surrounded by saints. My life did not really begin until I became a priest."

The bishop's wide face became even wider with a broad smile as he said softly, "And you believe your previous commitment does not matter?"

"I am not a Communist, and I will not serve you."

"It doesn't matter." The bishop dismissed the idea with a wave of his hand.

"When I made the commitment, I did not even know what the word *Communist* meant," Rolf said.

"Your training will guide you," the bishop assured Rolf. "With my help, you will do wonderful things for us."

"I serve only God now," Rolf said weakly.

The bishop now smiled fully, a gleam in his eye showing that he was warming to this challenge. "You don't believe in God, Rolf."

"My belief is irrelevant," Rolf said before he really knew he was saying it.

"As you were taught," the bishop said with a self-satisfied chuckle.

"My service is everything."

"Well said."

"And my service, now that I am old enough to make a valid commitment, is only to God."

"In whom you don't believe."

"I am talking now about my service."

"You serve the pope, right?"

"Yes," Rolf said proudly. "I serve the pope with all my body, heart, and soul."

"So it's not only God you serve."

"I will not help you."

"You owe us your life," the bishop said in a voice that made Rolf's skin crawl. "I covered for you when you failed with Father Novak."

"You killed him; I didn't," Rolf said.

"Have you told anyone about it?" the bishop asked.

"No," Rolf admitted.

"Not even in confessional?"

"No."

"You see?" The bishop clapped his hands in gleeful triumph. "That's your training."

"It's a very ugly memory."

"Still, if it weren't for that one decisive act, you would not be here today, serving the pope. You were eating out of garbage cans when we found you. You would have stayed there. You see, it doesn't matter what you think or feel. Are you ready for your assignment?"

"No."

"There is a certain visitor to the Vatican—"

"I cannot accept this assignment."

"It was accepted for you the moment you began to enjoy the hospitality of the state. There is a certain visitor to the Vatican. You will hear his confession."

"And?"

"That's all."

"You just want me to hear his confession?"

"That's all."

Rolf thought about the request for a moment. Could it really be that simple? "I would do that anyway."

"There you are." The bishop smiled. "You drew an easy one."

"Are you asking me to break the seal of the confessional? Because I won't."

"We shall see if you won't," said the bishop, smiling proudly. "You have had excellent training."

The bishop left.

Rolf was in turmoil. What should he do next? If he returned to Africa, they'd find him. Now that his position had some prominence, it would be difficult, if not impossible, to hide. There was no way out. He had to do what they said to do.

Rolf tossed and turned that night with sleepless dread, wondering how to extricate himself from the clutches of the most powerful dictatorship in the world. The memories, pains, and waking nightmares returned, making his head pound with excruciating pain. The smell of the rotting corpses of occupied Warsaw filled his senses. He requested sick leave from his duties at the secretariat and stayed in his room, trying to untie the knot in his brain. He found he could not manage a coherent thought.

After several days, Rolf tried to return to his duties. He was hearing confessions at one of the ornate confessionals at the Vatican, when, through the small opening, Rolf saw a man holding an object, and the red stones caught the light: a Judas cross.

"Bless me, Father, for I have sinned," the man said softly.

Rolf knew at once that this was the man the bishop had mentioned. "Are you Catholic?"

"Yes, Father."

"I will hear your confession." Rolf pinched the bridge of his nose and looked forward, listening intently.

"One, fifty-six, seventeen, and the color green," the man said.

"Is that your confession?" Rolf asked, but there was no answer. The man was gone.

That night, while Rolf was returning to his room, he encountered the Polish cardinal Karol, the man who had greeted him at the bronze door.

"Are you all right, Rolf?" Karol asked. "I heard you were ill."

"I think I had the flu," Rolf said.

"Yes, you do look pale," Karol said. "Do you fish?"

"No." Rolf hesitated, a bit confused by Karol's inquiry. "I never have."

"Then you will come with me some time," Karol insisted. "Best thing for you. I have a secret fishing spot. Nobody knows about it, only me and hopefully you, if you come with me. You must be careful around here; these Italian archbishops will fish any spot dry if they get a chance. But you'll come with me. You'll see."

"I can't be out in the cold and wet," Rolf lied. "Not until I have fully recovered."

"Oh yes, of course, my friend," Karol said. "You must recover your health first. But once you have done so, a fishing trip in the early morning air will have you feeling more robust than ever."

Rolf stopped at his room. "Thank you, Cardinal," he said.

"Please. Call me Karol. We're a couple of Poles, you and I."

"Sorry," Rolf said. "Karol."

"Until we go fishing then," Karol said.

Rolf entered his room and latched the door behind him. He went immediately to the basin to wash his face. When he stood back up, he saw the bishop standing behind him.

"One, fifty-six, seventeen, and the color green," Rolf said instinctively. He slapped his hands on the edge of the basin. His training had indeed been deeply engrained in him.

"That was easy," the bishop said.

"Will someone die because of this code I have passed to you?"

"No. One, fifty-six, seventeen, and the color green have no importance whatever. This has just been a test to assure me of what I already knew."

"What was that?"

"That your training makes you mine," the bishop said as he unlatched the door and left the room.

In a sudden panic, Rolf retrieved his suitcase from under the bed. He opened it, tossed it onto the bed, and began emptying his closet.

33

THE ROAD NOT TAKEN

Rolf left the Vatican that night. The Swiss Guard at the bronze door waved him through with a smile, since his comings and goings had been so frequent, and the archbishop tunic, Rolf found, hid much.

As he walked briskly to the cab stand, he looked back at St. Peter's Square to see if he was being followed. The most beautiful place on earth had quickly become a deadly trap.

How he longed for the slums of Calcutta, the villages of Biafra, or the labor camps of the American Appalachians, places where the starvation and suffering would have made most people uneasy. Those were the only places where he had ever in his life felt a belonging and a freedom.

When he hailed a taxi, and reached for the door, he turned again. He thought he saw a dark figure emerge from St. Peter's Square—a rotund figure that could have easily been the bishop following him.

Rolf sighed. He needed to get out of Vatican City immediately and then figure out how to get out of Rome altogether.

He quickly got into the taxi and asked for a ride to the Termini train station, thinking the station would provide the anonymity he needed. The station would be empty at that hour save for the occasional homeless person looking for a warm corner to sleep in for the night.

When he arrived, he located the bathroom. He pulled his pants, shirt, and loafers out of his bag. He removed and discarded his archbishop robes in the trash container. He then took off again in a different taxi so as not to be recognized.

He asked the cab driver to take him to an all-night pawnshop. When he arrived in a seedy part of Rome, Rolf didn't hesitate to open the door.

The pawnbroker barely moved, his watchful eyes following Rolf as he entered the store.

Rolf pulled out the Judas cross and gave it to the pawnbroker. "I'd like to sell this."

The pawnbroker examined the cross under the lamp, watching the brilliant red rubies catch the light. He tested the gold and then offered enough money for Rolf to plan his escape from Rome and secure passage on a boat to some obscure and distant port.

First, he needed to find a place to think and take time to calm down so he could figure out how the brainwashing he'd received in his adolescent years had now made a grown man a slave to the KGB.

There was a hotel across from the pawnshop. The dirty windows and the trash in front of the building were fine with Rolf. He walked up to the front desk just as the sun was coming up. The sleepy-faced hotel clerk checked him in without asking any questions.

Rolf sat on the bed and watched the sun rise over the alley and garbage cans behind his room. He thought about where to go and how to avoid being recognized or followed.

Not hearing from the Russians had somehow created a life absent all the horrors of his past. Now that life was lost, and Rolf felt more desperate than he ever had, even when he had been a homeless orphan in Warsaw. He thought about suicide for the first time in his life. Strangely enough, Rolf had never, until that moment, seriously considered not wanting to live.

Of course, the church considered suicide a mortal sin. Because Rolf could no longer pretend he did not believe in God, he struggled to understand how a loving or just God could allow his parents to be killed by monsters or allow the starvation and hopelessness that existed all over the world. Did any of it matter? How ironic to finally reach some peace through his work in the church and then have to run away from the very place that should have been immune to evil.

He tried to sleep but found only a restless sleep of about an hour. Rolf lowered himself to his knees and began to cry. He struggled to allow himself to pray for the first time from the heart and not just from the formality of the liturgy.

"Dear God," he said, "I want to continue good work. I—" Rolf jumped to his feet. Someone was knocking on the door.

"Cleaning service."

"Not now," said Rolf, but the knocking continued once more.

Rolf grabbed his wallet and jacket. His suitcase was open on the bed. For a brief moment, he thought about leaving it, but he scooped it up quickly and put the shoulder strap across his body as he ran to the window to escape. He crawled out the window just as the knocking stopped.

He walked across the first-floor roof, found a fire escape, and climbed down to the alley. He had already tied his tie by the time he emerged from the alley. He looked both ways, chose a direction, and walked briskly for a few blocks, regularly looking back to see if he was being followed.

Sure enough, a swarthy man in a tan topcoat followed for several blocks. Rolf started walking faster, weaving in and out of pedestrians on the busy city sidewalk now filled with the rush of lunch-hour activity.

The man in the topcoat continued to follow. Rolf made a sudden dash right out into the street. Cars honked wildly and screeched to a halt. Rolf made it to the other side of the street and looked back.

The man in the topcoat was nowhere to be seen. Rolf continued his walk up the opposite sidewalk, now going against the flow of pedestrian traffic. He dodged and weaved, narrowly avoiding one collision after another.

He looked back again and saw two priests coming up behind him, also walking against the flow of pedestrians. Rolf began to run.

The priests began to move faster too.

At the end of the block, Rolf quickly turned a corner to see if he could lose them, but he found himself surrounded by the crowds of the afternoon market in the Piazza Vittorio. Dodging and weaving the crowd, he looked over his shoulder again, and as he did, he lost his balance as his foot caught the edge of a fish vendor's bin. Rolf tried to right himself, but as he scrambled to avoid the fish bin, he tumbled headfirst into a young woman who held two grocery bags.

The young woman fell hard, first bouncing off Rolf and then falling backward and hitting her head on the pavement, where she lay still. Her grocery bags tore open as they followed her to the pavement. Tomatoes, mushrooms, canned goods, and loaves of bread spattered over the cobblestone.

Rolf's automatic instinct had been to drop and roll, and as he scrambled back up to his feet, he fought the desire to keep running. The young woman seemed to be injured, and a crowd had begun to gather. As she lay inert on the walk, Rolf looked down at the young woman's pale, soft face framed by flowing auburn hair. She wore a simple green button-up sweater with a wool skirt, attire that looked more American to him than Italian. Something about her reminded him of the Polish waitress in the library many years ago. Rolf had not been able to help the waitress that night as he hid in the rafters, and his inaction haunted him every time he heard her cries in his dreams. He knew he could not abandon this woman now, having been the cause of this accident, despite the danger of being seen.

As the crowd gathered around Rolf and the injured woman, Rolf looked up to see the two priests who had been following him making their way through the crowd straight toward Rolf. Just then, the old woman from the fish-vending cart pushed past Rolf and bent over to check the fallen woman's pulse.

"She is alive but unconscious!" yelled the old woman. "Someone take her to the hospital now."

Rolf quickly scooped the young woman up in his arms and hurried away from the market and back toward the piazza, where taxis were parked at the corner. He left the priests behind.

"We must get to the hospital immediately," Rolf told the taxi driver as he struggled to get the woman into the back seat. "She has been injured in a fall."

"*Oh merda, sì!*" the driver said as he started the engine. "The emergency hospital is very close. Just minutes from here, near the Piazza del Popolo."

Rolf sat in the waiting room of the Giamcomo hospital, which had been a short drive away, as the taxi driver had promised. The medical staff had responded quickly when Rolf walked into the emergency room with the delicate young woman in his arms.

"What happened?" the nurse had asked as the orderlies put the woman on a gurney.

"I don't … I ran into her, and she fell," Rolf had said.

The nurse had looked at him sharply. "What is her name?"

"I don't know. We are strangers."

"Where does she live?"

"I don't know."

The nurse had looked at him again, exasperated.

"I'm sorry," Rolf had said.

"All well and good," the nurse had said, pulling the curtain closed. "The waiting room is out there, down on the left."

He stayed there, mostly for his own safety to avoid the priests who had been chasing him but also because for some reason, he was curious and truly worried about the condition of the woman.

Late in the afternoon, the doctor who had taken charge of the young woman walked briskly toward Rolf with a concerned look on his face.

"Sir, this young woman you brought to us—you obviously do not know her, but do you think there was someone in the market who might know her? She has lapsed into a coma, and we must find a relative or someone she knows to speak on her behalf."

"I'm so sorry, but I don't know her or even if she lives in the area." Rolf was rubbing his eyes with both hands. "The accident happened at the Piazza Vittorio, so perhaps someone there knows who she is. I will go back to see if I can find someone who knows her."

As Rolf turned back to gather his belongings, the doctor extended his hand.

"I am Dr. Brunelli. You could have easily left after you brought the woman in. Instead, you have waited here a very long time. I can see that you are truly concerned for the woman. Ask for me when you return, and I will make sure the nurses keep you informed of her condition."

Rolf remembered the direction the taxi had driven and decided that walking back to the market would be faster than waiting for another taxi. The winter sun was beginning to set as he crossed the Piazza del Popolo toward the market. He was alone on the street this time and made it back to the Piazza Vittorio quickly. Although most of the vendors had already packed their remaining produce and closed their stalls for the day, the fish-cart vendor was still there, scrubbing the cobblestones around her cart.

"Pardon me, madam. My name is Heinrich. I was the man from earlier today who took the young woman to the hospital. They need to know who she is and how to reach her family. Do you know her?"

Rolf had quickly concocted the new first name, hoping that further inquiry on his identity would not be necessary.

The old woman dropped her broom and wiped her face with the tail of the soiled apron she wore. "Yes, I know her; she is my neighbor and my friend. Her name is Shannon. She does not have family in Rome. She came to Rome six months ago from America to work as a tutor for the Folonari family. She told me last week they are away on holiday. Will she be all right?"

Rolf was strangely relieved when he heard that this beautiful young woman was alone in the city. He was not sure why he felt that way. Perhaps it was simply that there would be no need now to deal with a family's anger over his carelessness. She was beautiful, and her beauty drew him in.

"The doctor said she is in a coma. It would be good if she had someone she recognizes there if she wakes up. Well, I mean when she wakes up. Would you come back to the hospital with me?"

On the walk back to the hospital, Rolf learned the old woman's name was Gianina Bruno, and she and her late husband had operated the fish cart at the Vittorio market for more than forty years. She was a small woman with physical strength that belied her size and her age, and she spoke simply in a matter-of-fact way.

"A young woman alone in Rome is no good. She is lonely. No friends her age. She always seems sad. And now this. No good." Gianina crossed herself, and as she did, she took a rosary from her pocket and brought it to her lips.

34

THE AWAKENING

The morning sun woke Rolf as Gianina pulled back the curtains from across the room. Rolf sat up, stretched, and rubbed the sleep from his eyes before he folded the blue hospital blanket and tucked it under the cushion of the couch that had been his resting place for three days. Gianina had come back to the hospital every morning to check on Shannon's progress. She had done the same thing every evening after closing the fish cart, and she and Rolf had spent many hours talking about Shannon and praying for her as they held vigil, waiting for Shannon to heal.

Dr. Brunelli had given permission for Rolf to stay in the family waiting room after Rolf had returned to the hospital with Gianina. He had been the doctor who'd cared for Gianina's husband as he lay dying in the same hospital just a few months before, and Rolf could see from their warm greeting that the doctor and Gianina had spent many days together through her husband's suffering.

"Wake up, Heinrich. We must pray our novena now." Gianina had started every morning with the same order to Rolf. She handed him a rosary and knelt at the makeshift altar she had set up in the waiting room.

At first, Rolf had been uncomfortable with Gianina's insistence that they pray. His experience of prayer, but for the brief time in the hotel room when he'd considered suicide, had always been for the purpose of ceremony, and as a priest, he had been the leader, not the led. Gianina's faith and fervent belief in the power of prayer intrigued him. He knew she had begun to trust him because he appeared to believe in God's power as well, and taking part in the daily prayers was important in order for him to stay close to Shannon.

"Glory be to the Father and to the Son and to the Holy Spirit. As it was in the beginning is now and forever shall be. Amen." Gianina recited the opening of the rosary every morning. She expected Rolf to lead the decades of the rosary prayer as they continued.

"Hail Mary, full of grace. The Lord is with you. Blessed art though among women, and blessed is the fruit of thy womb, Jesus. Holy Mary, mother of God, pray for us sinners now and at the hour of our death." Rolf whispered the prayer as he knelt on the floor beside the old woman.

They did not hear Dr. Brunelli come into the waiting room as they recited the fifth decade of the rosary. He let them know he was there with his loud "Amen," and they both stood up to see him smiling as he came forward with his arms outstretched to embrace them.

"Your prayers have been heard by our Father in heaven," Dr. Brunelli said as he squeezed both of them at the same time. "Shannon awoke just ten minutes ago, and although she is weak, and a bit confused about where she is, her vital signs are strong, and she asked for a priest to pray with her. I think the two of you should go see her now, and let her know that you've done enough praying for her in three days that a priest can wait!"

If they only knew, Rolf thought.

Gianina went to Shannon's bedside while Rolf waited at the door. His heart raced as he looked over at the woman he had yearned for while alone in the waiting room. The closed eyes of the angelic face he had seen in his dreams were now open and shone with a brightness that lit up the dreariness of the hospital room despite her infirmity. Rolf hoped she would remember him.

"Thanks be to God for your return, my dear child. Heinrich and I were so worried for you and prayed the novena of St. Rita of Cascia every day." Gianina wiped a tear before she wrapped Shannon in her strong arms.

"Gianina," Shannon said weakly. "What happened? Why am I here? Who is Heinrich?"

"Now, now," Gianina said. "We must thank God for your recovery. We will tell you everything that has happened in time. But first you must meet Heinrich."

Rolf panicked and turned to leave, but Gianina grabbed his arm and pulled him across the room to Shannon's bedside and then went around to the other side.

"This is Heinrich. Let the three of us pray now and give thanks for Shannon's healing. Heinrich, please begin." Gianina took Shannon's hand and nodded to Rolf to do the same.

After the trio had prayed a full decade of the rosary, Gianina announced that she was expected at the market, and after kissing Shannon's forehead and giving final instructions to Heinrich to look after Shannon until she returned, she marched out of the room.

Shannon looked up shyly at Rolf. Rolf retrieved a chair from the corner and pulled it close to the bed, anxiously watching her, immensely relieved when her eyes softened.

"I'm the reason you're here," Rolf explained shyly.

"You are?"

"Yes, I was hurrying in the market and knocked you to the ground when I tripped on Gianina's cart. I'm a man who doesn't look where he's going."

"Why? What do you look at?"

"I look back. Like Lot's wife."

She laughed softly. Her laughter was like music. "You don't look like a pillar of salt to me."

Now Rolf laughed. "All right. But I did put a healthy American woman in the hospital."

She stopped laughing and looked at him curiously. "I'm Shannon."

"Yes, I know. Gianina has told me about you. I am Heinrich."

"So you know about the Bible."

"Yes, a few things."

"What is wrong with me? Am I hurt?" she asked.

"There was some concern about a concussion because you hit your head when you fell on the pavement. And you lapsed into a coma," Rolf explained. "You have been here for three days. The doctor said that if you regained consciousness on your own, you would be all right, though."

"My head does throb."

"I am so sorry."

They looked at each other for a moment.

"Are you the one who brought me here?" she asked.

"Yes. But never mind how you got here," he stammered.

"Well!" boomed Dr. Brunelli, who had come back to check on Shannon's progress. "Welcome to the living."

"Thank you, Doctor," she said.

"How do you feel?" the doctor asked as he started to examine her.

"My head hurts," she said.

"You fell on it pretty hard. But other than the concussion, I see nothing else in the x-ray to be worried about. We are glad you are awake after a long sleep, though. Take this for the pain." He gave her two pills. "I would like to release you, but Gianina tells me you live alone."

"I do, and the family I work for went away for a month's holiday."

"Then I do not feel good about letting you go home for at least another day or two."

"I am sure I cannot afford to stay much longer."

"Perhaps there's a relative nearby? You need someone to look after you until the family returns. You must have rest."

"I could do that," Rolf said as his heart quickened at the thought of spending more time with her.

"He certainly looked after you here," the doctor said in support of the idea.

Shannon looked over at Rolf and smiled. "I feel I've put you out of your way enough already."

"I owe you that much," said Rolf. "Being that I'm the one who caused you to be here in the first place."

The doctor settled the matter, sealing the idea on prescription paper, and said, "Just for a day or so. I want to make certain. I will send someone to let Gianina know that you are taking her home. Maybe bring her in for another checkup tomorrow?"

Rolf promised the doctor he would look after her while Shannon was being dressed and prepared for hospital release. Within the hour, Gianina had returned, and they pushed her together through the hall in a wheelchair. Shannon rejected the wheelchair as soon as they were out the door.

She could walk but was a little wobbly and slow. Rolf and Gianina steadied her as they helped her into the taxi.

Soon they were at the front door of her home, which was in a crowded apartment building. Shannon opened the door, and Rolf guided her inside, allowing her to lean on his shoulder.

Rolf could see right away that Shannon was an ardent Catholic. In one corner, she'd turned a dresser into a shrine to the Blessed Virgin. It held an advent candle. There were many images of Jesus on the cross and of the Virgin Mary, and the words to the Hail Mary hung on the wall next to the kitchen table. A fleet of figurines of the Holy Mother, along with seven candles, filled the fireplace mantel.

Shannon asked Rolf to look in a drawer in the kitchen for a match, and she then asked Gianina to help her light the many candles around a makeshift altar.

"You should get off your feet," Rolf said. "I can do all of that."

"No, no," she said. "These candles are prayers of thanksgiving, every single one of them. Gianina will help me."

After Shannon and Gianina had finished the candle lighting, Gianina said, "Welcome home, Shannon. I must return to my fish cart. I will return to see you this evening. Heinrich will stay with you until then." And she was off.

"Are you hungry?" Rolf asked her.

She thought about the question for a moment and then smiled. "I feel as if I haven't eaten in days!" she exclaimed suddenly.

"Well, you haven't eaten since you were asleep for three days. Would you allow me to cook for you?" Rolf asked.

She made a confused face. "I never saw a man cook."

"Have you never seen a chef?"

"Well, that's different."

"Is it?" Rolf asked. He started opening cabinets and drawers until he found an apron. Then he surveyed the kitchen, checking the refrigerator and the cupboard and pulling out a few things, including spices, herbs, and seasonings.

"Heinrich, are you a chef?" she asked.

"I am, actually." The lie came quickly. It seemed necessary.

She made a confused face. "A German chef?"

Rolf laughed. "No, no, I am Polish. I am a Polish chef who lives and works in Paris. I come to Rome on buying trips. Watch the miracle that happens when I take your kitchen scraps and create a feast."

"Do you see any kitchen scraps?"

The refrigerator was quite empty. "I have to admit I'm not finding much."

"That's what I was doing when the accident happened. I had been to the market."

Rolf remembered the spilled groceries on the cobblestone street. Suddenly, he whipped off the apron and reached for his jacket. "I do owe you that," he said to himself as much as to her.

"But you've done so much already."

Rolf was already at the door.

"Please. I don't want you to be gone long."

Rolf stopped at the door and looked back at Shannon. She'd made her request sound personal. Rolf did not get personal with anyone. However, coming from her, the intimacy felt right. Her request was too kind to be a demand, but in her voice was the tone of the awarding of a badge of honor.

"I won't," he promised. Then he found himself saying words that felt strange to say. "Trust me. Now, get some rest. Please."

35

HOPE

When Rolf left, Shannon had to keep herself from leaping up with joy. Despite the pain she felt from her head wound, she was happier than she had been in two years. The loneliness and depression that had sickened her every day for the last two years was gone. This gentle and caring man with sincere dark eyes made her forget her heartbreak and truly forgive Phil's deception for the first time. *Oh, Phil.* She'd loved him truly, the way one could only love for the first time, and she'd wanted to marry him. It was too bad he'd been hiding a wife, as one of her guardians back home in Boston had discovered. It didn't matter now. Just an hour or two of Heinrich's company had made her feel cared for and secure, even in this foreign country. It occurred to her that he might not come back, and he might not be the person she thought at the first impression. Her depression might return. She wanted to trust him but worried he might have a family in Paris. She remembered her embarrassment and heartbreak in Boston, when she had fallen for a married man and had no idea he was married. However, for the moment, all she could do was praise God for the respite, no matter how brief.

Heinrich did return. He came back within a half hour, after seeing Gianina at the fish cart and gathering produce from Gianina's fellow vendors, including wine and flowers. After sharpening Shannon's knives, he made a show of cutting and chopping. Quickly, he had a delicious soup ready for her. He presented it on a tray with the yellow daisies he had found in the market. She looked at the flowers and found that words failed her. She wanted to say thanks for them but realized that a thank-you wasn't enough. This kind—and handsome—man was going out of his way to be nice to her and doing it with a flourish. She loved the way that felt.

After dinner, Rolf lit a fire, and they enjoyed the wine. Rolf watched Shannon fall asleep on the couch. Lying about being a chef had come naturally to him. Of course, he had done his share of cooking, but he was not a chef. He just wanted to protect her and stay with her. Rolf closed his eyes. When the time came, this problem would solve itself. So far, he hadn't seen any priests, and no one there knew who he was. If he just stayed low, he could blend in with the other tourists, just as he'd told Shannon he was.

When Gianina stopped by after closing her cart, she helped Rolf find some covers for Shannon, and they both sat and watched her sleep.

Rolf nervously broke the silence. "Gianina, would it be improper for me to stay here to keep an eye on her?" He knew that if Shannon had been under Gianina's watchful eye for all this time, Gianina would tell him the truth. He was worried she would send him away.

"That is fine. You have shown yourself as a trustworthy man. I will check back tomorrow morning. Take care of her." With that, Gianina handed Rolf another blanket and left.

He watched Shannon sleep until well into the night, never taking his eyes off her and never losing interest, sitting upright in a chair.

He wanted to touch her more than he'd ever wanted anything, which was a confusing, strange sensation for him. Since his time alone in the library in Warsaw, he had always been distant and avoided getting close to others. He had been able to lead a life designed to spare him any need for intimate relationships. The desire to be close to another had never happened to him before, but at about three o'clock in the morning, he realized there was nothing in his life he would not have traded for the opportunity to know all about her.

He must have fallen asleep while sitting up and thinking that thought, because just a little after sunrise, she was putting the blanket that had fallen to the floor back in his lap. She smiled when he blinked.

"It seems a strange man has spent the night in your apartment," he said. "I meant to leave shortly after you fell asleep. This would seem like impropriety, but Gianina said it was okay. I hope you are not mad."

"Are you married?" she asked him point-blank, seemingly out of nowhere.

"No," he said. "I never married. I am concerned. I don't want you to get a reputation with your neighbors. I shouldn't have stayed." He stood up.

"You were well behaved," she assured him. "Besides, Gianina rules this building with a strong hand. What she says goes, and you did promise both her and the doctor you would look after me. I am feeling a lot better."

The doctor agreed when he saw her later that day. She had made a complete recovery, although she would need to regain her full strength after having been in bed for so long. After the hospital visit, she said she felt good enough for a walk. She went with Rolf to the market to buy more produce for dinner.

"You have healed me with your fine cooking," she said playfully to Rolf as they looked over the produce.

"After first inflicting the problem," Rolf said. "It was the least I could do."

"You have healed me of more than just a bump on the head," she said, and Rolf wondered to himself how that was possible. She explained, "You've healed my loneliness with your company. I have been very much alone."

"You are a long way from home," Rolf said.

"Yes."

"And you don't know anybody?"

"I do now."

"Well, I don't live here."

"You don't?"

"I visit often."

"Where do you live?"

"Paris."

"Oh, that's right. You told me last night—a Polish chef who lives and works in Paris. Are you going back soon?" She was close to tears.

"What brought you here from Boston?" he said, buying time to invent the right lie.

"I was a fourth-grade teacher there at a Catholic school. St. Joachim."

"And you're here on vacation?"

She paused, and they walked in silence for a moment. She pressed her lips together in a thin line, and Rolf could see she was suppressing a lot of emotion.

"My heart was broken," she confessed at length. "I fell in love with a man who turned out to be married. I couldn't function at all after that; it hurt so badly. Everything I looked at reminded me of him. Father Yeager—he's the pastor at St. Joachim—got me a job as a private tutor with an American family in Rome so I could get away and forget about the whole embarrassing thing."

Rolf was still back at the words "I fell in love with a man who turned out to be married." He could now understand why she'd questioned him so bluntly about being married. He felt a thrill all over, a sense that this beautiful young woman was as attracted to him as he was to her. Rolf juggled this new emotion. As they crossed the street, he looked over his shoulder for the men who had chased him the day before. All was clear. However, he knew he might be putting Shannon's life in danger for just being seen with him.

"I can't believe how easily I just told you that," she said.

"If you'd rather change the subject," said Rolf. How did one deal with emotion?

"It's been so long since I've had anyone to talk to like this," she said, clutching his arm with her soft hand. "I am so grateful that you're here, Heinrich."

"Tell me about your family."

"I have none. I was orphaned as a small child. The nuns took me in. I was raised at the St. Joachim Convent in Boston. I had no brothers or sisters to play with. I never really had friends my age. The closest person to family I ever had was Sister Blandine, who raised me. She did everything she could to make me happy. She taught me catechism. I miss her more than I can say. I write her every day."

"I'm sorry," said Rolf, thinking Shannon's life was much like his cover story about being rescued and educated by nuns. Her loneliness was like what he'd experienced in his actual life. He gave her his hand, and she held it.

"What about you? Where is your family?" she asked.

"I was an orphan like you."

"You were?"

"I lost my entire family when I was six years old."

"How? I mean, if you don't mind."

"In 1939. The Nazis."

She stopped and put her arms around him. They held each other. Rolf closed his eyes. Being close to Shannon was not like being close to Natasha. Shannon felt soft and right.

"You know about being alone too," she said.

Rolf leaned his head against hers and asked, "Can I tell you something?"

"You can tell me anything."

"There's only one time in my whole life when I didn't feel all alone."

"When was that?"

"Right now."

She pulled away a bit and looked at him.

"You did say I could tell you anything."

"I did."

They kissed. It was an intense experience. He had never come close to kissing anyone since his adolescent encounter with Natasha. He held on to her, leaning in, hoping he would never have to let go. She pulled away quickly and turned her face away from him, all the while holding him closer. Suddenly, she caught her breath, pulled away, and asked him a difficult question.

"When do you have to go back to Paris?"

His pause before answering seemed to agitate her.

"I suppose the next time there's an emergency at my restaurant," he said.

She smiled.

He put an arm around her and turned her around to walk back. "I'll make lunch," he said.

She put her head on his shoulder. He did not want to leave her side for even a moment.

Back at her flat, she lit candles while he sliced carrots on the cutting board. There was a knock on the door. Rolf started to take off the apron, saying, "I'll get it. Get off your feet."

"Really, I'm fine," Shannon replied.

She went to the door and opened it.

Rolf went back to slicing but kept an eye on Shannon at the door.

"Please. Come in," he heard her say.

Shannon backed away from the door. Rolf glanced up. Into the apartment came the bishop.

36

An Assignment

Rolf was instantly brought back to the reality of his secret KGB life. Then, instinctively, he tightened his grip on the cutting knife. As the bishop came in and put a hand on Shannon's shoulder, Rolf hid the knife in the back of his pants and approached.

"I'm Father Blut," the bishop said, "the new chaplain at the hospital. This is a routine home visit, Shannon, just to make certain you are well taken care of."

Rolf moved in closer.

"Very well," Shannon said. "I am in excellent hands."

The bishop cast an eye toward Rolf, who stood ready for anything.

"Please, Father. Sit. Would you care for some lunch?" Shannon said.

The bishop would not take his eyes off Rolf. "Who is this man?" he demanded, pointing at Rolf.

"He is my friend," she said. "This is Heinrich."

"Heinrich," the bishop repeated.

"Father," Rolf said, tight lipped, his breathing ragged.

"Why is he here?"

For a moment, nobody said anything.

"Because he is my friend."

Rolf looked at her with a lot of admiration. *She's not ashamed*, he thought to himself. *She's not ashamed of anything, so she can't be intimidated.*

The bishop's eyes narrowed as he looked at Rolf as one would have looked at gum stuck to a shoe. "I think he should leave."

"I don't want him to leave, Father," Shannon said.

"Did he spend the night here?" the bishop demanded.

"It was innocent," Rolf insisted.

"Nothing happened, Father," Shannon said.

"I am pleased to hear you both say that," the bishop said, "but his being here this long has the appearance of impropriety, wouldn't you say?"

"He's a very good man," Shannon said.

"I hope you're right." The bishop shrugged. "But you really don't know."

"I do know." She had a way of insisting without sounding disrespectful or unpleasant.

"Shannon," the bishop said.

"That's enough," Rolf said sharply and firmly. Rolf looked directly into the bishop's eyes. "I'll go with you."

"Don't go," Shannon said. "We haven't done anything wrong. You know we haven't."

Rolf put his hands on her shoulders and looked into her eyes. "He's right," Rolf said. "It's time I left. Even though it's only the appearance of impropriety, I have too much regard for you to allow even that. But I promise I'll be back."

"When?"

He had no idea. He didn't want to lie to her, but more than that, he didn't want the bishop to suspect him of sending her any secret messages.

"Soon. I promise, Shannon."

She really did not want him to go, and he enjoyed knowing that. He tried to smile in a special way, a way that might show her how he felt and maybe even who he was. But how could he do that? He didn't even know who he was. He had never so much as made a real friend before. There certainly were reasons why, but looking at Shannon made him forget the reasons. He left with the bishop.

Once they were outside the apartment building, the bishop looked around to make sure no one was near and then spoke softly but firmly to Rolf. "Go back to your quarters at the Vatican, and wait while I go back in there and clean up another of your messes."

Rolf responded to the bishop's threat by grabbing the bishop's hand and swiftly pulling his arm behind his back while pushing him against the wall of the building. Then he quickly disarmed the bishop by pulling an ice pick out of the bishop's robe.

"What is this? You were going to kill her? I won't let you," Rolf said.

Rolf released him when a pedestrian walked by, and Rolf and the bishop pretended to be conversing friends. The bishop shook his head and laughed. "Rolf, you really are giving me headaches."

A black sedan pulled up. The bishop opened the door and motioned for Rolf to get in. Rolf shook his head.

"I think it would be beneficial to both of us for you to step into the car," the bishop said.

"So you can kill me? I think not."

"If all I wanted to do was kill you, why would I bother with the rest?"

Finally, Rolf got in, if only to keep the monster away from Shannon. The bishop followed. Once they were in the car, the driver took off in the direction of Vatican City.

"We're going back to the Vatican?" Rolf asked.

"Check your bag," the bishop said. "Make sure we retrieved all of the items you left behind in the market and at the train station." He turned to the window.

Next to Rolf on the seat was the suitcase he had lost in the confusion at the market. Rolf opened it and saw, along with his other things, the archbishop's clothing he had discarded, and the Judas cross he had pawned.

The sight told him everything the bishop did not have to say: he would never get away, and the KGB had him in their sights the entire time.

"And if I make an accurate report of your behavior over the last few days, my next assignment will be to kill you," the bishop said. "You didn't tell her anything, did you?"

"No," said Rolf.

"You see?" The bishop smiled. "That's your training."

"It's not my training. I simply didn't want her to know."

"Otherwise, I will have to kill you both," the bishop said.

"I assumed," Rolf said.

"I see you are very fond of her! I think I've figured out a way to make everyone happy," the bishop said.

Rolf rolled his eyes. When had anyone ever mentioned the idea of making him happy? "How is that possible?"

"You have progressed to the exact position in the Catholic church where you can help us the most. We get few operatives this close. To kill you would be failure—a waste of training and expense, not to mention a blot on my record. In fact, the assignment I'd get to kill you would be the last assignment of any consequence I'd ever get. But now I see how I can hold you in place with the help of this woman. You'll get to have the woman, and I'll keep my operative in place. I'll make all the arrangements. I'll even finance the affair. And in return, you go back to the Vatican and do your job. Is that idea appealing?"

Rolf was astonished at how acceptable the idea was to him. Having Shannon was all that mattered; he'd figure the rest of it out in time.

"You must be very careful with her not to blow your cover," the bishop added. "She must never know who you really are."

"Yes," Rolf agreed.

"I'll even guarantee her safety."

"Yes, this does appeal to me."

"And of course, if you ever disobey me or try to run away again, I'll guarantee the opposite."

Rolf silently cursed himself for putting her life in danger. He now knew he had to keep up his end of the bargain no matter what.

"Keep in mind if the KGB or the Kremlin find out about our arrangement regarding the woman, we're both dead. You can't marry her. You know that you are expected to keep up the pretense of your devotion by keeping the vows. Frankly, the celibacy thing is broken all the time by our comrades. Those indiscretions go unnoticed, but marriage would not."

Rolf thought about his conversation with Dmitri, the one in which he'd promised to be celibate. Back then, it had been an easy promise to make. Now the bishop only asked for secrecy, not celibacy. And Rolf didn't care.

"I know," Rolf said.

"You really are my responsibility now," said the bishop.

37

FISHERS OF MEN

Three days later, an hour before the sun came up, Rolf left Vatican City in a Vatican car driven skillfully by Karol. From Rome, they took the Cassia north toward Viterbo and then toward Orvieto. After a short drive from the grandeur of the Vatican, they were now on the flat summit of a gigantic butte of consolidated volcanic ash rising above the practically vertical faces of tuff cliffs.

As the sun rose, they arrived at Karol's secret fishing spot via a dirt road that turned onto a small path winding along an impenetrable set of cliffs. They abandoned the car and proceeded on foot, bearing rods and tackle, up a steep tree-lined grade for about twenty minutes and then climbed over a short wall the Etruscans had built out of tufa stone in the third century before Christ. Karol had talked nonstop about the history of the area during their early morning drive.

Even though Karol was older than he, Rolf was doing most of the heavy breathing. Anything but breathless, Karol, after talking the whole way about fishing and hiking as a boy in Poland, began a history lesson.

"In the seventh century BC, this was the location of a Villanovan settlement whose huts were built on stilts over the lake using reed platforms, hay roofs, and cobbled floors. About four hundred years later, it was settled by the Etruscans after they fled the Roman attack on Velsna, which eventually became known as Volsinii, now known as Bolsena."

When Rolf saw the spot at the top of the climb, he understood the reason for secrecy.

Lago de Bolsena was a clear and beautifully serene lake. The early light of dawn made it even more ethereal. It was a sheltered world, a large lake formed in an extinct volcano crater. The area was uninhabited that morning but for the fish and the two of them. Karol kept a rowboat there. As he explained to Rolf, Karol had originally discovered the lake during one of his many hikes into the mountains surrounding Rome.

Karol made it all so easy, as if he had been planning for quite some time for the day when he would bring his first guest to his secret spot. He provided the extra rod, the tackle, and the boat and even insisted on doing the rowing.

Rolf could see that Karol had timed everything for effect. By the time the sun came up, Rolf found himself anchored in the clearest water he had ever seen. He could see the stones on the bottom of the lake.

"The water of Bolsena is so clean," Karol said softly, as if reading Rolf's mind, "that it's considered perfectly safe to drink. No development mars Bolsena's shores or its views. And the gentle slope of the surrounding land limits the amount of spill-off or soil erosion that can affect the water's transparency."

Surrounded by the clear water and the extreme quiet of dawn, Karol and Rolf sat as still as statues in the rowboat. Each had a line in the water. Each line was brilliantly illuminated by the sun and visible all the way down.

Rolf realized that in clear water like this, the fish would be visible before even biting on the hook. *Nothing could possibly hide in these clear waters*, he thought. *Where all is visible there can be no lies and no deception. Karol has brought me to a place where there are no lies. At least it was a place without lies before I came to it.*

Just as Karol had brought the extra rod, Rolf would bring the lies.

Out of the silence came a soft voice: "I've read your book."

"Have you?" Rolf asked, trying vainly to sound disinterested.

He was used to hearing people react to his writing. He knew that if they liked the book, they would start with "Great book!" or "I simply loved your book." When someone started with a simple "I've read your book," it was an invitation to receive criticism. Rolf made it a habit not to take the bait, but it was clear Karol had something to say.

"I found it very moving," Karol said. "Your description of your early life. The deaths of your parents and your own childhood battle for survival in the face of near starvation were riveting. Spiritually, how have you come to grips with that entire trauma?"

"It has shaped my life," Rolf answered. "I personally experienced extreme hunger, so I made it my life's work to address world hunger."

"Yes," Karol said. "Brilliant."

"I also am an amateur chef," Rolf said, moving quickly off the subject. "If we catch any fish—"

"We will."

"I can cook them."

"What about God, Rolf?"

"What?"

"There's no mention of God in your book."

Rolf paused. It was a criticism he had not heard before. It cut right to who he was. God was not in the book because when he'd written it, he had not believed in God. But as a priest, that was something he could never admit to anyone.

"It's a book on world hunger," Rolf replied, "not theology."

It was then that Rolf could see through the clear water several fish investigating his bait.

"You don't think God is relevant to world hunger?"

Much to Rolf's relief, the trout started biting one after another. First, they bit on Rolf's line, but they bit on Karol's too. The stillness gave way to hurried activity, the offering of quick suggestions, and the teamwork it took to land so many large catches.

"This is almost as good as Peter did on Gennesaret," Karol remarked at one point.

When they made it to dry land and lifted the boat up upon the rock that was its resting place, they trailed a large catch of healthy brown trout, many fish on a line.

"You had a good day," Karol said. "We both had a good day, but you had an exceptional day."

Scaling the tufa stone wall and climbing down was much easier than the hike up. The joy of the fishing, the clear water, and the perfect morning was another new experience for Rolf.

On their return to the Vatican, toting their catch, Rolf felt hopeful for the first time in weeks. He suggested they go to the rectory kitchen so they could feed their fellow priests. On their way to the kitchen, Karol said, "Did I tell you I'm going home soon?"

"We're home now," Rolf said.

"I mean Poland," Karol said. "The Gdansk Shipyard. Come with me."

Rolf became interested in the pots and pans and changed the subject. Karol talked away while Rolf threw on an apron and filleted and breaded the fish they had caught.

"How long since you've been home?" Karol asked him.

"Home?" Rolf asked.

"Poland."

Rolf counted back in his mind to the untimely death of Father Novak. "More than twenty years."

"Why is that?"

"Poland carries very bad memories."

"Things have been bad there for a long time."

"For my whole lifetime," said Rolf. "The country was always under attack. Always under the boot of a foreign dictator."

"There's a new spirit at home, Rolf," said Karol. "It's called solidarity. Have you heard of Lech Walesa?"

Rolf made a vague gesture. "I heard something."

"Come with me, Rolf. You must see for yourself the courage of these men and women to form a nongovernmental union."

"In Poland?" Rolf asked. He'd had no idea such a thing was going on.

"Come see for yourself," Karol said. "It would make you so proud."

Rolf muttered something about his duties at the secretariat.

Karol frowned just a little. "I'll be making other trips," Karol assured Rolf. "Eventually, I'll get you to come with me on one of them. You'll see. I was right about the fishing, wasn't I? It did improve your mood."

Rolf smiled in spite of himself. It was a warm smile. Karol had been right. Fishing had made him feel better.

38

ANOTHER ASSIGNMENT

Rolf had taken extra precautions to prevent surprise visitors in his room when he returned to the Vatican from Shannon's apartment, such as putting in a new lock and requesting and installing a door brace. Apparently, none of those precautions had paid off. Rolf found the bishop sitting in a chair, waiting for him, when he returned to his room. The message was clear: the bishop could find his way into Rolf's bedroom in the Vatican anytime he wanted to.

"Where were you?" the bishop asked.

"Fishing," Rolf told him. "With my friend Karol."

"That was a test of your training," the bishop said. "We already knew where you were. You were followed. We have decided that Karol is a very good friend for you to have."

"He is my friend because I like him."

"All the better. If he decides to go fishing again, see that you are invited to accompany him."

"I want to see Shannon."

"Why not?" The bishop smiled. "You've earned it.

That started the pattern. The sight of the bishop's bloated face was enough to bring back the migraines, depression, and nightmares, but that same face could also arrange for him to see the one face he longed for, the one person in the world he really wanted to see. Instead of letting the anxious feelings send him straight to bed for days on end, he would contemplate an encounter with her. In Rolf's mind, Shannon justified everything. It was the most logical, acceptable, and enjoyable arrangement he had ever experienced. She waited at the end of his suffering, so the suffering was justified. He'd never thought he would see the day when his suffering would be justified, but here it was.

———◇———

Later that day, Rolf dressed in a new suit, picked up flowers and a gift box, and rang Shannon's doorbell.

"Heinrich!"

She crushed the flowers by running into his arms and kissing him. He came in, closed the door, managed to set the flowers aside, and took her into his arms.

She kissed him ardently but then pulled away. She blushed and quickly walked to the kitchen to retrieve her shawl.

"This is so overwhelming," she said, trying to catch her breath. "Could we just go for a walk or something?"

Shannon pulled her wrap from the back of the door and motioned for Rolf to follow her. She led Rolf on a long uphill walk near her neighborhood, Gianicolo. High on the top of Janiculum Hill, one of the seven hills of Ancient Rome, was a lush garden park full of carnival attractions, including bumper cars and pony rides. As they strolled along a path lined with shooting galleries and Punch and Judy shows, there was an electricity between them that kept them touching, either hands or shoulders.

They came to a rose garden with a panoramic view of the entire city below, and he laid out his jacket for her to sit on.

"Do you think God has a purpose for us, Heinrich?"

Ah, he thought. *That question.* He had known she would bring God up at some point. Her apartment was a shrine to the Virgin Mary. He was sure she attended Mass every morning. He did not want to tell her another lie if possible.

"I've never in my life had an honest conversation with anyone about God," he admitted.

"But you believe in God?"

"I sometimes doubt."

"Heinrich, you mustn't."

"But I do. The first part of my life taught me to fear evil but not to believe in God."

"How can you not believe in God?"

"I saw my parents shot to death by demons in a church. At that time, I believed the church to be a safe place, but it was far from it. I became a child facing the future without any family, and then I began to doubt that there was a God. The loving God I had been taught about certainly would not have let such horrible things happen."

Shannon swallowed, seeming not to know what to say. Rolf pulled away. A sad silence stopped them both for a moment, and then Shannon reached to touch his face.

"Heinrich, I believe that God has brought us together."

"I'm not sure what brought us together, Shannon." Rolf wanted to change the subject, so he stood up and walked to a line of rosebushes. After plucking a rose, he walked back to Shannon and, handing her the flower, sat back down beside her.

"At the hospital, you prayed the rosary with Gianina at my bedside, and Dr. Brunelli said that your prayers had healed me."

"Yes, I did pray with her every day." Rolf shrugged. "It is not an easy thing to say no to Gianina. I have never seen anyone with so much faith, and it seemed important to her that I pray, so I did."

"If you have no faith, then why do you carry a cross with you?" she asked abruptly.

"What?"

Then Rolf noticed that as he had laid out his jacket, his Judas cross had come out of the pocket. He quickly stuffed it back in.

"Could I see it?" she asked.

He nervously took the cross back out of his pocket and let her hold it for a moment.

"That's the strangest cross I've ever seen," she said. "What does this odd skull with all these rubies represent?"

"It's a good-luck piece," he explained, hastily stuffing it back into his pocket.

To try to change the subject again, he shifted closer to her on his jacket. Looking at her intently, he moved to kiss her, but she turned away.

"This is moving very fast for me," she breathed.

"I think of nothing but you," Rolf told her, taking her hands.

"I've come into your life for a reason," she said. "I am clear that I am here to bring you closer to God, Heinrich, but these other feelings I am having are more confusing."

"If anything could make me believe in an all-powerful, loving God," he said, "it would be you."

"Will you promise me that you're not already married?" she asked. "You know why I need that promise, don't you?"

"I promise," he said tenderly. "I am not married."

Then she let him kiss her.

39

SISTER LUCIA

The bishop was waiting for Rolf in his room again.

"Have you ever been to Portugal?" the bishop asked Rolf.

"No."

"Are you certain of that?"

"You've kept a steady eye on me. Wouldn't you have known if I'd ever been to Portugal?"

The bishop smiled. "Have you ever met Sister Lucia de Santos?"

Rolf remembered the Spanish priest with the film can under his arm who'd spoken at the Jesuit school where Rolf had taught. The film had been about Our Lady of Fátima, and when Rolf had seen it, he'd known he was a part of the evil she'd warned against in her message to three Portuguese children. That had been the start of the headaches and his fight with depression.

"Oh yes," said Rolf. "I've heard about it. But no, I've never met her."

"Then why has she invited you to visit her?"

"She hasn't, at least not that I know of."

The bishop handed him an envelope whose wax seal had already been broken.

"This was slipped under your door late last night," the bishop said. "Do you read Portuguese?"

"Some," Rolf said, looking at the envelope, which appeared to bear a stamp for Portugal. He worked to control his anger at yet another of the bishop's intrusions. "She wants to speak to me on an urgent matter," said Rolf after reading the letter.

"I've reported this to Moscow," the bishop told him. "Anything that concerns her is of the utmost importance. She has been a major factor in the church's anti-Soviet stance. There are those who would like to see her dead. There are others who believe she is harmless, since she never goes anywhere and has been a Discalced Carmelite for forty years. She's old. They say her eyesight and hearing are almost gone. She hasn't published a memoir or any writings in many years, and she speaks to no one ever. This is why we find it strange that she would send for you."

"I don't see how I can get away."

"You get away to see the girl."

"That's different. That is my agreement with you."

"You will go on this journey. Mention at the Secretariat of State that Sister Lucia wants to meet with you, and they will let you go. I will travel with you. When you have met with her, you will tell me everything she says. If for any reason she knows who you really are—"

"How could she?" Rolf asked. "How could she know anything?"

"There are those in the KGB who fear her very much. There was a rumor that she wrote a letter, which was later lost, stating that there were Soviet spies in the priesthood. Somehow, they believe she finds out these things. What I am telling you is that if she has found out about you, you are to tell me right away. If that turns out to be the case, it may be that your next assignment will be to silence her personally."

Rolf did not ask another question, knowing fully that he was not going to be spared the order to kill.

A week later, Rolf and the bishop traveled by plane and train to Coimbra, Portugal, and took a cab to the gates of the Carmelite Convent of St. Teresa. Rolf had read about the place. In the sixth century, Discalced Carmelite monks had built a walled-in area in 250 acres of the forest in which to cultivate trees and exotic plant species from all over the world, some five hundred of which could still be found there.

Rolf got out of the cab.

"I'll be waiting at the gates when you return," the bishop said.

Rolf didn't answer. He shut the door and went up the walkway, past the gates. He was shown into the monastery and to a small sitting room just off the foyer.

The room was furnished with a couch and three chairs, and there were two end tables beside the couch. Sister Lucia awaited Rolf in a room lit only by candles.

The nun watched him as he took a seat on the chair opposite the couch.

"Would you pray with me?" Sister Lucia asked.

"Yes," Rolf said. He was struck by her large black eyes. They looked not at him but straight ahead at some invisible focal point. She appeared to sense his presence rather than see him. It seemed to Rolf as if she were looking directly into the eyes of another, but no one else was in the room. Knowing what he had heard about her visions of the Blessed Virgin, Rolf imagined that perhaps she was seeing the Virgin at that moment or was pretending to. Rolf had always silently assumed Sister Lucia was either insane or lying. He'd never taken reports of apparitions seriously. But sitting there in her presence, he found either possibility hard to believe. Those large black eyes seemed all-knowing, not delusional or dishonest.

Rolf knew all about going through the physical motions of prayer for the benefit of others, having done it several times daily since entering the priesthood. By the time she was finished with her silent prayer, he was crossing himself.

"I want you to know that you have a very important calling," she said to him after a moment of silence.

Rolf was unsure if she had any idea who he was. "How did you know of me?" he asked directly.

"I did not," she answered. "I do not now. I can hardly see or hear you. But I know that you are here, and I know that I invited you to be here. She told me to."

"She?" Rolf asked politely. "You mean—"

"Yes," she said, seeming to know what he was about to say. "Once, I only spoke to her on occasion, at times when she appeared to me. Now she is my entire life, and I am much more in the next world than I am in this one. We are in very frequent contact. I have no interest in this world. Spiritual matters occupy my mind fully. From time to time, she tells me what I must do, and I do it. She told me to tell you that you have an important calling."

"I have been called to serve at the Vatican," Rolf said.

"You have not heard your calling yet. You do not hear it now. You think of me as a crazy person."

"No, Sister."

"Do not try to tell me otherwise; there is no time for that. I do not indulge in idle conversation. You do not yet believe. I have been told that. The important message for you is that you will believe. You will hear your calling, and you will know that it is God calling you. There will be no mistake about it. I am to tell you to find the courage to answer God's call. It will be dangerous, and you will suffer. But that suffering is nothing compared to the evil that will unfold if you do not heed God's call. Much has gone wrong, and you have a very important role to play in setting things right."

Rolf could see there was no point in arguing with her. Calling her stubborn would have been an understatement. "What is my role?" Rolf asked.

"You will know."

Then she seemed to go deeply into a trancelike state and said nothing more. Rolf sat there and spoke her name a couple of times, but she gave no awareness of it. After a while, he got up and left the room.

At the outside gate, he found the bishop and a taxi waiting for him.

"Get in quickly," the bishop said. "I've just gotten word of your new assignment. We must go. Quickly."

Rolf got into the taxi, and the driver sped for the train station.

"Your new friend the fisherman?"

Rolf nodded.

"He's going to Poland soon."

"Yes," Rolf said. "He told me."

"You must go with him. This is a very important mission. Much will be asked of you. You will want to be observant."

They rode in silence as Rolf tried to comprehend what was involved in being observant.

"What did she want?" the bishop asked. "Do you think she knows who you really are?"

"She never called me by name. At times, she didn't even seem to really be aware of my presence."

"Did she say anything?"

"Yes. She said that I have a very important calling."

The bishop waited for more and then laughed. "That's all she said?"

"She said I had a very important role to play in setting things right."

"Did she explain what she meant?"

"No. She went into some kind of meditation, and I could not get her to answer my questions."

The bishop thought for a moment. "You're not leaving anything out?"

"She did tell me that she lives more in the next world than in this one."

"Yes. I've heard that about her. How did she know about you?"

"She said she didn't know me at all. The Blessed Virgin told her that I had an important calling and that she should pass that along to me."

"Is she crazy?" He laughed, although hesitantly.

"Maybe."

"You think she read your book and got your name and your so-called calling from that?"

"That kind of thing happens when you publish a book."

The bishop shook his head and laughed again. "Too bad we wasted our time on this," he said at length. "You've got a very important assignment waiting."

ʃ

40

THE CALL EXPERIENCE

Several days later, Karol easily persuaded Rolf to return to the secret fishing spot. In the stillness of the lake, with lines in the clear water, Karol asked Rolf a question he'd been asked once before.

"What was the moment like when you knew that God was calling you to enter the priesthood?"

What a coincidence, Rolf thought. *Sister Lucia told me I had a calling.* Suddenly, Karol was reminding him very much of Sister Lucia. Certainly Karol was more matter-of-fact in his conversational style, more of that world, and more responsive to the present moment, but he and Lucia were the same in some way that Rolf could not quite account for. In the presence of both of them, he felt a strong sense of his mother and father. Normally when he thought of his parents, he thought of people who were victims—people who'd been unable to stand against the onslaught and who'd left him defenseless. But in the presence of Karol and Lucia, he was reminded of feelings about his parents he had not felt since early childhood, since the days when his mother had taught him about Jesus and his father had taught him how to pray. Those feelings of calm and acceptance called out to him to become something wonderful, as opposed to his days of starvation, which had turned him into a wild animal, or his days with Dmitri, who'd turned him into an assassin.

Even with all of those thoughts going through his mind, he did not take long to answer Karol's question about the moment God called him to the priesthood. Having almost lost his shot at the priesthood when he was previously asked that question at the cost of one human life, Rolf was careful to let no time elapse between the question and the answer. However, Karol interrupted him before he could start the first word.

"For me, it was the death of my father," Karol said. "It was 1941. I remember I was working as a laborer in a limestone quarry at the time to avoid being deported to Germany. My father was dying in my arms, the worst thing I could imagine, and God was sitting right next to me. I felt no fear. I knew I would serve Him and never gave it a second thought."

"I know that when I was called, I was having pastry and coffee in a small kitchen on a very cold morning," Rolf said quickly. "More prosaic perhaps than Paul on his way to Damascus but very specific and clear and more unforgettable a memory than the invasion of Poland in 1939."

"A call is a call," Karol told him.

Rolf was immensely relieved that Karol seemed to believe him. He wasn't sure why he cared that Karol believed him even in the lie. It was a hard-won lesson on lying: be specific, and let the mundane rule the day.

"By the way," Rolf said, "is the invitation still open? Gdansk Shipyards?"

"You'll come?" Karol was overjoyed.

Karol made all the arrangements, and within a few days, Rolf and Karol sat next to each other on the plane, sipping coffee. They wore ordinary street clothes so they could pass into Soviet-controlled Poland as two secular gentlemen.

Rolf could not help but appreciate the irony of being a man pretending to be a priest pretending not to be a priest.

"When you were starving and hiding as a boy, did you pray?" Karol asked Rolf.

Rolf didn't feel he could be completely honest with his friend on that subject, but surely the truth would suffice in this case. Why would he have to lie about a time in his life that he'd already truthfully described in his most popular book? Rolf was discovering that he wanted somehow to communicate.

"My father told me to look at the cross on the wall," Rolf said. "An instant later, the wall came down, cross and all. Within a few minutes, the priest and my parents were all dead."

"You're angry at God for letting it happen," Karol suggested.

"It was a long time ago," Rolf said.

"The savage attack on your home and your loved ones—that made you doubt," Karol said.

"Who said anything about doubt?" Rolf asked.

"What you are about to see at the shipyard, Rolf," Karol said, "will change you. It may remove your doubt."

The thought of seeing Poland again brought Rolf's deep depression to the surface. He was holding on to sanity by a thread, desperately trying to quiet his mind by focusing it on doing the job that would bring him back to Shannon.

"You've seen it before, of course," Karol said as the plane was landing.

"Seen what?" Rolf asked.

"The Gdansk Shipyard."

"No. Never."

Situated on the left side of the Martwa Wisla and on Ostro Island, the shipyard in Gdansk was the largest in Poland. The moment the bus pulled to a stop and he and Karol got out, Rolf was impressed by the vast array of green cranes looming overhead and the glowing welding torches, which looked like fireflies against a massive hull.

What he saw was beautiful, a monument to Polish workmanship and shipbuilding. The expected depression did not engulf him. He was not going to encounter his past there.

They were met at the gate by a Soviet security guard. Karol and Rolf presented the guard with the fake papers that had been sent to Karol, falsely identifying them as members of the Soviet-controlled longshoremen's union. The guard quickly accepted the fake papers at face value without so much as a cursory glance at the writing on them.

Once they were inside the gates, Karol said, "I hate to have to lie, but what can one do?"

Rolf noted the irony. Clearly of the three of them, Rolf, Karol, and the Soviet guard, Karol was the one who was telling the least amount of lies—and the only one who was really being fooled by lies.

As impressive as the shipyard seemed, Rolf couldn't help but notice the scarcity of workers.

"It's so deserted," Rolf observed. "Is this a holiday?"

"Just wait," Karol said. "It's anything but deserted."

The vast array of masts and spires that made up the great shipyard quickly grabbed Rolf's attention. Karol could see that his countryman was impressed with the shipyard, and that brought out the historian in him once again.

As Karol proudly escorted Rolf along the docking, he gestured at the vastness of the port.

"During the war, this was all part of the Danziger Werft, a German shipbuilding company founded in 1921 on the site of the Kaiserliche Werft Danzig, which was closed at the end of World War I. During World War II, the Danziger Werft built forty-two Type VII U-boats for the Kriegsmarine. By the end of that war, the shipyard was badly damaged by bombing raids. It was then taken over by the Polish government and a Polish shipbuilding company and renamed the Gdansk Shipyards," Karol explained, loving to enact the role of tour guide in his native land. "Now it goes by the rather odious name of the Lenin Shipyard."

They came to a vast ship, one used more for display than anything else. Rolf had never seen anything like it.

"That's a Polish ship?"

"It's a fuel and oil tanker. The SS *Soldek*. She's the first ship built in Poland after the war, meaning under the Soviets."

The idea that the Poles had built such an impressive ship was amazing to Rolf. He was even more impressed when, suddenly, a gangplank appeared, and Karol led him on board the great ship.

As Karol led Rolf down through the ship's four holds, past the anchors and cargo handling gear with steam-propelled engines, past the life-saving equipment and emergency steering gear, and down to the lower deck, Rolf began to sense a teeming humanity aboard the ship. When they reached the bottom deck, past several manned checkpoints, they saw hundreds of Polish longshoremen gathered at the feet of one man on a makeshift stage. It was the largest secret meeting the shipyard had ever hosted.

Rolf gasped as soon as they came into that bottom room.

"Every man or woman who has gathered has done so at great personal risk," Karol whispered to Rolf. "If the Soviets even knew this meeting was happening, there's not a person here who would not be in mortal danger."

Rolf made a mental note that in this crowded basement of the retired ship called the SS *Soldek*, many courageous Poles were gathering to change a history of subservience to first the Russians, then the Germans, and finally the Soviet Communists by declaring the formation of a real union and fighting for an independent Poland. The dock workers were mesmerized by a round-faced, broad-shouldered man with a large mustache named Lech Walesa as he spoke.

"In '76, I was fired and blacklisted for collecting signatures to build a memorial for the workers killed in the strike," Walesa said. The workers cheered every time he paused for a breath. "For the last two years, I have lived in hiding, supported by friends in the struggle and by the church. Now, along with Andrzej Gwiazda and Aleksander Hall, I have founded the Free Trade Union of Pomerania. I believe we will see the day when our own union, free of Soviet control, will, along with the mother church, win back the soul and freedom of Poland."

The place went wild with raucous cheering. Rolf became afraid for everyone gathered there—young men, old men, men with families and futures—knowing well how the KGB would react to such a demonstration of independence.

Walesa motioned for silence. The crowd of dockworkers and their families and their priests responded to Walesa's every gesture. Silence came at once.

"Please, do not make too much noise," Walesa said. "We risk being shot on sight."

"We live that way anyway!" one dockworker bellowed. There was some cheering. Walesa smiled and nodded.

"The next speaker," Walesa said, "is a man who knows all about that risk. First, let me tell you a few things about him. He's a playwright, actor, and athlete and is fluent in many languages, not counting his own. When the Nazis ran Poland, he entered the underground seminary, and when the Communists took over, they forbade Jagiellonian University to grant him his doctorate. And yet he leads the fight for our liberation today at the Sacred College of Cardinals. Our very own Cardinal Karol Josef Wojtyla."

Walesa stepped down to great applause. Karol took the stand. Rolf was impressed that so many of them recognized Karol on sight.

"The Lord be with you," said Karol with both arms raised.

"And also with you!" was the booming response.

To open, Karol led the workers in a Hail Mary. He went on to petition the Blessed Virgin for strength, courage, and freedom from Soviet oppression. Then he spoke with enthusiasm and conviction.

"I encourage each of you to pray the rosary. As we know from the miracles at Fátima, the Holy Mother stands with us in our fight against Soviet oppression. She predicted that Russia would spread her evil, and the Polish people have experienced that evil firsthand every day for the last thirty years."

The mention of Our Lady of Fátima caused Rolf's heart to beat faster, and his mind raced with questions he was trying to suppress. The recent experience of being face-to-face with the dark eyes of Sister Lucia intensified his reaction. He tried to discipline his mind to focus on his assignment, which was to observe the faces of those present. Deep breaths calmed him, and he looked around the room at the people gathered there.

"There will be a revolution," Karol announced, "and as sure as I stand here, it will be a peaceful revolution. We do not need to engage the oppressor in the violence that is his nature. We are free men and women who love God and fear nothing. The world will see us for what we are and will recognize our independence. The Soviets will be forced by the entire God-loving world to recognize it as well."

The crowd cheered.

"Do not be afraid to change the image of this land and promulgate your faith!" Karol exclaimed.

Rolf was impressed to see such brave men and strong leadership for the Polish people. The spirit of that combination gave him a counterbalance to his childhood memories. The mere presence of the workers, as led by Karol and Walesa, made him feel he could stave off depression in the future by remembering that day.

On the way back to Italy on the plane, Rolf started to look at Karol in a slightly different light. He had known Karol as a nice, friendly, and patriotic man. He knew Karol liked him (or at least liked the person Karol thought he was); Karol liked to fish; and Karol had a sharp, intuitive mind. But Rolf had not known that Karol had the heart to inspire that many men and women to risk their lives in the hopeless quest of overcoming Soviet oppression.

"So?" Karol asked him on the plane. "Was I right? Did Gdansk ease your doubts?"

"It changed me," Rolf admitted. "I never thought I'd see Poles in such a state."

"We are a proud people," Karol said.

"This is the first I ever heard of the solidarity movement," Rolf said.

"Now you have more than heard of it. You have seen it."

"Yes."

"A revolution in the making."

"And you seem to be the one who is making it, Karol," Rolf said. He regretted the accusatory tone of his statement and quickly added, "You're the lightning rod for the Polish stevedore."

"I can see why you have done well at writing books," Karol said. "You flatter me with a poetic metaphor. The lightning rod is God. I was hoping you would see that."

"You were hoping I would see God?"

"I was."

Rolf chose his next words carefully. Karol still spoke with warm friendship, but the question of belief versus doubt still hung in the air.

"I began to see that God might return to Poland," Rolf finally said.

"God never left Poland," Karol assured him.

Rolf had to be careful now. The absence of God in Poland was a staple of Rolf's belief system, one proven by his experiences. He took a chance and changed the subject.

"I had no idea you were fluent in eighteen languages," Rolf said.

"It's an exaggeration," Karol said. "Only sixteen. My Farsi is extremely limited, and who counts Latin anymore?"

Rolf laughed agreeably.

"You speak quite a few languages yourself, don't you?" Karol asked.

"Maybe six. It's the word *fluent* that slows me down. Knowing a language and having absolutely no difficulty with it are two different things."

"I know what you mean," Karol said. Then he leaned toward Rolf. "God was there, Rolf. He was there on the *Soldek* with us."

Rolf nodded. He didn't believe it, and he feared that Karol knew he didn't.

"You'll see," Karol assured him, sitting back in his seat. "You're a part of it too now, Rolf."

"A part of what?"

"The Polish revolution."

"I haven't been a part of anything like that."

"Just being there with me made you a part of it. Every one of us on that ship could now be a marked man, so we are all taking the same chances. That makes us all brothers."

Rolf knew that it didn't, that he was the only one there actually following orders, but he could tell now that Karol was convinced of Rolf's own commitment to the Polish cause. That relieved him. It was important that he keep his cover for the bishop. But he was troubled. His growing friendship with Karol was taking on a new importance to him, and he worried about the harm that might come to Karol because of it.

41

REFUGE

Shortly after his return to the Vatican, Rolf sat in his room opposite the bishop. The bishop showed him photographs one after another. Rolf looked at them and had a response to each one.

"No, I didn't see him," Rolf said. "Don't recognize him. Or him. Or him. But him. Yes, he was there. And this man—he was the main speaker. Walesa."

"What did he speak about?" the bishop asked.

"Forming an independent union of dockworkers."

The bishop fanned out another stack of photos before Rolf. "And you say these men were there?"

"Yes."

"Did your fishing friend speak as well?"

"I had no idea he was fluent in eighteen languages."

"So I've heard."

"That's impressive. Can you even name eighteen languages?"

"What did he say at this secret meeting?"

"Same. Independent union."

"Very good."

The bishop was about to leave, but Rolf stopped him.

"I want her now," Rolf said. "I want her right now."

The bishop gave a mock sigh. "Ah, young love," he said sarcastically. "I'll have a car for you waiting in St. Peter's Square." The bishop handed him some money.

It was a late hour by the time Rolf got changed and made it to Shannon's door.

"It's me—Heinrich," Rolf announced from outside.

She threw open the door and held her robe together. "I wish I weren't so glad to see you," she said.

"Are you?" he asked eagerly. "I hope?"

She let him in, and they embraced.

"It would be so much better if you came during the day," she said, knowing full well what he had come for that late at night, and she wouldn't be able to turn him away this time.

"Because of the neighbors?" he asked.

"No. I don't care about the neighbors. It is because my faith says we should wait until we are in a union blessed by God and the church."

They held each other in silence for a moment, and then Rolf, by the way that he held her, couldn't help but make it clear why he had come.

"You're not in Rome on business tonight?" she asked as she pulled away from Rolf.

"I'm here to be with you tonight."

"I don't think we should," she said vainly.

"Please don't ask me to leave tonight."

"I wish I could, but I cannot, Heinrich."

He lifted her off her feet and pressed her hungrily to his chest. Although he moved with urgency, he was gentle in everything he did. Rolf walked with her in his arms toward the bedroom and paused at the door. He brushed the hair from her forehead and looked deeply into her eyes. She gazed back at him with passion in her eyes.

Neither spoke as he gently laid her on the tousled bedspread. He untied the belt that held her bathrobe, and as he softly stroked the curve of her neck, she let out a feeble groan as if to stop him. He untied her hair, and it glistened in the light from the window.

They both lost their virginity that night. For a moment, after they made love, Shannon cried quietly.

Rolf stroked Shannon's hair as she awoke the next morning. Now deeply connected to this woman, he was trying to figure out a way he could escape from the KGB and marry her without putting her life in danger. She was the one who broke the silence.

"I love you," she whispered.

"Yes," he said, taking her hand. "This is a truly miraculous moment. I love you and absolutely nothing but you."

"Do you think we belong together?"

"Yes. I want nothing more than to be with you."

Rolf could sense she wanted assurance, just as he felt he could sense her very nature, but he didn't know what to do about it.

He didn't know what assurances to give or not to give, and the realization reminded him of the newness of what he was feeling and the potential for it. *If she could only wait*, he thought to himself. Then he had the sad realization that he had refused to wait another moment for what he wanted from her. He had forced the issue by being unable to wait another moment to make love to her.

She broke the silence again. "What is your life in Paris?" she asked.

He groaned with the weariness of having to lie to her. "I run a restaurant that drives me insane with minutiae. I don't like to think about it when I'm with you."

"I would go there," she said.

"You would not be happy there—believe me."

Shannon was quiet, and he wondered what she was thinking. He reached out and continued to stroke her hair.

"Heinrich, are you married?" she asked for the second time since they'd met.

"No," he said.

"I only ask because it already happened to me once. I couldn't bear it again. Not with you."

"I've never been with a woman before."

Shannon sat up quickly and pulled her robe to her chest. "Are you making fun of me?"

"I'm telling you the truth. You are the only one."

She relaxed again and kissed him on the forehead. "When, or if, the time ever comes that you wonder whether I would be willing to give up my job and apartment and come to you there, the answer is yes. I would."

Rolf said nothing. His stare became a blank stare.

"I can see that the time hasn't come," she said sadly. "I won't mention it again."

42

THE TRUTH

The next time Rolf went with Karol to the secret fishing spot, the ride to the lake was silent. When they sat in the rowboat in the middle of the lake with their lines in the water, they sat in silence. When Karol broke the silence, he did so with a pained voice.

"I have been trying to find the words."

Rolf looked up.

"The news that has reached me," Karol said. "I can see that you have not heard."

"What?"

"The labor meeting at the shipyard—remember?"

"Of course."

"Ten dockworkers who attended were shot down like animals in the street."

Rolf felt a shock wave run through his entire body and shuddered.

"Ten dead," Karol said.

Rolf looked at the water. He could see all the way to the distant bottom of the cratered lake.

"I'm saying a memorial mass for those who were murdered in the city. Would you say it with me?"

Rolf nodded. He would do it because there was no way to get out of it. He would do his job well, as he'd been trained, and he would say a memorial mass for the brave dead men whom he himself had marked for death. It was the first time since the death of Father Novak that Rolf was a murderer, one who'd survived by taking the life of another.

A few days later, in a small cathedral not far from Shannon's neighborhood, Rolf stood shoulder to shoulder with Karol as both said the mass in unison. During his homily, Karol singled Rolf out to the mourners as one who had risked his life to be there at the shipyard. He extolled Rolf for his brave participation as one who had marched with Karol and Walesa for the cause of Polish independence.

The first wave of people lined up for communion. Rolf and Karol stood at opposite ends of the communion rail, each delivering the Host to a long line of worshippers who had come to honor the murdered Poles. Rolf's mind wandered, as it often had during his years of saying Mass by rote.

He thought about the lies, the first lie being that he was a priest of God. That lie had become two lies. He was no priest, and there was no God. The third lie had split into four lies. He was saying a memorial mass for ten dead Polish dockworkers. He didn't mean the words he was saying in general. He didn't believe they'd died for a successful cause. He was their murderer. He would bring more death every day he was alive.

While Rolf was lost in his thoughts and robotically delivering the sacrament, a young woman came into the church through the far door.

With her hands folded together, she slowly came down the aisle closer to the altar. Rolf suddenly looked up and saw Shannon, and at that moment, she saw Rolf, known to her as Heinrich, dressed as a priest and placing the Host on the tongues of the faithful. The look on her face said it all. She not only had fallen in love with a priest but also had been the one to cause him to break his vows. She was full of shame and disbelief.

Shannon screamed and then fainted and fell hard on the stone floor of the church. Rolf gasped, wanting to go to her, but he was blocked as everyone crowded around her to see what had happened. Several men nearby picked her up and carried her outside. Rolf could do nothing but continue the mass. Nobody seemed to know that her fainting had a connection to him.

As soon as the mass ended, Rolf hurried to Shannon's apartment, not taking the time to change into street clothes, because now his secret life had been revealed to her. There was no longer a reason to try to hide from her that he was a priest. And why, after that revelation, should he not try to tell her that he was not a real priest after all? As much as he believed that he loved her, he had recklessly put her in harm's way in order to be near her. He had allowed some dangerous men to know about her and follow him to where she lived. Those same men were probably watching him right now as he knocked on her door.

She came to the door in tears, trying to sound angry but only sounding hurt.

"How could you? How could you just destroy my life and break your own vows for your own selfish pleasure? How could you lead me into such sin?" she asked Rolf in a tone that told him he would never get near her again.

"I'm a much bigger liar in church than I am here," he told her, but he knew his explanation would not count for much.

"I wish you were married," she sobbed. "I wish you had lied to me about that instead of lying to me about being a priest. This is the most horrible thing that could have happened."

"Please. Could I come in and explain?"

She shut the door in his face. He heard it latch. His one solace was that maybe if he never saw her again, she would be safe from the KGB. As long as he continued to do their spying and could convince them that Shannon had not found out about his being a priest, maybe she would be safe.

The bishop was waiting in Rolf's room when he returned to the Vatican.

Rolf could not look directly at the bishop; he was overwhelmed with distaste for the flabby face of the man and everything he brought with him. Now that there was no Shannon for him, nothing made their arrangement acceptable to him. There would be no comfort and no solace. There would only be the dread that if he disobeyed the murderous instructions the bishop smilingly gave, Shannon might be killed, tortured, or both. Rolf knew he would have to keep the agreement for her sake. He would have to cause the deaths of many innocent people just to keep her from getting hurt. It was a miserable thought, and it brought back the dread that had engulfed his life before he had met Shannon.

"Did I cause those men to die?" Rolf asked the bishop, feeling he was about to explode.

"People die." The bishop shrugged. "Who knows the reason?"

"They were all men whose pictures—"

The bishop interrupted Rolf to say, "I'm talking to your training now; I'm not talking to you. We have a 247 situation."

The sudden clarity Rolf felt was like ice water in his veins as he met the bishop's eye.

"Somewhere in your training, did you ever hear that expression?"

"You want me to kill someone."

"We want you to eliminate a threat to us."

"No. I won't."

"But your training says you will. In fact, your training enables you to take a man's life on cue, using only your bare hands, and then arrange the body so that murder is not suspected at all."

"Who is the target?"

"Your fishing friend," the bishop said.

Rolf was immediately filled with an outrage that had been building since childhood. "No. I won't."

"What do you think will happen to Shannon if you don't?"

Rolf's response was quick and a testimony to his excellent training. With a lightning-quick spin of his body, Rolf cracked the side of the bishop's head with his right elbow. The bishop fell, fumbling for something in his sleeve as he went down. His weapon was not there. Rolf already had it, and he drove it deep into the bishop's chest and heart as they crashed to the floor. Rolf pulled back the bloody ice pick.

The bishop was dead.

Rolf went to work straightening the room and wrapped the bishop's body in the coverlet from his bed. He waited for the bell calling the priests to vespers, hoping none of the other priests would miss him that night.

Rolf lumbered down a back hallway with the bishop draped over his shoulder. Downstairs, the giant furnace that warmed the massive building had a blazing fire inside. Rolf swung open the heavy iron door and gave everything he had to loading the bishop's body into the burning furnace. The bishop was a heavy man, and Rolf could not push his body over and in. At first, he could only get the bishop's torso over the side of the furnace, dangling in the flames, bent at the waist. Then Rolf hoisted the dead man by his ankles and flipped him over the side. The flames engulfed the corpse immediately. Rolf closed the huge furnace door, not knowing if he had just closed the door on a terrible part of his life or just made it far worse.

Rolf walked quietly back up the hallway to his room, free of his burden. He bolted the door behind him and cleaned up in his sink. He looked into the mirror and wondered if the KGB knew about Shannon. The bishop had promised he wouldn't tell them and would keep the affair a secret. But how much could one trust the word of a KGB assassin? And why did they want Karol dead?

BOOK 4

THE MAN OF GOD

43

THE POPE

A month went by. Rolf lived in a perpetual state of anxiety, paranoid that someone would show up looking for the bishop and know that he had been the last one to see him. But nobody came for him. Nobody was waiting in his room when he got home. Nobody said or did anything about Rolf's secret murder. There was no death reported. There was no investigation. No one came looking for the bishop. After a while, to calm his nerves, Rolf began to convince himself once again that he was out of danger—that the bishop had become a rogue operator and would be neither missed nor asked after.

After another month had passed, Rolf once again entertained the hope that his connection to the KGB was now somehow severed. This hope was all he had to combat the deep depression that followed him everywhere, resulting from the loss of Shannon.

She had made the pain of living a double life worth it. She had justified his suffering. Now she felt betrayed by him, and Rolf knew better than to try to contact her. His love for her was real, but he knew she would be safer and happier without him in her life. He knew that anything he could do to ensure her safety he would do, and that thought was the only way he could feel good about himself. If the KGB knew about her and came to him again with assignments, he would have to accept those assignments.

Rolf continued to go fishing with Karol and drew what peace and tranquility he could from the quiet, the clear water, and the odd reassurance he took from Karol's congeniality. Even though Karol regularly encouraged Rolf to love God and Poland in a more active way, Karol was never harsh or critical toward Rolf. Rolf had the strange feeling that Karol accepted him for who he was. Of course, it couldn't be true. Karol didn't really know him. If Karol were to find out about Stalin's plan and the role Rolf played in it, he would feel differently. How could Karol ever accept a person with the stain of murder on his hands?

But they both enjoyed fishing together.

Rolf's job at the Secretariat of State became more demanding because of the Del Vado inheritance. Renato Del Vado was an Italian billionaire who had been living in Denmark. He died with no family survivors and left his considerable estate to the Vatican. The Danish property taxes were high, and Denmark's tax code was labyrinthine. The paperwork involved in transferring the Del Vado holdings to the Vatican was immense. Much of it fell onto Rolf's shoulders because of his mastery of languages. The complex inheritance took up more and more of Rolf's time, and Rolf welcomed the extra work. It helped keep his mind off his hopeless longing for Shannon.

On the day of the Feast of the Transfiguration, Rolf was sifting through another in a series of high stacks of paperwork on his desk, when he first noticed a bell ringing somewhere outside. Then other bells, some of them closer, began ringing.

Rolf looked up from his work. The bells seemed to have significance, but he did not know what it was. Suddenly, Karol came into his office, agitated.

"The Holy Father has expired!"

When Rolf heard those words, fear took hold. Somehow, he thought at first Karol was talking about the bishop. "What?"

"He was at the papal summer residence," Karol said with a halting voice and tears in his eyes. "There was a mass being said at his bedside several hours ago."

Rolf realized who the deceased Holy Father was, and then Karol's explanation snapped him out of his personal fear and into the present realization that the whole world was about to be shaken. Rolf knew, as did practically everyone in Vatican City, that Pope Paul had been at Castel Gandolfo for three weeks in poor health. Rolf had even heard it said that the pope might not ever return to the Vatican.

"After he became agitated," Karol said haltingly, "he received one last communion. Then he lost consciousness and died of a massive heart attack."

As Karol momentarily lost the ability to speak, he and Rolf crossed themselves.

"He thought so much of you, Rolf." Karol was barely able to get the words out. "He was so proud of your accomplishments."

As Karol again lost the thread, Rolf remembered the first time he had met Pope Paul in Africa. It had been an odd meeting, for the pope had been dumbfounded by Rolf's youthful appearance. Then, years later, the pope had called him to the Vatican. Rolf realized that not only had the church lost its leader, but also, he had lost an ally.

"Thank you for telling me," Rolf said. "I was too buried in my work to heed the bells."

"Still working on the Del Vado papers?" Karol asked, dabbing his eyes.

"Yes," Rolf said, handing Karol a handkerchief. "It's never ending. I suppose it's time to put down the work now, however."

"Yes," Karol agreed. "No one will blame you for that. It's time for prayer. I won't be seeing you for a while, Rolf. I'm called to be with him in Castel Gandolfo, along with the other cardinals in Rome."

"I will be praying for you," Rolf said, knowing that whenever he spoke of praying, he lied.

"Pray for us all," Karol said.

Rolf locked his desk drawer and the office, and he and Karol went to join a grieving world in prayer.

The bells rang out for a long time, bringing mourners from all over the world to St. Peter's Square. Throughout Rome, the old saying "Peter does not die" was repeated in prayer and conversation, meaning that the papal line was unbroken by death. Yet Karol and Rolf both had known the pope as a man, and they could not help but grieve his departure from the world.

During the brief time between the death of Pope Paul and the electoral conclave, French cardinal Jean Villot, the camerlengo, or church's secretary of state, took charge of all things at the Vatican. Leaders of the church, Karol among them, gathered at the pope's deathbed and then held a formal meeting at the Vatican to arrange his funeral and set in motion the election of his successor.

The pope's body was brought back to Rome from Castel Gandolfo to lie in state at St. Peter's. A memorial mass was sung at St. Peter's that night. Later, a requiem mass was held. Rolf, Karol, and the entire population of Vatican City, as well as a host of heads of state from all over the world, attended.

In a tradition dating back six hundred years, Mass was celebrated for the repose of the deceased pope's soul for nine consecutive days before the funeral, a tradition known as the *novemdiales*. According to the dictates of the Universi Domini Gregis, the apostolic constitution, the pope's body was to be prepared for burial between the fourth and sixth day after his death.

During that time, the camerlengo was charged with the duty of destroying two of the pope's most vital possessions.

A group of cardinals, Karol among them, gathered around a giant communion table. Cardinal Villot, a short man with dark hair and green eyes, held high the papal ring to ensure the others could see it and confirm it had been the pope's.

It was the Fisherman's Ring with the papal seal, the symbol of the pope's authority.

The cardinal took out a razor, showed it to the others as well, and then used the razor to chip away at the ring, defacing it. Cardinal Villot then took a large hammer, showed it to the others, and smashed the ring to bits. Then, with the same hammer, Villot smashed the papal seal as well. This custom of papal succession dated back to the early days of the church, when the death of a pope might have been concealed and the papal ring and seal used by the church's enemies as false proof of delegated authority.

Cardinals, dressed in violet, not red, prepared the body of Pope Paul for public display. They laid out the body in a white cassock, surplice, chasuble, and pallium and red slippers adorned with a gold brocade. On his head was a gold-colored miter.

The pope's body was brought to the Vatican basilica in a procession that formed in the Clementine Hall of the apostolic palace and proceeded to the great bronze door.

The great bronze door opened, and the procession of the casket and all of the cardinals emerged into public view. The pope's body was then placed on the altar of confession, on a simple catafalque. A quiet throng of mourners lined up for days to pay homage to their spiritual leader.

When the bronze doors closed again, the inner sanctum was closed to the public. Behind those doors, history would soon be made, as all the outside world knew. That quiet, beautiful place was sealed but was the object of the unblinking world's eye.

Pope Paul VI was finally laid to rest in the crypt of St. Peter's, along with many other popes, including his two immediate predecessors, John XXIII and Pius XII.

All flags flew at half-mast. The ringing of the bells faded away. Network television cameras gathered at the outer gates.

44

ELECTORAL CONCLAVE

Gregorian chants set the mood as a torch-lit procession of eligible cardinals dressed in red and led by the helmeted Swiss Guard passed by a group of archbishops, Rolf among them. Rolf's and Karol's eyes met briefly as the procession of cardinals passed. They were entering the conclave to elect a new pope.

The proceedings began with a mass celebrated at St. Peter's Basilica by the cardinal electors for divine guidance in their task to elect Pope Paul's successor. Six hours later, the cardinals proceeded to the Sistine Chapel as the chapel choir sang "Veni, Creator Spiritus." Archbishop Virgilio Noe, the papal master of ceremonies, gave the command *"Extra Omnes!"* The doors were locked, and the conclave began.

The cardinals filed into the beautifully ornate voting chamber. Because this was the largest electoral conclave ever assembled, the traditional canopied thrones had given way to twelve long tables.

There were no open windows, and the summer heat was intense from the beginning.

Discussion began. A tall, thin Italian cardinal named Cimaglia raised Karol's ire early on by suggesting that they elect an Italian pope, given the influential papal role on Italian politics. Although most of the cardinals agreed, Karol felt it was necessary to rebut.

"I think the nature of the man is more important than his nationality," said Karol, receiving a dirty look from Cardinal Cimaglia. "I would like to suggest Cardinal Lorscheider, a proud Brazilian who has fought hard for the welfare of his people."

Karol made a point of mentioning a non-Italian who had battled hunger and poverty, just as his friend Rolf had. Lorscheider modestly looked up at Karol and smiled. He was well respected, but Karol knew he was known as a liberation theologian. That fact, coupled with his lack of Italian status, would no doubt keep him out of the election.

The talk turned to worthy Italian candidates, and the two names most agreed upon seemed to be cardinals Siri and Benelli. Siri was known to be a curial bureaucrat and a staunch traditionalist, and Benelli was more of a moderate with autocratic tendencies.

Then Cardinal Cimaglia made an impassioned plea to the College of Cardinals for the election of a dark horse named Cardinal Albino Luciani. "There is only one among us who really deserves to be elected," Cardinal Cimaglia said.

Immediately, Cardinal Benelli surprised everyone who thought he might be the front-runner by agreeing that Luciani should be the next pope.

Karol was surprised that Luciani's name was being taken so seriously. He was a good man and a faithful servant of God, but he was shy and self-effacing, and his health problems were many and serious.

After minimal discussion, the cardinals took a preliminary vote. During the balloting, because of a drawing of lots, Cardinal Villot chose Karol to serve as a scrutineer.

The cardinals, Karol among them, proceeded to place their ballots in the giant golden chalice. After the votes were counted, Cardinal Villot had to read from the scroll the announcement nobody wanted to hear: "Insufficient for election." The voting was extremely scattered.

Outside, the mourners crowding St. Peter's Square saw gray smoke emerge from the chapel, signifying that the preliminary vote had failed to select a new pope.

Again, there was brief discussion, which included a lot of silent impatience with the stubbornness of others, and another vote took place. The gray smoke again emerged to signal to the gathering faithful that they were still without a pope.

The next day, the cardinals were ready to find a compromise candidate and end the world's suspense. Discussion was again brief, except for Cardinal Cimaglia's third exhortation in favor of Cardinal Luciani.

As the cardinals once again proceeded one by one to place their ballots into the golden chalice, Cardinal Luciani was limping badly. Karol was next behind him. When he saw the pain with which Luciani walked, Karol came to his aid, taking his arm to help him along.

"Are you all right?" Karol whispered.

"My feet are so badly swollen I can hardly wear shoes," Luciani whispered back.

Luciani stumbled, and Karol caught him, but two other cardinals—Cardinal Cimaglia and a short Czech cardinal named Boesch—came running up to assist Luciani, practically shoving Karol out of the way.

"Albino!" Cardinal Cimaglia blurted out, making a show of helping the man. "Let me help you!"

Cardinal Boesch was at Luciani's other arm, panting out, "Can I assist? Here—take my arm!"

Luciani was humiliated by the attention they drew. "Please, please," he protested, pulling away from both men. "I am fine."

On his way back to his seat, Luciani stopped to whisper rebelliously to Karol, "I voted for your man Cardinal Lorscheider each time."

Luciani was in much pain through the counting of the votes, and his walk back to his seat from the chalice was labored. Mostly, he looked down to make sure he would not trip on the uneven stone. When he arrived at his seat and looked up, he saw several cardinals standing in front of him with grim, serious faces.

"Cardinal Luciani, do you accept your election?" asked Cardinal Villot.

Luciani was shocked and incredulous. He looked at the other cardinals. He stared straight at Cardinals Boesch and Cimaglia, who seemed pleased at the outcome of the vote. He said directly to the two of them, "May God forgive you for what you have done."

The other cardinals looked at him expectantly.

"I accept," Luciani finally said with tears in his eyes.

"How do you wish to be called?"

After a moment, Luciani said, "Pope John Paul."

The throngs gathering outside the Vatican gates were waiting to know. The smoke that first appeared looked dark because some cardinals had deposited their ballots and tally sheets into the stove, darkening what was supposed to be white smoke.

Cardinal Felici, the ranking cardinal deacon, came out onto the balcony of St. Peter's Basilica and delivered the habemus Papam announcement in Latin, declaring the election of Pope John Paul. Then John Paul himself appeared on the balcony, and the onlookers were treated to the joyous sight of the white smoke issuing from the chapel chimney, telling them for certain that a new pope had been elected. A new age for Catholics everywhere was about to begin.

After John Paul shyly withdrew, the crowd's applause remained so loud that he was compelled to appear again.

Bells rang all over the world as, for the first time ever, a pope with two first names greeted a waiting world, a world that soon found out that the two names signified his desire to combine the best qualities of his two predecessors.

Cardinals Cimaglia and Boesch led the cheering that day.

45

A CONSULTATION

The most influential cardinals sat around the conference table with the new pope seated at the head of it, surrounded by his attendants. Among the cardinals at the table were German cardinal Boesch and Italian cardinals Cimaglia and Bellini, all of whom had gained influence by openly supporting the election of the man who had become pope. Karol was there too. His influence was also on the rise simply because the new pope admired him and valued his honest counsel.

However, the discussion was not going according to Karol's counsel at all.

"There are so many ways that we must enter the modern world," said Cardinal Cimaglia, "but this is the main way."

As he almost always did in these meetings, Cardinal Boesch backed up his good friend Cardinal Cimaglia, saying, "If we offer the olive branch, certainly the Russians will respond in kind."

Karol, as was happening more and more, found that he could not keep silent. "Would you offer a branch to Satan himself?" he asked.

"Do you mind?" said Cimaglia. "We are trying to have a civilized discussion."

"Civilized," muttered Karol. He could not hide his disgust for what these cardinals were trying to get the new pope to do.

"The days when Cold War reactionaries ruled the Vatican belong in the past," said Boesch.

"If we are not about the business of world peace, what are we doing here?" demanded Cimaglia.

Luciani nodded. "Yes, I take your point about world peace."

"We have waited so long to hear those wonderful words," said Cardinal Cimaglia.

"What a glorious day this is," said Cardinal Boesch.

"All we need to do is recognize the legitimacy of the Soviet Union, and a great dialogue can begin," Cimaglia said. "And we can make some inroads into a part of the world where we have not been since 1917."

"Your Excellency, may I speak directly to you?" Karol asked the new pope.

"Certainly," Pope John Paul said, giving Karol the floor.

"With worshipful respect, I must point out that the Soviets have murdered and imprisoned many innocent people."

"Of course, now we must consider the interests of Polish nationalism," Cardinal Boesch said, interrupting. He said the words *Polish nationalism* with such sarcasm that Karol said a silent prayer for patience.

"Consider the interests of all Catholics in Eastern Europe!" Karol demanded, drumming the table with the flat of his hand in exasperation. "Or the inhumane treatment of all workers. Consider the tens of thousands of priests who have been summarily lined up and executed for practicing their faith. Consider the interests of the hundreds of thousands of innocent, brave men and women suffering in the gulags for the crimes of praying, attending Mass, or simply writing some lines of poetry. In my country, the workers are risking their lives and dying in order to stand up to the tyrants, and they are doing it because they think we are on their side! If we support the oppressor at a time like this, can't you see what that would do? It would give them permission to continue with their murder. It would establish God's church in the eyes of the world as endorsing atheism, brutality, and unrestrained imperialism! We must isolate the Soviets, condemn their actions, and tell the world what evil really is!"

After he spoke, there was an uncomfortable silence. Karol was out of step with the general desires of a few powerful cardinals in the room. They had no use for his passion, yet they were all shamed by it.

"You are very eloquent, Cardinal," Pope John Paul told Karol, "but we are talking about improving relations, not endorsing."

"I love the way you think, Your Excellency," said Cardinal Cimaglia.

46

THE DEL VADO INHERITANCE

As life at the Vatican began to normalize under the leadership of the new pope, Rolf remained buried in the mountainous and never-ending paperwork involved in the Del Vado inheritance. He was not unhappy to be inundated with tedious and prosaic tasks. The paperwork enabled him to escape thoughts of depression and fears of reprisal by occupying his mind and his time in service to the Vatican in a way that no one could question his true identity.

Furthermore, the work kept him out of sight of just about everyone but Karol, with whom he still went on regular fishing excursions and who frequently sought him out at his office within the Secretariat of State offices. Out of sight meant out of mind, or so Rolf was hoping. Rolf knew, because Karol kept telling him, that there was controversy brewing at the Vatican over the church's relations with the Soviet government. Rolf wanted to avoid any such discussions. The personalities involved might be undercover KGB agents who could either press him into unpleasant service or settle with him for his treatment of the late bishop.

Karol knocked at Rolf's office door and entered Rolf's office, and sure enough, he found Rolf poring over another stack of papers, which was backed by another stack of papers.

"Rolf, I have just tried to gain an audience with the Holy Father, and he was unable to see me."

"Has his health improved?" Rolf asked, not looking up.

"He doesn't complain, but when I last saw him, he looked like he was in a good deal of agony."

"I will pray for him," Rolf said automatically.

"He seems so fragile," Karol said. "Also, I am concerned. He continues to receive counsel in favor of improving the Vatican's relations with the Soviet Union."

"Well—"

"With all the respect for him in the world, I have been doing everything I can to dissuade him. I'm afraid I haven't changed his mind. Those two obsequious cardinals, the Italian and the German, flank him at every opportunity. They have his ear."

Karol stopped talking and looked at Rolf. Rolf could feel his glare and finally looked up from his work.

"Would you help me, Rolf?"

"What could I do?"

"Talk to him. Plead the case for Eastern Europe."

"I haven't even met His Excellency. He doesn't know me."

"I could change that in the next fifteen minutes," Karol told Rolf, "assuming we could get in to see His Excellency."

Rolf felt a pang at the base of his stomach. Karol wanted him to get involved in the controversy.

"I can get you an audience with the Holy Father—if not right now, we can wait until his schedule opens up," Karol assured him.

"But this Del Vado inheritance is a mess. I'm way behind as it is."

"It might not take long," Karol said.

Rolf repeated his question. "What could I do?"

"Tell him about what the Soviets have done to our land, the destruction of the churches, and the oppression of our people. He needs to hear of this from someone other than me."

"What credibility have I got? I am an expatriate. The only time I have even visited behind the Iron Curtain was that one visit to Gdansk with you."

"Exactly." Karol clapped his hands with renewed enthusiasm. "Tell him about that. Tell him about the brave workers who gave their lives. Tell him how it felt to see that these freedom fighters gained their courage from the support of the church. Tell him how you felt when you found out the Soviets murdered ten men who were there with us, just shot them down in the street."

Rolf was cornered. If he weighed in on the issue, he could draw attention to himself from the wrong corners. For all he knew, the cardinals who were arguing in favor of the pope's recognition of the Soviets were undercover priests for the KGB just as he was. Rolf didn't know who the other agents in the priesthood were. However, that didn't mean those other agents didn't know who he was. He didn't know whether or not he was being watched. As long as he stayed buried in the Del Vado affair, no one bothered him—only Karol. Now Karol was trying to get him involved.

Rolf was desperate for an idea, but nothing came.

"I will, of course, do what I can," Rolf replied lamely. He could only hope the pope was too busy to see them right away. Then Rolf could claim he needed to get back to work and thus forestall the inevitable.

"Come with me then," Karol said. "Right now."

Rolf was just getting out of his chair, when a knock on the door seemed to save him. "Please come in!" Rolf called out.

Rolf's supervisor, an elderly, frail archbishop named Gianelli from Genoa, entered. "Archbishop Wozzak?"

Rolf looked up. "Yes?"

"Good news. I have just received word from the Roman Bank that a large portion of the Del Vado inheritance may now be brought from the Roman Bank to the Vatican Bank."

"That is excellent news," Rolf said, trying not to show Karol how truly relieved he was.

"Some of it can now be done with a simple wire transfer," Archbishop Gianelli said. "But there is a sizable amount in bearer bonds. An employee of the Del Vado estate, an Italian attorney named Travani, is ready to transport the bearer bonds from the Roman Bank to the Vatican Bank and has requested a personal envoy."

"Of course." Rolf turned to Karol apologetically. It was always Rolf's job to provide such envoys because of his command of languages. "I'm sorry."

"He wants you to meet him in front of the First Bank of Rome," said Archbishop Gianelli, expressing the urgency. "He's waiting there now, and he hasn't much time. He has sent a car for you."

"Of course," Karol said, managing a smile and a pat on Rolf's shoulder. "Be careful with it. But come see me as soon as you get back, please."

"I will," said Rolf, hoping that in the meantime, he could come up with a reasonable excuse.

Rolf promptly left the Vatican. A chartered car was waiting for him at St. Peter's Square and dropped him at the front steps of the First Bank of Rome, and he leaned against one of the building's eight columns.

Although Archbishop Gianelli had said the attorney would be waiting, there was no one there when Rolf arrived. After about ten minutes, a middle-aged Italian man wearing an expensive suit and carrying a briefcase approached.

"Archbishop Wozzak?"

"Senior Travani?"

They shook hands.

"There is a matter I would like to discuss with you before we go in," Travani said. "Could you step inside the car for a moment?"

A black limousine hovered by the curb. A chauffeur opened the back door for Rolf. Inside the limo was a group of men.

"I thought we were making a withdrawal," Rolf said, backing away.

"I already have," Travani said. "I've got the bonds in the car."

"How? You just got here. I've been waiting."

In that instant, Rolf knew he had been tricked. They had known about his preoccupation with the Del Vado inheritance and had used that preoccupation as a way of drawing him out where he could be taken.

Rolf took off running, crossing the narrow cobblestone street and heading toward an alleyway. The man named Travani jumped into the limo, and it took off, weaving through traffic, trying to keep up with Rolf. Pedestrians screamed and scattered in all directions to get out of the way as the limo took the curb and blocked Rolf's path.

Two large men got out of the limo and tried to grab Rolf.

He slipped out of their grip by twisting his arm. Then Rolf decked one of them with a right cross to the temple and nailed the other one with a spinning kick to the jaw.

"That's enough," a voice said.

He saw two more men with guns pointed at him. He thought about rushing them—they were out of shape and slow—but a sudden pain in the back of his head led his world into darkness.

47

FALLING SCALES

When Rolf opened his eyes again, he found himself in a private gated garden with four men standing around with their guns pointed his way.

The man called Travani stood over him. He showed Rolf a Judas cross.

"This was clumsy, I know," Travani admitted. "It's just that we have no time."

"For what?" Rolf asked.

"Don't play stupid. I know who you are. I work for Dmitri as well."

"Why do you say I work for Dmitri? I was informed that you were an attorney for the Del Vado estate and needed an envoy," Rolf said, feeling the sizable and painful bump on the back of his head.

"There is no time for this," Travani said. "Listen. We have a situation here. When was the last time you heard from your contact?"

Rolf took a moment to think and then decided he could drop the act a little bit but not all the way. "A month and a half," he admitted. "Maybe two months."

"At that time, were you given your assignment?"

"At that time, I completed an assignment. I gave a report to him about a meeting I attended at a Polish shipyard at his behest."

"And nothing since?"

"Nothing."

"Did you not think it odd? A month and a half with no contact?"

"He once went more than twenty years without contacting me."

"But with everything going on?"

"Around the Vatican, everything is about the new Holy Father."

"The new pope is the problem exactly."

"I've only heard good things," said Rolf in a practiced way.

"Apparently, there's a cover-up. The people around him know he has a failing heart and could die at any minute."

Rolf was worried now. "You want me to target the pope?"

"No. Believe me, no," Travani said. "This is finally someone we can work with. He wants to improve relations with our government. There's never been a pope like this. Our best heart surgeons have gathered in Rome even now, just in case they can make a difference. But our intelligence tells us that we may be too late. It will most likely not be long before the pope is dead. This is why you have to complete your assignment by seven o'clock tomorrow morning."

"I have not been given an assignment."

"My patience is running out. When you play stupid, it's highly unconvincing. It's all about time now, so let's speak plainly."

"I have not been given an assignment," Rolf insisted.

"I find it interesting, as do certain KGB officers, that your contact disappeared at exactly the time he was sent to give you your assignment."

Rolf said nothing at first and then said, "There was no assignment."

"There certainly is now," Travani said. "You must now do as you are told, and if not, you will be executed for both the murder of your contact and the treason implicit in the act."

Nobody said anything for a moment. Rolf was listening hard to see if this man knew anything about Shannon.

"Once you have completed your assignment, all suspicions about your part in the bishop's disappearance will drop. You will be accorded the highest honors we have and the life of comfort that goes with them. So, Priest, you now have a choice between heaven and hell."

Then came the words Rolf had been dreading: "Also, I understand there is a young woman in this city whose health and welfare are a concern for you. Is this not so?"

Rolf closed his eyes. "What is the assignment?"

"You insist on this charade?"

"Tell me," Rolf said simply.

"A 247. It is to take place at your fishing spot. The man who takes you fishing is your target. Do not assume, with your contact out of the way, that we don't know your secrets. Deal with him in the boat, but see that he does not fall into the water. There will be two men dressed as fishermen waiting at the landing rock at seven o'clock that morning. They will prepare the corpse and provide you with an escape vehicle. If you can't manage it with your bare hands, use this." Travani handed Rolf an ice pick. "Keep the blood to a minimum. Many of us believe the future of the Soviet Union is in your hands. This man must not become the next pope. We simply can't take the chance that he might. You will be a great hero in our eyes."

Rolf looked blankly, remembering a time in his youth when he'd wanted nothing more than to have Dmitri see him as a hero.

"And you'll be walking back to the Vatican," Travani added, pulling a gun on Rolf. "So I'd start right now."

"I will be asked about the bearer bonds," Rolf said.

"With a clever mind like yours, I'm sure you'll come up with a convincing story. I believe the disappearance of your contact is your fault. And since it is your mess, it is up to you to clean it up. Your survival, and that of the young woman, will depend upon your effectiveness in proving your loyalty to the skeptics who think your training will fail you. Get up."

Rolf got up. Two of Travani's men showed him to an open gate. Rolf was a little light-headed, but he walked away.

He walked a few blocks, his mind repressing his fear and formulating around a singular concern. The Polish waitress flashed into his mind. What the Germans had done to her—he could not allow them to do that to Shannon. He leaned against a wall, trying to catch his breath. He had to focus, and he closed his eyes, using his training to calm his breathing.

Rolf looked back the way he had come. Three men were following him, but they were different from the ones in the garden. These men looked more like working-class men than the ones in the garden, who'd been in suits and vestments. He thought he recognized the butcher from the market where he had shopped for dinner on the first night he cooked for Shannon. The man was still wearing his apron. The other two were dressed as dockworkers, with rough gray pants and vests.

Rolf pushed away from the wall and turned to the street that led to Shannon's apartment to try to tell her that she was being watched and that her life was in danger. There wasn't much he would be able to do to help her other than tell her to get far away from Rome as soon as possible.

Rolf looked back at the men as he as knocked on Shannon's door, knowing now that there were many spies to avoid. The door opened as wide as a small chain would permit, and a frightened old man looked through the opening. The old man saw a priest, so he unlatched the door.

"Shannon?" Rolf questioned softly.

The old man shook his head. "Gone."

"How long?"

"A month."

"Could I come in?"

"Yes, Father," the old man said. "She left you a note."

The old man let him in, and Rolf latched the door behind him, worried that the three men would follow him in. He didn't want harm to come to the old man. The old man disappeared into the back room for a moment and then came out with an envelope.

"Is your name Heinrich, Father?" the old man asked to make sure. Rolf nodded, and the old man handed him the sealed envelope. Rolf broke the seal.

> Heinrich, for I will always think of you as such, my heart is glad that you are a man of God but deeply sorrowful for helping you break the vows you made to Him. I have atoned in the only way I can. I have entered the Mount Holy Oak Convent in Boston. I will pledge my life to God and serve the poor. I will never love another in the way we loved. I will pray for you every day. I cannot judge you, but I realize that you are struggling in your faith. If you are ever lost and need to know which road to take, read Acts 9:17–18. Yours in Christ, Shannon

Rolf looked up from the letter. He dug a pen out from his pocket, quickly wrote some words on the back of the envelope, and showed them to the old man. The old man's eyes widened when he saw the words Rolf had written, words that tried to describe the trouble that would come Shannon's way if anyone ever saw the letter.

"Could we burn it?" Rolf whispered.

The old man ran to the kitchen and rummaged through the drawers. Finally, he found a pack of matches. The old man grabbed the note from Rolf, and they watched as Shannon's note burned in the sink. Rolf crumpled to his knees.

As the note burned, Rolf thought about the fire Shannon had kindled in him. He thought about her faith and her tender love, a love that had led even him to imagine the existence of a divine Creator. He thought about the unconditional acceptance she seemed to have for him still, even though she knew he had been dishonest with her as well as with the church she loved so much. As he thought about her, he knew instinctively that she would be happier with a life of sacrifice to God, and he would never see her again.

Then he remembered her words: she'd told him many times that she had come into his life for the purpose of bringing him to God. As soon as he remembered those words, he knew she was right—and he knew she had succeeded. He knew, just as he had known doubt and fear a few moments earlier, God was real, and God was right there in that room with him, the old man, and the ashes of Shannon's note.

He felt the arms of God holding him. *This must be what Karol felt when his father died.* The turmoil of the last few hours stilled further with a certainty. He knew he was being called by God. The large black eyes of Sister Lucia and her words came to mind: "You will know." He did know. He knew that Sister Lucia was an agent of God, and he knew why she had sent for him and what he should now do to rectify the past.

He realized then that in spite of his denials, he always had believed in God. When he'd been a teacher and the Spanish priest had come to school and spoken about Our Lady's predictions about Soviet evil, Rolf had had his first realization that he was part of that evil. It must have been God telling him that. The two people in his life for whom he had felt real love, Shannon and Karol, were people who not only believed in God but radiated God. Rolf could now see that God had brought those two people into his life. Rolf now knew that God had been with him all his life. It was only the training by the Soviets that had told him otherwise.

"Do you have a car?" Rolf asked the old man.

The old man nodded.

When Rolf emerged from the apartment and closed the door behind him, he only looked alone. For him, the world had changed with the loving reminder in Shannon's letter of a piece of scripture he had been assigned to memorize in the seminary about Ananias visiting Saul. It had meant nothing to him then, but it meant the world to him now.

He looked down the street. The three men who had followed him there made themselves visible again, crossing the street toward Shannon's building but stopping at the corner under the streetlight. One of the men lit a cigarette and then flicked the match in Rolf's direction. Rolf sat on the stoop in front of the apartment house and recited the verse from the book of Acts: "Then Ananias went to the house and entered it. Placing his hands on Saul, he said, 'Brother Saul, the Lord Jesus, who appeared to you on the road as you were coming here, has sent me so that you may see again and be filled with the Holy Spirit.'"

The men were now crossing the street toward Rolf. He smiled, and his eyes filled with tears.

"'Immediately something like scales fell from Saul's eyes,'" he said to the men. "'And he could see again.'"

Rolf stood up and walked away from the apartment house. The three men followed him closely. Rolf was memorizing the street, buildings, cars, pedestrians, and smells drifting out from open windows. He knew that Father Novak and Karol had been right. From then on, he would always be able to describe in detail the moment he was called by God.

"'He got up and was baptized,'" Rolf said to himself. "Yes, Lord. I do. I hear you calling. Finally."

All the fear and dread Rolf had felt every moment since the Nazis exploded his world in 1939 left, just as the scales had fallen from Saul's eyes. He felt once again the unconditional love of his parents. He remembered his mother, who'd taught him to read. He remembered his father, who'd died trying to save him.

He remembered the cross on the wall. He remembered that his father's last words had been to keep looking at the cross, to never take his eyes off the cross.

48

THE TOLLING OF BELLS

At sunrise, Rolf was once again fishing in a small boat with Karol at the secret fishing spot, floating on the clear waters of the great cratered lake. Rolf's eyes scanned the shore. He looked at his watch.

"You are quieter than usual today," Karol said softly. "Something imminent troubles you."

"Will you hear my confession?" Rolf asked. "It is something terrible."

"Where better than here?"

"Bless me, Father, for I have sinned," Rolf said.

"Tell me."

"You know of my early life, the murder of my parents."

"Yes. And I know that you hid and survived."

"What you don't know, Father, is that I was taken by the Soviets and turned into something base, a young man who could kill when ordered by the KGB. At sixteen, I shot and killed a defenseless man at point-blank range. I was assigned, after my training, along with over a thousand others over the years, to become a Catholic priest to spy on the West and destroy the church from within. Not long ago, I broke my vows and took a lover, lying to her about who I was. I believe that act of the flesh ruined her life. A month ago, I received an assignment from another undercover priest. One that I didn't like. I killed him and burned his remains. I have lied to everyone always. I am not a real priest but a Soviet spy."

Karol just smiled at him, not seeming the least bit surprised.

"The Soviets believe you will lead the Polish people against them," Rolf said.

"They are correct," Karol said.

Rolf gripped the ice pick in his right hand. He knew what he was supposed to do, and he had already figured out exactly how to do it. A quick movement with his legs would cause the boat to capsize, and a quick thrust with the ice pick would take Karol's life easily. Then Rolf would have completed his assignment. The contradiction of the two lives he had been living had now collided. He had been warned that to spare both his life and Shannon's, he must take Karol's. The compulsion to be effective and fulfill his training gripped him, just as it always had. He felt a blinding pain, one that could only be assuaged by decisive action. Once again, he sensed that he was about to find himself helplessly following orders.

However, something new had been added. He felt the presence of God in the boat with him just as surely as he felt Karol's presence. He knew that God would help him survive the pain.

"I have been sent here today to kill you." Rolf displayed the ice pick. "With this."

Rolf began to raise the ice pick but then slowly loosened his grip and dropped the ice pick into the lake, and they both watched it slowly sink into the deep, clear water. Then Rolf pulled something else from his sleeve and handed it to Karol: the Judas cross.

"This is the Judas cross. Every pseudo priest of Stalin has one. It is the sign we use to know each other. There are over a thousand of us. It was Stalin himself who devised this plan to control and eventually destroy the church from within."

"We must see that each one of them is rooted out," Karol said, taking the Judas cross and looking at it. "Do you now renounce your sins and sincerely wish to atone for them?" Karol asked.

Rolf nodded.

"Will you perform the act of contrition?"

"Oh my God," said Rolf, feeling the words of the familiar prayer for the first time and speaking them to the presence of God. "I am heartily sorry for having offended thee, and I detest all my sins because of thy just punishments but most of all because they offend thee, my God, who is all-good and is deserving of all my love. I firmly resolve with the help of thy grace to sin no more and to avoid the near occasion of sin."

"For your penance," said Karol, "you must set your life right. I absolve you in the name of the Father, the Son, and the Holy Ghost."

"How is it possible that I can truly be forgiven?"

"I believe that you repent. You are absolved. God forgives you, and I forgive you."

"I understand about God, but how can you?"

"I knew it all along, Rolf."

"How is that possible?"

"I come to this spot because it makes me feel close to God. I have been given many gifts from God. One of them is the ability to read people's hearts. That is why I brought you here to my secret spot—to bring you closer to God."

"I was plotting your death."

"They have made many attempts on my life. There will be many more."

"But how can you forgive a friend who—"

"Because I am forgiven. I know that God has forgiven my sins. When I accept that forgiveness, I am filled with joy. Forgiving those who sin against me or God is my response to the miraculous gift of grace. It is the result of my gratitude."

Rolf was deeply perplexed, trying to find a way to understand Karol's pure, unconditional love. "But I am responsible for the murder of the ten men you told me about. I left that out of my confession."

"The Soviets are responsible," Karol said. "You are just a terrified Pole who, like many of us, survived atrocities committed by one dictator after another. But we will throw them off our backs. Wait and see."

"What gives you that assurance?" Rolf asked. "God?"

"God and you," Karol told him. "This is an important moment in our struggle. Today you have come back to God. You are now a soldier for good and for God."

Rolf broke down into sobs. Karol wrapped his arms around him.

When Rolf opened his eyes and looked over Karol's shoulder, he saw movement on the shore.

Three men dressed as fishermen but carrying weapons emerged from the trees at the rock where they'd docked the boat. They were looking at Rolf and Karol through binoculars.

"Can you swim underwater?" Rolf asked his friend.

"I was once a champion swimmer."

"Follow me. Quickly."

They looked at each other for a silent moment and then dove into the cold water, Rolf leading the way, just as bullets started to fly above their heads.

The bullets put holes in the rowboat, but Karol and Rolf weren't in it anymore. It slowly began to sink.

Rolf and Karol stayed underwater as long as they could, emerging three times each to breathe and hearing the shooting every time as Rolf led Karol to the far shore of the lake. When they emerged, dripping wet and cold, Rolf felt changed, baptized by the water. He felt as if he'd been immersed by John the Baptist himself.

A faded old car came bumping through the trees and over the rocks toward them. The old man now living in Shannon's apartment was at the wheel. The car came to a stop where Rolf and Karol stood shivering and wet. The old man got out but left the car running. He handed a towel and dry clothes to Karol.

While Karol used the towel, the old man handed Rolf a handgun wrapped in a cloth rag.

"Change clothes quickly," said Rolf.

While Karol was changing, Rolf said, "The woman's name is Shannon Maher. She has returned to the Mount Holy Oak Convent in Boston, Massachusetts, where she grew up. I don't want them to hurt her. Please, Karol, see that she's looked after."

"Of course," Karol promised him. "You and I both will."

"I won't be there to see. And you must make sure she finds out about me. She believes she sinned by causing a priest to break his vows. She must be told that I am not a real priest, and it was all my doing. She is blameless. She must be absolved, as you have absolved me. If something happens to me, Karol, and I fear it will, see that Shannon knows that she brought me to God."

Karol put his hands on Rolf's shoulders and said, "You are the rock upon which I will build my church, and the gates of hell shall never prevail against it. Have faith, Rolf, for the church that is that rock still reigns. And you are standing on the rock with me."

Automatic fire thudded softly in the dirt nearby as one of the KGB agents emerged from behind the trees. Rolf took quick aim and shot the man through the heart. He fell to the ground.

"Get in!" Rolf ordered Karol. "Stay at the Vatican! Don't come here again!"

The old man got into the driver's seat. Rolf opened the passenger door, shoved Karol into the car, closed the door, and then slammed the side of the door with his hand, shouting, "Go!"

The car pulled around and took off the way it had come.

Three more men with automatics emerged from the trees. They opened fire at Rolf, who took immediate cover behind the closest grove of trees.

Karol watched through the rear window of the old man's car as they sped away. The sight filled him with great sadness and fear for his friend.

The old man was driving fast. Receding from view was the scene of Rolf drawing fire in a gunfight. The farther away they got from the shooting, the more they could hear a powerful but distant tolling of the bells.

"We have to go back for him!" Karol exclaimed.

"He said I shouldn't," the old man said. "Anyway, there's no time, Cardinal. I must get you to the Vatican. The pope is dead."

"We still grieve," Karol said, "but we have a new Holy Father now."

The bells were getting louder.

"That's the one I mean," the old man said. "The new pope. He's dead."

"No, no, I'm sure—"

"John Paul. They just announced it this morning. That's what those bells are. I have to get you to the Sacred College!"

"John Paul is dead?"

Karol prayed for the souls of his two friends, one a sickly man who'd never seemed to want the immense responsibility that had been placed upon his shoulders by the College of Cardinals and the other who was offering up his life for the cause of freedom.

As Rolf jumped out from the cover of a stand of low oaks, he drew immediate fire from the three men. The bullets went wide, hitting the trees.

Rolf rolled to his left, squatted low, and ran for cover near a rock. He waited three seconds, put his gun up, and fired twice. Both shots were direct hits. Only one assailant was left standing.

The third shooter came into view and walked toward him—a familiar face. The sight of Dmitri sent a quick shiver through Rolf's bones. He couldn't help thinking about his nightmares and was amazed that the solution to the horror he had experienced for so long was so close at hand. Now that the presence of God filled Rolf, he knew he had nothing to fear from this brutal man. Rolf knew that for the first time in his life, his way was clear.

"You told me I would not see you again," Rolf said to his old mentor.

Dmitri looked as if the years had not been good to him. In camouflage clothes, a low hat, and sunglasses, he looked more like an old man hiding in the bushes than the soldier Rolf remembered.

"They sent me because there's still some hope that you will listen to me and come to your senses. We can still accomplish our plan. I can save you," Dmitri said.

"I've already been saved," Rolf said.

"You must come with me."

"For most of my adult life, I have struggled to reconcile what you taught me about the evils of the Catholic church with my own experience. The compassion and purity of actions I've encountered all over the world from the real priests and nuns of the church contradicted the hate you instilled in me. I now realize that it is only through God that I may be set free from Russia's torment." Rolf lowered his gun. "And you can be absolved as well, Dmitri, despite the horrors of the past. If you repent, God will forgive you for your sins as well."

"God?" Dmitri snorted. "Do you really think I suffer from self-condemnation in any way? I am not weak like you, Rolf."

"Dmitri, we've committed murders and damaged people's lives all for one man. And for what? Stalin is not even alive anymore, yet this plan of his festers in your heart. I beg you to come to God."

Dmitri laughed a low, rough laugh as he walked toward Rolf.

Rolf didn't move.

Dmitri raised his gun and fired. Rolf's body twisted to the right as the bullet slammed into his chest, and the force of the bullet knocked him to the ground.

"I now have my repentance, Rolf!" Dmitri yelled as he rolled Rolf over with a kick of his boot in Rolf's side.

"Father, forgive me," Rolf whispered as he fired his own gun when Dmitri bent over him. Dmitri landed on top of Rolf with a thud.

With blood flowing from the wound in his chest, Rolf gasped for breath as he rolled Dmitri's body away from him. He struggled to his knees, and with fading strength, he made the sign of the cross with a trembling hand just as the sunrise burst through the trees.

"In the name of the Father, the Son, and the Holy Spirit. Oh my Jesus, forgive ... us our sins. Save us from ... the fires of hell. Lead ... all souls to heaven."

49

THE POLISH POPE

In a dressing area, Karol donned, for the first time, the papal vestments. He held two items in his hands, and he took time to examine them both.

One was an envelope containing Sister Lucia de Santos's description of the third prophecy of Our Lady of Fátima, handed to him only moments before by the late pope's personal assistant. He had heard for many years that this prophecy was a closely guarded, highly controversial secret so upsetting that Sister Lucia had for decades refused to describe it or commit it to paper. Now, upon reading it for the first time, he found it unexpectedly benign and strangely bland. He wondered what all the fuss had been about. There was something in it about a vision of a bishop dressed in white who had been shot, stumbling across a field strewn with corpses. He felt the bishop in white could be him, in reference to the earlier assassination attempt. Then he wondered if it could refer to another such attempt that awaited him.

He looked with great concern at the other item he held, the Judas cross Rolf had given him at the lake, remembering that Rolf had said there were more than a thousand Catholic priests in the world who carried that cross and took orders from the KGB.

He put the Judas cross in a drawer and went out to the great balcony to wave at the cheering throng. It was a historic moment watched on televisions all over the world.

Throngs once again gathered outside the Vatican gates, waiting to know who the new pope would be.

As he waved to the masses, the new pope shed silent tears for his friend

Rolf, who was now a Polish martyr after enduring life as one of Stalin's priests. He knew now that Rolf had died saving his life, giving him the opportunity to don the papal robes and lead more than one billion faithful followers. Rolf had given his life to expose a grave and sinister plot to destroy the holy church.

Karol resolved to uncover and put down the coup and help free his Polish people from the yoke of Soviet Communist oppression. He would be strengthened by Rolf's sacrifice. Karol knew he would succeed.

50

THE LEGACY

In a food kitchen run by St. Joachim's parish in Boston, a pregnant young woman was serving food to homeless families at the soup kitchen. Shannon was carrying the child of the man she had known as Heinrich. The Mount Holy Oak sisters would care for her during the pregnancy and then accept her vows after the birth of the child. The sisters had agreed to allow her to raise her child at the convent, just as Sister Blandine had raised her. Sister Blandine now stood next to Shannon, serving food to a line of hungry people. Shannon felt secure and happy to be back in Boston, back with Sister Blandine, and set on a new, more purposeful path.

Two Jesuit priests brought a portable television into the soup kitchen and turned it on.

"All right now," Sister Blandine called out, setting down her serving spoon. "Let's all stop what we're doing and have a look at the new Holy Father."

Everyone in the soup kitchen gathered around the small television screen to watch the jubilant celebration in the piazza of the Vatican. Shannon and Blandine crossed themselves and prayed for the new pope.

"He's chosen the name John Paul II," the television announcer said. "He's the first Polish pope."

Shannon immediately thought of Heinrich. She wondered if he knew this new pope personally. As the television camera zoomed in close on the new pope's face, Shannon recognized him as the other priest who had said the memorial mass for the murdered dockworkers. That same day, she had discovered the heartbreaking truth about Heinrich's double life and realized that the father of the child she carried was a priest.

Then something else made her think of Heinrich: one of the two Jesuit priests who had brought in the television suddenly reached out to turn up the volume, and as he leaned down, a cross dangled from the fold of his robe, its rubies catching the light and turning it red. It was the same strange-looking cross that had fallen out of Heinrich's pocket in the rose garden high up on Janiculum Hill.

Author's Note

The visions of Fátima have fascinated many ever since Lucia, Jacinta, and Francisco first reported seeing the Virgin Mary in 1917. She appeared to them six times, and one of the visits did include a specific request for the consecration of Russia to her Immaculate Heart. The story of their inquisition is fictionalized here, but it is based on events that occurred.

Jacinta and Francisco died within two years of the apparitions, as the lady had promised to "take them to heaven soon," and Lucia really did enter a convent in Spain. There were three messages, as this book mentions, but they were three parts of a single vision and were called secrets. Sister Lucia wrote the first two down on the direction of her confessor. These were published in Sister Lucia's memoir in the 1940s. These two parts of the vision were a vision of hell and a prophecy about the rise of Communist Russia, its forthcoming persecution of the church, and how it would spread its errors throughout the world unless it was consecrated to her Immaculate Heart by the pope.

The third secret, perhaps because it was not written down until well after the other two, has been the source of much speculation. Lucia herself stated that the third secret was so horrible that she could not bring herself to write it down, and did not, until after a serious illness in 1943, and only after a direct order from Bishop de Silva to do so. She wanted the secret delivered to the pope. It was to be kept in a sealed envelope and not revealed until 1960, when Lucia said that Our Lady felt the contents would be better understood. The third secret is believed by many to prophesy a great apostasy within the church itself, something that would shake the very foundations of the church. Coincidentally, it was in 1960 that the Second Vatican Council was being planned to help the church "better embrace the modern world". Indeed, dramatic changes would come to the catholic church as a result of that Council.

Pope John Paul II instructed, in 2000, that the full contents of the third secret be revealed to the world by then Cardinal Joseph Ratzinger, who later became Pope Benedict XVI. Accompanying the revelation of the secret was an explanation that asserted that the third secret was the prophecy of the assassination attempt of Pope John Paul II. Some in the Catholic Church claimed the secret he revealed was not the secret Lucia gave the bishop in 1943. You can read the secrets of Fátima yourself, including photocopies of Lucia's handwritten papers, at http://www.vatican.va/roman_curia/congregations/cfaith/documents/rc_con_cfaith_doc_20000626_message-Fátima_en.html.

Russia was the first state to have the objective of eliminating religion, and the persecution of the Russian Orthodox Church is well documented. Stalin implemented many measures against the church, including confiscating property, killing priests, instituting onerous taxes, and running propaganda campaigns. The plan to infiltrate the church, fictionalized for this novel, has been revealed and documented by many former Communists in Europe and the United States. The authors, in this work of fiction, have taken creative license and speculated that perhaps the third secret could have included a warning about the infiltration of the church by atheists and Communists intent on destroying the church. Interestingly, Pope John Paul II did consecrate all nations and humanity during his visit to Fátima in 1982, a year after he was shot, but he never specifically mentioned Russia. The authors have wondered, given the horrible scandals in the church over the last four decades, was the failure to specifically and directly consecrate Russia to Mary's Immaculate Heart the catalyst?

It is the authors' hope that readers will be drawn to learn more about the miraculous events that occurred in Fátima one hundred years ago and be touched by the message from Our Lady of the Rosary.